THE AMAZING FARTZINI III

Finale

SHANE ROBINSON

Other books by the author:

The Amazing Fartzini: An incredible story about an incredible boy who found magic!

The Amazing Fartzini II: The magical adventures of a boy wizard continue …

ISBN: 978-1-9162356-6-3

DEDICATION

I dedicate this book to my wife Angela and son Jake for helping to make my life magical!

CHAPTER ONE

LAS VEGAS, NEVADA

"The Amazing Fartzini" stood in position, feeling very alone on the biggest stage he'd ever performed. Now, a famous magician, headlining at a Las Vegas casino resort, he was about to demonstrate the most dangerous magic trick stunt of his entire twenty-five-year-old life, attempting to catch a live bullet between his teeth! Facing him was an armed marksman, pointing an old-fashioned musket at him, loaded with a deadly bullet with his name on it!

The extremely-dangerous magic trick stunt I'm referring to is infamously known as "The Bullet Catch" – infamously because the daredevil stunt has already tragically claimed the lives of many magicians since the time of its invention. The most famous of which was "Chung Ling Soo" – otherwise known as William Ellsworth Robinson. He was shot dead on stage at the Wood Green Empire Theatre, London, 1918. It remains a mystery to this day as to whether it was an accident, suicide, or murder!

One month earlier, on a sizzling hot Monday afternoon, The Amazing Fartzini – otherwise known by the less flattering name of Eric Fartz was sitting at his dressing table in his dimly-lit backstage theatre dressing room. He was talking to his Jewish American showbiz managers reflection in the mirror, who was standing right behind him, dripping in gold as well as sweat, about his magic act.

"You need to find a finale trick that will really make people sit up and take notice – something that will scare the living crap out of 'em!" advised his straight talking, no nonsense, brash manager, as he lit his big fat Havana cigar, completely ignoring the "No Smoking" signs backstage.

One of the many bulbs which framed the large make-up mirror was flashing; causing the very overweight, fifty-something, bald man to blink as he spoke – sweat pouring off his unsmiling face.

When The Amazing Fartzini first appeared in Vegas, or "Sin City" as it's otherwise known, about six months ago, he had initial success. But recently the number of people coming to see his show had dropped as sharply and as dramatically as his "Guillotine Illusion" blade. As his manager worryingly put it: "You're not getting enough bums on seats, Son – and the resort is losing money!" Not helped by the fact that a brand-new luxury casino resort had recently opened opposite, with a rival cutting-edge magic show. And to add to the theatre's problems, the air-conditioning unit had packed up earlier in the day and the searing Nevada desert heat had unwelcomely invited itself in.

"… Why don't cha perform that famous bullet catching trick as your finale?" There was silence. "No one's doin' it anymore!"

"Yeah, and there's good reason for it," thought Eric, raising his eyebrows as he listened to his overly talkative manager ranting on, while he skilfully rolled a quarter repeatedly across the backs of his fingers. "Is he trying to get me *killed?*"

"At least, no one's doin' it using a marksman firing an old-fashioned musket, that is," his manager continued to add while blowing out a big puff of thick acrid smoke.

"Do you think I'm *crazy?*" finally responded the handsome, blonde, blue-eyed magician, coughing. The coin accidentally fell onto the floor. "Twelve magicians have lost their lives performing that trick – and I don't want to be the thirteenth!"

"Well, obviously, you will need to take all the necessary precautions," said Mr Goldberg as he wiped his sweaty brow with his already sweat-drenched hankie.

"What? Like, duck out of the way!" thought Eric. He then spoke. "… What's wrong with the 'Impalement Illusion' I already close the show with?" then asked the young illusionist, slightly puzzled, as he swivelled on his stool to face his stressed-out manager.

The over-sized manager stubbed out his over-sized cigar and removed his expensive, designer, mohair jacket and cradled it over his arm, saying, "Sure, it's a good illusion, Son, but it's not scary enough. The audience knows that it's just an elaborate illusion and that no harm is *really* gonna come to ya. What the audience *really* wants to see is the magician risk his life – that is what will bring the punters back to the theatre!"

Eric listened closely and thought that his manager had a good point. "Let me think about it Mr Goldberg."

"Just call me, John."

"Sorry, John."

"Well, don't take too long about it. The casino resort management have already been busting my balls about it – and these aren't the sort of people you wanna mess with, if you get my drift!"

"I understand," said Eric, looking slightly nervous and worried. He knew exactly what he meant. An image of "Don Corleone" from *The Godfather* movie suddenly popped into his head.

His manager turned and walked towards the door. "I didn't become as successful as I have by not knowing a good thang when I see it!"

"*Oh,* Mr Gold–John!" Eric called out. "I am still waiting for my paycheck for the last two mon—" But Mr Goldberg didn't answer and disappeared in a puff of smoke.

Eric had been asking the same question for a while now, and all he seemed to get from his manager were excuses, or he was always in a hurry somewhere.

But money doesn't grow on trees as they say – even for a magician. And Eric was starting to feel the pinch. He had never been particularly good with money and had already foolishly squandered most of what he had either on bad deals such as real estate, which turned out wasn't real after all, boozing, or losing at the blackjack tables. The casinos were the real magicians of Sin City –– they made everyone's money disappear! And the shows and attractions, along with the cheap "all-you-can-eat" buffets, only really exist to lure people inside to gamble.

What was worse was that Eric had racked up huge gambling debts with the very same type of people Mr Goldberg was referring to in the dressing room – and the highly extortionate interest was mounting up! And he was counting on his paycheck to pay these "Goodfellas" back.

But Eric still loved to perform magic, and Las Vegas baby is the magic capital of the world – indeed, there are more live magic shows performed there than anywhere else in the world!

But as he slumped forwards and rested his

elbows on his dressing table to support his weary head, the mirrors reflection exposed someone longing to be somewhere else. Anywhere but Las Vegas. He had come to realise that fame was not all it was cracked up to be, and it came at a cost. Not in a monetary sense, but he felt a bit like the oil that greased the machine. The same cold, heartless machine that had no feelings whatsoever for all the misery and upset that it caused when the punters lost all their money. He found it was becoming a bit soul destroying, not to mention he was missing his family and friends back in England.

"I wonder what Em, Jack and Gary are doing now?" he thought as he let out a sigh.

"Ten minutes till showtime, Mr Fartzini!" hollowed the assistant stage manager as he rushed past his open dressing room door.

Eric immediately sat bolt upright and finished applying his pancake makeup, so he didn't look too pale and washed out in front of the bright stage lights. He noticed it had started to get noisier backstage as the dancers walked past in their skimpy, sparkling leotards, carrying their headdresses and feathers, and chatting excitedly to one another.

"Hi, honey!" called out Gloria as she whizzed past, still getting dressed, trying to catch up with the other eleven glamorous showgirls on their way to get into their positions on stage.

"Hiya!" quickly called back Eric, slightly less enthusiastically.

Gloria was an African American from Detroit, and the friendliest out of all the dancers. Most of them were from the US, though one, who had recently joined the troupe, was from the UK. Eric found some of the troupe to be a bit cliquey, especially, Candy – who was also African American – Rhonda, and Samantha. They were from the wealthy part of LA and could be quite catty sometimes. Mind you, worst of all was the choreographer – a youngish, very camp, tall and skinny guy with short black hair named Ruben. He strutted around like he owned the place. And annoyingly, always seemed to be clapping his hands for no reason – like his garish, multi-coloured lycra leggings didn't get him enough attention already. He'd already had the young newcomer from the UK in tears.

The show was called "Merlin's in Town", Starring, The Amazing Fartzini' and lasted for about an hour (the corny title of the show was the brainchild of the show producer, which Eric hated). It was the showgirl's job to top and tail the show, as they say in showbusiness, while The Amazing Fartzini filled in between performing his magic show. And the cast performed three times a day and seven days a week. Everyone was utterly exhausted.

There was a knock at Eric's dressing room door. It was the compère with a bourbon in his hand. An ageing, potbellied guy from Texas, who had a long drooping moustache. "Howdy, Eric. Just checking if there is anything else you want me to say?"

"Hiya, Jim. No, I can't think of anything — but thanks for asking."

"Hey, how's your luck at the tables?" There was a silence. "I guess that means you lost again last night, huh." Eric's face said it all. "Can't you magically conjure up a few blackjacks — and while you're at it do the same for me!" joked the jolly compère, laughing as he left. Eric could cheat at cards, but only used his card sharking skills for entertainment purposes.

They were about to put on a matinee performance, starting at 3 pm. Eric quickly put on his long flowing medieval robe, attached his long flowing white beard, and finally fitted on his long flowing white wig, and then made his way along the corridor and up the short flight of steps to the stage wings.

On each side of the wings, were all his magic props; all ready to be brought out on stage by a couple of the dancers who doubled up as magicians' assistants. Gloria was one of them, and the other one was Laura.

Eric quickly went and checked his magic props one last time to make sure that they had been set up correctly.

The show hadn't started yet, so after checking his props, he decided to go and have a quick peek out into the auditorium to see how many "bums on seats", as his manager put it, there were. Over by his station on stage left, the stage manager, who was wearing cans and communicating with the sound and light techs at the back of the showroom, saved him the bother of looking. "It's less than half full again!" he called out in his usual miserable, monotone voice.

The stage managers name was Dirk Rollinson. And he had made it quite clear to Eric from the start that he hated working with magicians because they always caused him and his crew a lot more work than other types of shows and were nothing but a hassle to him.

Having heard how few people there were again in the auditorium, Eric's expression immediately changed to one of disappointment.

"Chin up! The show must go on!" called out Gloria, after seeing Eric looking a bit forlorn, while at the same time trying not to knock her headdress off as she stretched. Eric smiled at her, and then went and squeezed himself into one of his cabinet-style boxes ready to make a surprise appearance as "Merlin the Wizard". The idea was once he'd made his appearance, he and his assistants would whip off their medieval costumes revealing themselves dressed in modern hip-looking one's and carry on like this.

It was so hot because the air conditioning still wasn't working that the dancers were sweating before they'd even kicked their legs in the air.

"*Hey!* Mind where you're sticking those feathers!" Gloria yelled to Candy behind her while bending over and speaking to her through the gap in her legs.

"Well, if you didn't have such a *big fat butt*, it wouldn't be a problem, would it!" snapped Candy – who was far from sweet.

Gloria moved towards her with her hands firmly placed on her hips. "How dare you say that to me, ya bi—"

Ruben suddenly *jetéd* out from the wings, clapping his hands quickly together. *"Girls! Girls! Ssstop* that at *once!"* he said, raising his affected lispy voice angrily. "We have a show to put on – ssso get back to your places *now!"*

Suddenly the overture began and he quickly *jetéd* back the way he came to get out of the way, clapping his hands again, saying, "Remember gals! Teeth, tits, and tush! Teeth, tits, and tush!" Politeness wasn't one of his strong points.

Meanwhile, The Amazing Fartzini was standing hidden inside a tightly confined, pitch-black box, desperately wanting to scratch his itchy nose, caused by his fake nylon beard, struggling for air, hoping they'd hurry up and get on with the show.

The tabs then opened to thumping music, revealing twelve beautiful showgirls revealing more than their fathers would have liked, with fixed smiles on their faces, baring their gleaming pearly whites amongst other things.

On cue, the dancers kicked their legs high in the air and shook their wobbly bits to the delight of the sparse audience – mostly sad old men sat on the front row, getting some respite from the gaming tables.

The sweat-drenched dancers finished their sizzling routine to scattered applause and hurriedly made for the wings as the compère walked out onto the hot and steamy stage, smiling broadly, and greeted the audience. He then began telling the same old corny jokes he'd been telling for years.

"Why is it compère's always stay on too long?" thought Eric, still self-imprisoned inside his sweat box, desperately wanting him to finish so he could be introduced.

"Ain't it hot in here, Marylou?" said an elderly lady in the audience to her friend sat next to her, frantically fanning herself.

"Yeah … I blame it on the climate change!" her friend replied.

"What a load of cra-nonsense!" said a guy sat on the adjacent table, having overheard their conversation. "The reason it's hot in here is cause the air-conditioning ain't working! I'm outta here!"

Finally, at last, the compère finished his long-drawn out routine and announced to the now even fewer audience members that remained, "… Ladies and Gentlemen, prepare to be amazed – *Merlin's* in Town!"

The lights dimmed, and mysterious music started playing as two of the dancers, dressed in medieval costumes, wheeled out a tall black box covered in silver stars and moons from the wings and positioned it centre stage. Then after spinning the box around at dizzying speed a couple of times, followed by a bit of prancing about, they opened the doors to show the interior was empty. The girls then took their positions on either side of it, slipping on the moisture-laden stage as they did, and gesticulated towards it. Suddenly, smoke began to appear inside the box and completely fill it.

The anticipation was building, and as the smoke dissipated, standing motionless inside the box was The Amazing Fartzini dressed as Merlin. The audience began to applaud as stage pyrotechnics exploded at the front of the stage, but suddenly the wizard collapsed and fell out of the box! One of the assistants then screamed in horror, "HE'S DEAD!"

CHAPTER TWO

KNOCK! KNOCK!

The tabs closed twice as quickly as they opened, and the stage manager, who was trained in first aid, rushed onto the stage, quickly followed by the rest of the cast.

"Get back! Give him some space!" the stage manager yelled to everyone who was leaning over Eric's limp body, distraught. "He's just fainted, that's all!"

He quickly removed Eric's fake beard – his wig had already come off when he fell to the stage – and checked his breathing, then loosened his shirt and elevated his legs to increase the blood flow.

"It's *too* hot to perform!" said one of the dancers at the back. Everyone agreed.

Then, after a few moments, Eric's eyes opened. "Where am I – what happened?" said Eric, dazed.

"You fainted," answered Gloria, helping him up.

"Will a couple of you help him back to his dressing room," said the stage manager.

There was then an announcement made over the PA system. "Ladies and Gentlemen. We do sincerely apologise, but due to there being an air-conditioning fault, the management have decided to cancel the shows for the rest of the day. If you would like to rebook to see the show on a later date or have a refund, please make your way now to the box office. Once again, we are very sorry for any inconvenience this may have caused! Thank you for your kind attention and understanding!"

Gloria and Jim helped Eric back to his dressing room and sat him down on an armchair in the corner.

"I'll go and fetch you an iced tea!" said Gloria (they didn't serve hot tea).

"Could I have milk with my tea, please?" asked Eric.

"*Milk!*" exclaimed Gloria.

"*Milk!*" then exclaimed Jim.

"Milk!" both then exclaimed in unison.

"That sounds yuk to me, but alrighty if that's what choo want, honey," said Gloria, still in disbelief as she started to leave, thinking, "I guess it must be a Brit thang!"

Eric smiled and said, "Thanks!"

"Hey, you should faint more often," said Jim, "then we can have more time off!"

Eric laughed. "We're all treading on thin ice as it is here, Jim. Best not give them another reason to get rid of us, eh?"

"Yeah, I was just joshing with ya," said Jim, smiling. "… Are ya gonna be okay then Eric?"

"Yeah, I'll be fine."

"Well, I'll be off then. I've got a date with a sweet, strawberry blonde, called Bourbon, waiting for me at the new casino across the Strip," said Jim, smiling and licking his lips. "… And their air conditioning works!"

Eric laughed again. "Sounds good – maybe I'll see ya later!"

Soon after Jim left, Gloria came in with an iced tea with milk. "There ya go, handsome!" she said, cringing as she handed it to him.

"Ta!" said Eric as he took the drink from her hand. Both their hands touching.

"… Don't I get a kiss then?" She unabashedly straddled him where he sat and puckered her lips. Eric chuckled and gave her a friendly peck on the cheek. Then, holding her hips, prised her off himself – which was not easy because she was the strong alpha female type – making it clear that he wasn't interested in anything else except friendship. "I'm only messing wit choo!" she said, laughing as she removed herself from his lap, inwardly disappointed.

She clearly had the hots for him but knew only too well that he had a fiancée back home in England, called Emily, and he wasn't interested in anyone else – he didn't stop talking about her, so how could she forget. Not that that stopped her from flirting with him, though.

"Well, you seem much better now Eric!" said Gloria, pleased.

"Yeah, I'm fine – it was just being in an enclosed place for too long in the heat. Next time I'll get in the box much later," he said as he took a big slurp of his weird concoction of a drink.

"Oh, I just *love* your British accent! Where abouts in England did you say you were from again?" she asked, still flirting and making eyes at him – but from a safer distance.

"Sheffield in the North originally. Then my mum and dad split up and my mum and I moved to Ramsgate in the South-East."

"… Hey, now that we've got the night off, d'ya fancy coming out for a drink at the new casino resort?" asked Gloria, flashing her eyelids once more. Eric hesitated. "There's a big group of us going. *Come on* – it'll be *fun!*"

"… Erm … okay, sure! You go on ahead, and as soon as I've packed my magic props away, I'll come and join ya!"

"Cool! See ya later, honey!"

"See ya!"

Eric then went backstage to pack away all his magic props. He never liked to leave his magic props exposed for people to discover his secrets or meddle with them – and it wouldn't be the first time.

By now, there was nobody left backstage. Even all the stage management had abandoned it. And the only people in the auditorium were a few waitresses still clearing away empty glasses and the sound of someone vacuuming the carpet.

Once Eric had wheeled the "Merlin

Appearance Illusion" back into the wings and packed everything away, he went back to his dressing room and closed the door behind him. How nice and peaceful he thought it was for a change: no loud music blearing out; no screaming and shouting – mostly from Ruben; no cattiness – also mostly from Ruben.

He sprayed deodorant under his armpits, put on a clean white short-sleeve shirt, combed his long wavy blonde hair, and put his pack of cards in his trouser pocket – he never went anywhere without them – all ready to go out and enjoy himself.

Suddenly, there was a loud, knock, knock, on the door. "Who could that be?" he thought. It startled him a bit. "Oh, it's probably just Gloria again. I must make it clearer to her that I'm not interested!"

Eric opened the door and four huge, muscle-bound men burst in, forcing him back into the room. He knew instantly who they were. "I'll get you the money as soon as I can, don't hurt me!" he pleaded, holding his hands up.

The scar-faced, Italian American Mafioso in front, grabbed Eric by his shirt, ripping it, as he pulled the powerless magician to within a few inches of his mean and angry looking face.

"I didn't know you cared!" joked Eric, who's wit was even sharper than their Italian designer suits.

Mistake! The mobster clearly didn't have much of a sense of humour and punched him in the stomach, winding him, and shoved him away. Then, rapidly like a Tommy gun loaded with foul language, the Mafioso let him have it.

"… I just need a bit more time!" tried to explain Eric, now in pain and feeling very scared.

"What?" said the mobster doing all the talking. "Say dat again." He then turned his head to one side, showing one of his ears was missing.

"HE SAID, HE NEEDS MORE TIME!" yelled one of his huge "heavies" right behind him. (A "heavy" is a Mafia term for someone packed, carrying a weapon.)

"What the …" The mobster pulled an even uglier face and covered his only ear. He then started gesturing with his hands flying about all over the place, and saying, "There's no need to *shout*, ya moron! What's da matter wit choo, huh? Are you crazy? *Jeesh!*"

"Sorry, Boss!" said the heavy.

The mobster boss then turned back towards

Eric, and as he began to remove his pistol, said chillingly, "It's too late, kid!"

"Do you accept PayPal?" quickly said Eric desperately.

The mobsters all laughed.

"We've got a comedian here!" said the Mafia Boss, sweating profusely along with everyone else. Then after a little bit of thought, said, "Okay, I'm a reasonable man. I'll give ya anuda week." He then started wagging his half-finger. "But no more excuses wise guy! Either cough up the $50,000 ya owe us in cash, or you'll be wearing cement shoes at da bottom of da river! Capeesh?"

"Yes!" just answered Eric, breathing a sigh of relief, even though he didn't know what "capeesh" meant.

"But we're in da middle of da desert, Boss!" advised another of his heavies behind him.

"Shut up, or you'll end up joining him!" he shot back. "Boy! Is it *hot* in this joint or what?"

"I suppose we could dump him in The Venetian Resort Hotel river!" his heavy then said, trying to be helpful.

"I said shut up, didn't I!"

"Yes, sorry Tony–er–Boss!"

"Hey, what 'ave I told ya about not

mentioning my name in public, huh!" He then slapped the heavy across the head.

"*Ouch!*" screamed the heavy.

"I hardly touched ya! Stop being such a cry-baby!"

The Mafia Boss was known as Anthony "Tony One Shoe" Garibaldi on account of him only having one leg – he lost it to a shark, and I don't mean the kind that swims around in the deep blue sea. Anyway, even though he now has a prosthetic leg and wears a pair of shoes, the nickname stuck ever since.

Eric then went to put his hand in his pocket to remove something. Suddenly all four mobsters pulled out handguns and pointed them at him.

"*Slowly!*" said the crime boss in case he was about to pull out a gun. "Take it easy!"

"*Don't shoot!*" called out Eric, cowering in fear for his life. He continued very slowly reaching into his pocket and removed his pack of cards. "It's *just* a pack of cards!" His trembling hands removed the cards from the case and fanned them out, saying nervously, "Pick a card!"

But his pack of flimsy paper cards was no weapon up against the cold steel of their guns and even colder hearts. The crime boss knocked the cards out of Eric's hand, causing them to fly everywhere. "I *hate* card tricks!" he said. He then pointed his half-finger towards him. "Remember! *One* more week!"

With that, Tony One Shoe turned and limped out the door, followed one by one by his heavies, leaving Eric visibly shaking and panicking as to where he would get that kind of money in time.

He waited a bit longer, then quickly went over to the doorway, poked his head outside, and peered left and right to make sure they were gone. Thankfully, they had. He then swivelled back inside, resting his back against the wall, and allowed himself to slide down to the floor. He then put his hands on his head and shook it, thinking, "How did I get myself into this mess?" When he initially borrowed the money, he had no idea it was the Mafia he was dealing with.

He thought back to all the good times he'd had back in England with his friends Em, Jack, and Gary, and all the fun adventures they used to have together. He really missed them and started to feel down.

He hadn't seen any of his family and friends since his contract in Las Vegas started six months ago: it was too expensive for any of them to come and visit him. But he did communicate with his mum and Em by phone and Skype regularly. Though being in showbusiness often meant travelling by one's self far away from home for long periods, and even before this contract, he'd lost touch with Jack and Gary and hadn't seen them in person for a long while.

Sure, he had gotten to know some people in Vegas that he got on quite well with, like Gloria, but there was no one he could call real friends, as such. He found it hard to tell who his real friends were, as a lot of people were as false as the promises of winning big money in Vegas. They pretend to be friendly to your face but would stab you in the back the moment it's turned.

And, although at first, he jumped at the idea of performing his magic show on a Las Vegas stage, like some of his magic idols, Siegfried and Roy, David Copperfield, and Penn and Teller, it was proving not to be the glamorous life he had thought and hoped it would be. Having to live out of a suitcase, and deal with unscrupulous entertainment managers, prima donna choreographers, not to mention the Mafia.

Eric had come to realise that the real pleasure one gets from performing magic wasn't the money and the fame – because just like a mirage in the desert that can all quickly disappear – it was the joy one gets from seeing the smiles on people's faces by making them feel happy. But to be able to make other people happy, one must first feel this way themselves. And for Eric, that meant being close to his loved ones and friends.

But, as of right now, he couldn't just quit his contract and go home, he had debts to clear – Mafia debts! And these weren't the type of people who were in the habit of writing-off one's debts.

"Enough of this maudlin," thought Eric. He got on his hands and knees and started picking up all the fifty-two playing cards that were strewn all over the floor.

As he was picking them up and reassembling the pack, he started to reminisce fondly about one of the many adventures he had with his friends when he was about fourteen or fifteen and going to St. Bartholomew's C of E school in Ramsgate, Kent. It happened during the summer holidays when they all joined the circus.

CHAPTER THREE

ROLL UP! ROLL UP!

"Eric! Are you doing your homework?" called out his mum, Ingrid.

"... *Yes*, Mum!" he called back from his bedroom. He was telling porkies as usual: he was on his hands and knees at the time, picking up all the playing cards he'd accidentally dropped on the floor while practising card manipulations.

His mum opened his bedroom door to find Eric on the floor with his back to her searching for something on the carpet.

"What on *earth* are you doing down there?" asked his mum. "It doesn't look like you're getting much homework done to me?"

There was a pause. "Oh, we are doing a biology project on fleas, and I was just checking if we had any in our carpets," he answered sheepishly as he quickly sat on his cards. It was the first thing he could think of to say.

"*Fleas!* We don't have *fleas* in this flat!" exclaimed his mum, offendedly.

"No, I don't expect we do, but it's part of my homework study and I have to check – and I am pleased to report that I have found no fleas thus far!" said Eric, smiling.

"Oh, good!" she said, relieved to hear it. "Anyroad, I came to tell you that the Russian State Circus is coming to town!"

"Oh, cool! I can't wait to go!" he replied, excited. Eric loved the circus.

"Well, I'll let you get on with … whatever homework study it is you're doing. Carry on," said his mum, scratching herself at the thought of fleas as she left.

As soon as his mum left, Eric phoned all his friends to tell them the exciting news that the circus was coming to town.

The following week the school broke up for the summer holidays and thanks to Emily's dad, who used to perform in a travelling circus himself many years ago as a knife-throwing act, he was able to get them free tickets.

It was a lovely hot summers day and the unmistakable sight of the big top could be seen from quite a distance. The Russian circus had set up on a large open field in Ramsgate. As they approached, they could hear lots of families with excited children making lots of noise, queuing up to enter the big top. The four excited friends raced across the field towards the entrance with their tickets aloft. Eric was the fastest, followed closely by Jack, then Emily, and as usual, trailing lastly behind was Gary.

"C'mon, Gary!" the others called out; slightly peeved that they had to let others past them while they waited for him to get there, and panicking, in case they didn't get a good seat. Gary eventually arrived, panting heavily, and as soon as they showed their tickets to the ticket collector, all four made their way inside the big top in search of seats. It was already nearly full.

"Over there!" called out Jack, pointing to four empty seats in a row. The seats were high up, but they were still in the centre section. But just then, they spotted a family of four climbing up one of the aisles and looking as if they were heading straight for them.

"Quick!" said Eric. And the four eager children raced them up the adjacent aisle to try and beat the family to them. They dashed up the rickety steps in their quest to get good seats, and then along the row of already taken seats, quickly brushing past people's legs and stepping on their toes in their desperate attempt to get their before the others. Finally, they made it, and plonked themselves down on the uncomfortable wobbly plastic seats before anybody else could.

"Where's Gary?" said Emily, noticing he wasn't with them.

"I might have known," then said, Jack. "Look, there his is down there!" Gary was still at the bottom, queuing up to buy candy floss.

A little while later, up he came, stuffing his face with candy floss, causing each row of people to experience what seemed like a major earth tremor with each step he took.

Gary squeezed past people along the row, and then just about squeezed into the empty seat next to Emily, while still blissfully devouring his candy floss. He looked like he'd just grown a pink beard!

"Don't get any for *us* then!" said Emily, sullenly.

"I couldn't carry anymore," replied Gary, muffled by the big wad of candy floss covering his entire face.

Suddenly the lights went out in the audience. "Stop arguing, you two," said Eric. "The shows about to start."

The spotlight shone on the ringmaster in the centre of the ring, a tall handsome figure, wearing the traditional top hat and tails.

"Ladies and Gentlemen, children of all ages. Welcome to the greatest show on earth! Sit back, relax, and enjoy yourselves. The show is about to commence!" announced the ringmaster.

The music began and out came the first of an incredible line-up of talented circus performers. And what a show it turned out to be. The delighted audience witnessed: acrobatics, juggling, clowning, tightrope walking, plate-spinning, hand balancing, the high-flying trapeze, and a wonderful finale parade with all the artists.

The four friends left the big top buzzing with excitement and couldn't stop talking about all the wonderful acts. But their favourite act of all, was the four clowns – they thought they were hilarious and couldn't wait to go and see them again.

In fact, the four children went to see the circus many times during that summer. So much so that they knew the clown's comedy routines almost off by heart. Emily's dad managed to get them the occasional job there, helping with the menial tasks, like collecting tickets, selling popcorn and candy floss (which was Gary's favourite job), and clearing up and so on. They loved working there and got to know the ringmaster and most of the circus performers quite well. And when Eric wasn't working, he would amaze them with his magic tricks.

Well, one time in the height of the summer, not long before the matinee show was about to start, the four children were out the back having fun, learning juggling skills, when the ring master suddenly came running over to them panicking.

"Oh, there you! Thank goodness!" said the ringmaster in his broken English, Russian accent, sounding desperate. "I need all of your help!"

"Whatever is the matter?" asked Emily,

concerned.

The ring master caught his breath, then explained. "The clowns have been drinking too much vodka and are now incapa-incapaci-incapacita—"

"*Drunk*, you mean?" said Eric, with a slight grin.

"Yes, all four of them are – how you say – crashed out in their caravan, sleeping it off."

"Well, how do you expect us to help?" asked Jack.

"I need you to go and put clown make-up on now and take their places," said the ringmaster with great urgency. "The show is about to start in twenty minutes!"

Emily laughed. "Well, these three are already clowns!" she joked.

"*Oi!*" responded Gary.

"Well, I don't know about that Mr Ivanov?" said Jack, sounding very doubtful.

"Oh, *come on* Jack. It'll be a great laugh!" said Eric, always the performer.

"*I'll* give it a go," said Emily, excited.

"Yeah, okay," then said Jack, apprehensive.

Gary went noticeably quiet. "What about you, Gary?" asked Eric.

He looked terrified at the thought. "Erm,

erm. I don't want to do it," he finally answered nervously.

"You'd be *really* funny, Gary!" said Eric. The other all agreed.

"But what if other school kids recognise us?" said Gary.

"They won't – because we'll be in clown make-up and costumes!" then said Eric trying to persuade him to do it.

"*Please,* I need your help, or I will have to cancel the matinee show!" almost pleaded the ringmaster.

Everyone looked at Gary. "… No, I can't." he uttered, shaking his head adamantly.

"I'll give you all free tickets for the rest of the season and as much candy floss as you want!" said the more and more distraught Russian.

"*Okay then!*" said Gary immediately, upon hearing the mere mention of confectionary.

"Wonderful! Wonderful!" said the ringmaster, now with a big smile on his face. "I can't thank you enough. Come with me quickly – there is still time!"

So, the four children quickly followed the ringmaster. As they went past the clown's caravan, they could hear all of them snoring their heads off.

"I don't mind dressing up as a clown as long as I'm not made a fool of, and people laugh at me!" said Gary at the back, being serious.

"Well, that's the *whole* idea of being a clown!" said Emily shaking her head, never ceasing to be amazed at what Gary comes out with.

"Yeah, and if we forget the routines – so what. We'll just make it up!" said Eric, who was the most eager up front.

"Yeah, and at least we don't have to learn any lines!" said Jack, now starting to feel more confident.

Gary suddenly started to smile, "Yeah, and we'll get to frighten all the little children!" he said to no response, except raised eyebrows from all the others.

They followed the ringmaster through an opening at the rear of the big top, and there inside the backstage area were the rest of the circus performers warming up. Some were still applying their stage make-up, while others were either juggling clubs in the air or throwing themselves into the air. One strong looking guy was balancing his partner upside down above his head using only one hand!

"That looks dangerous!" thought Eric. "I hope he doesn't suddenly sneeze or need to go to the loo!"

All the circus performers were very friendly and said hello to the new clown recruits as they welcomed them into their world.

The ringmaster then asked them to sit down on some stools. He then said something extremely fast in Russian to some of the performers, and the next thing they knew was their faces were being smothered in white greasepaint. Next came the rouge applied on their cheeks. Then the fixed raised black eyebrows were painted on higher up on their foreheads, followed by the exaggerated bright red lips. And lastly, which no clown would be complete without, they attached the classic comical-looking red nose. The children all looked at each other and laughed.

While they were having their make-up applied, it gave them a chance to go over the clowning skits and routines and decide who was doing what.

"Five minutes till curtain up!" called out one of the stagehands.

The children's hearts began to beat even faster at the sudden realisation that the show was about to start, and they were going to be a part of it. They quickly got into their colourful and comical clown costumes, and then slipped on the enormously grotesque clown boots.

"Don't forget the clown wigs," called out one of the helpers.

And each of the children quickly grabbed hold of a clown wig from out of an old basket, and put them on, causing much further hilarity between them. *"Bagsy* the rainbow coloured one!" yelled Gary. By this time, they were already getting into the spirit of pranking one another and being silly.

"They're going to be just fine!" said one of the acrobats to the ringmaster.

"Where are all the clown props?" Eric asked the ringmaster.

"The stagehands have already placed them by the entrance," he replied, pointing.

Eric quickly rushed over and picked up the French horn, "That's always gets a laugh," he thought.

"I wanna drive the clown car!" said Jack, excited.

"Shotgun!" Emily quickly called out, equally excited.

"Shot—" started to say Gary.

"Beat ya to it!" said Emily.

"Oh! I wanted to ride shotgun!" Gary

declared, looking disappointed; but his face soon lit up when he saw the over-sized camera which sprayed water. He grabbed hold of it and pretended to take a snap of Emily.

"Don't you dare!" she said, moving away sharply. "You can have a go in it after me."

Amongst the other clown props, was a large rubber club, a plank of wood, several buckets filled with water and another with confetti, and a line of custard pies, which the children remembered causing much hilarity and mayhem.

The ringmaster then gathered the newly transformed clowns around him. "Just go out and enjoy yourselves and have fun. And remember, when you are doing the – how you say in English – oh, yeah – the "Wash Day" routine. *Only* throw the bucket of confetti at the audience – *not* the bucket of water! Have you got that?"

"Yes!" said the children, buzzing with excitement and nerves. They could hear the noise from the audience out front – the atmosphere was fantastic.

"Vrup!"

"Oh, *Gary*, you haven't?" said Emily.

"Fraid so!" he answered, grinning. The

others quickly moved away, holding their rubber noses.

Emily had a quick peek out at the audience, seeing lots of families with small children with excited looks on their faces. "It looks *packed!*"

The music started, and the ringmaster adorned his top hat, straightened his bow tie, and picked up the radio mic ready to make his entrance and to walk out into the spotlight and greet the excited crowd.

The opening act were the jugglers, and they too moved near to the entrance ready to make their appearance.

The curtains parted and the ringmaster walked proudly out into the spotlight towards the centre ring. "Ladies and Gentlemen, children of all ages. Welcome to the greatest show on earth! …"

Meanwhile the children rehearsed their clowning skits and routines as best they could remember. It was the clowns' job to entertain the crowd while the stage crew cleared away the props of the previous act and prepared the stage for the next act. And later in the show they were given their own performance spot.

The ringmaster introduced 'The Voznesensky Brothers', who came quickly running out to the up-tempo music and the roar of the crowd, throwing juggling clubs back and forth to one another at lightning speed, and getting the show immediately off to a thrilling start.

"Get ready,' said the ringmaster to the novice clowns waiting anxiously behind the curtain as he went back out to take the jugglers off.

The Juggling act took their deserved bows to thunderous applause from all around the big top and made their exit. Then as the ringmaster was in the middle of speaking, and the stage crew quickly went about setting up for the next act, a comical looking open-top car suddenly came driving out, noisily beeping its horn, with two clowns sat in it, smiling, and waving at the crowd – namely Jack and Emily. And right behind them was one mischievous clown – namely Eric – chasing another – namely Gary – around the ring, squeaking a horn close to his backside and making him jump.

Then, after continuing to chase Gary around the ring several more times, Gary had to pause to take a breather, so Eric then went up behind the ringmaster and made him jump, much to the amusement of the youngsters in the crowd.

And as Gary was sat down at the edge of the

ring getting his breath back, he heard a little girl say out loud, "Look at that *fat* clown, mummy. Isn't he funny-looking?" pointing to him as she said it.

Gary immediately turned around and pulled a scary face at her, frightening the little girl and causing her burst into tears. He then got up and pretended to take her picture. *"Smile!"* he said, then squirted water at her. He then quickly moved away and continued to play the same prank on other poor unsuspecting souls around the ring.

Meanwhile, the clown car continued driving around in circles, beeping its horn, while driving the ringmaster mad. And despite the ringmaster's best efforts to make them stop and get rid of them, he eventually gave up and walked off stage shaking his head – which was all part of the act of course.

The crowd were loving it and thought the clowns were hilarious – well, apart from the distraught little girl and her angry parents.

Then after a little while longer, the ringmaster came back on and finally ushered the clowns off to hearty applause, putting a stop to the mayhem, and then began introducing the next artists.

The four novice clowns had done extremely well for their first time, and as they came off stage all the other artists congratulated them. "That was fun!" said Gary.

And after a couple more appearances, performing hilarious slapstick skits in between the other acts: chasing one another around the ring, bashing each other over the head with a large rubber club; accidentally smacking one another in the face with a plank, kicking each other up the backside, stepping on one another's toes; pushing each other over on the floor; throwing custard pies at each other, and generally being violent and getting away with it, the time had arrived in the programme for the clowns main slot.

The ringmaster, with some trepidation, then introduced the clowns once again. Out they came, laughing and joking to lots of cheers and applause from the audience. Eric and Jack were carrying an old-fashioned, tin, washing tub between them. Gary was carrying a bucket full of water in each hand. While Emily was carrying a laundry basket overflowing with colourful and comical-looking clown clothes under one arm, and an over-sized scrubbing brush in the other. They were about to perform the classic clown Wash Day routine.

They set everything down in the centre ring, and everything started quite civilised. Gary first poured water from one of the buckets into the tub. Then Emily dunked an enormous pair of spotted underpants into the water – holding her nose for comic effect as she did – and started scrubbing away.

But it didn't take long before the clowns started flicking water at each other, and before you knew it, one thing led to another, and a water fight broke out – much to the sheer enjoyment of the crowd. Emily quickly grabbed the remaining bucket of water and tipped it over Gary's head, soaking him. The audience howled with laughter. Eric and Jack quickly looked at each other as if to say, "She seems to have enjoyed doing that a bit too much." Then Jack pushed Eric backwards into the tub of water, not noticing Emily creeping up behind him. She tapped Jack on the shoulder, and as soon as he turned around, she pushed him backwards into the tub on top of Eric.

Meanwhile, Gary had sneaked off to get another bucket of water. And it was at this point that things started to go disastrously wrong! He was supposed to pick up the bucket of confetti to throw at the audience, but something switched off in his brain, and he picked up the bucket full of water instead. He then immediately started chasing Emily around the ring determined to get his own back on her. The crowd by now were rolling up with laughter.

After being chased around the ring a few times, as rehearsed, she then stopped right beside the front row of the audience, with her back towards them, pretending to get her breath back. Gary then did a run-up and threw the bucket of water towards her. She immediately bent over and dodged the water as it went all over the front row of the audience, soaking them. Mostly landing on the same little girl he squirted water at earlier. She immediately started crying her eyes out again, and both her extremely angry parents, who were also soaked, then climbed over the barrier, and started chasing Gary the clown around the ring. All chaos had broken loose.

The audience thought it was all part of the act and were in hysterics as they watched the clown chased by members of the audience and slipping all over the place.

The other clowns looked on, motionless, not believing their eyes. "What happened to the confetti?" Jack asked Eric, who were still stuck in the tub.

"Your guess is as good as mine!" replied Eric, just as bewildered.

The music started and the Ringmaster and stage crew came immediately running out. "I can't believe what he's gone and done!" said the ringmaster. He then spoke into the mic as some of the stage crew joined in the chase, trying to stop the parents from killing Gary.

"Ladies and Gentlemen. Let's hear it for the clowns!" said the ringmaster, trying to carry on as if nothing untoward had happened.

Meanwhile, as the ringmaster was trying to restore some order and calm on the mic, Gary was still running for his life – which is not the easiest thing to do with enormous, big clown boots on – and Emily was helping Jack and Eric out of the tub.

The stage crew managed to catch up with the furious parents and stop them just in time before they collared the rogue clown. They were then unhappily escorted back to their seats. "That clown's a *psycho!*" said the father. "He's had it in for us from the start!" Gary meanwhile had quickly darted threw the stage curtain and made his escape, running all the way home dressed as a clown.

The three remaining clowns smiled and waved goodbye to the audience as they made their exit. And as soon as the stage crew had cleared and prepared the circus ring for the next act, the ringmaster quickly introduced them; then made a beeline for the disgruntled parents and their child, who were heading for the main entrance to leave. The ringmaster tried his best to appease them with his limited English vocabulary, offering to give the child a free stick of candy floss. The parents promptly told him where to stick it and said they would never come to their rubbish circus again.

Suffice to say, the four children didn't get asked to be clowns there again, and Gary certainly didn't get any free candy floss. But the fun they had that summer more than made up for it!

CHAPTER FOUR

A RUDE AWAKENING!

As Eric picked up the last remaining playing card from his Las Vegas showroom dressing room floor, his smile faded, as did the fond memories of the fun times he once had with his friends, as the dire reality of his current situation came flooding back to him.

He squared the now less than perfect pack of cards, still feeling shaken by his uninvited Mafia guest's ultimatum, and put his loyal fifty-two cardboard assistants safely back into their own little box of a dressing room. Right now, they felt like the only real friends he had out there. He got up from the floor and changed his shirt again for one that wasn't soaked from sweat or ripped – a blue one this time, which reflected his mood. He then left, closing the door behind him, and made his way through the unusually quiet and abandoned showroom and into the bustling and noisy atmosphere of the casino.

He no longer felt in the mood to meet up with the others and decided he would get a taxi to his apartment instead. He was renting a ground floor apartment in an area called Flamingo Heights, which was only about ten minutes' drive from the Vegas Strip. It had a swimming pool and jacuzzi and was somewhere quiet he could relax.

As he walked across the casino floor, beeping slot machines seemed to surround him and beckon him closer from all directions, tempting him to come and pull their handles. He resisted, but the blackjack tables he was about to encounter could be too much of a temptation.

Should he gamble the last $1,000 cash he had and turn it into $50,000, so he could pay back the money he owed to the mobsters, he thought. He was a magician after all. Just focus on the gleaming brass door handles ahead of you, and keep walking straight out the building, he kept saying to himself.

It wasn't much cooler in there either, evident by the sweat still oozing from out of every pore. All he had to do was get past the row of blackjack tables and it was a home run. Surely, he could manage that this time.

"Hiya, Mr Fartzini!" called out one of the drop-dead gorgeous female dealers, stood sticking her chest out behind one of the tables. It was the same dealer that took $500.00 off him at the blackjack table a couple of nights back – he recognized the alluring voice. "Hi, Jasmin!" he said, offering her a quick glance. His pace quickened. Two more tables only to pass, he reassured himself.

"… Hi, can I get choo a drink?" asked the waitress.

"Sure! A JD and Coke, please," said Eric as he removed his wad of cash from his hip pocket and made himself comfortable at the blackjack table.

Six hours – and too many JD and Coke's to remember the minutes – later, Eric finally persuaded himself to leave the casino and go home. It was almost midnight, but you'd be mistaken for thinking it was daytime with all the neon lights lighting up the sky.

And with just enough money to afford the cab ride home, he hailed a taxi on the Strip and got in.

"Hey, your face looks familiar to me," said the cab driver, trying to puzzle his brains as to where he'd seen him before. The clue was the massive poster of him smiling away on the billboard right in front of them, with the name The Amazing Fartzini written above his head.

"Oh yeah?" Eric just replied.

"Yeah! I just can't put my finger on it," he replied. "Anyway, where to boss?"

"Flamingo Heights Apartments, please."

The bright yellow cab pulled away and headed north along the Strip. "You sound like you're from Australia," said the chatty driver.

"Close! The UK," said Eric jokingly, slurring slightly, and thinking, "Why do the Yanks always think Brits are from Australia?"

"I'm Joey, by the way."

"Pleased to meet you Joey."

"… Oh, I know where I know you from. Aren't choo that magician fella performing at the Excalibur?" said the driver, convinced he'd nailed it.

"No," answered Eric. "You must be mixing

me up with some one else." He didn't feel much like talking after losing heavily again at the casino.

"Well, you sure do look and sound just like him! Isn't that strange – I could have *sworn* it was you! I watched him perform a while back – are you sure that you are not him? What's his name? He's got a weird sounding name – *Fartzini!*"

"You mean, The *Amazing* Fartzini," said Eric, correcting him as they passed the magnificent Bellagio fountains on the left.

"Yeah, yeah, that's the one!" The driver glanced at his mirror again, staring at his disheveled passenger. Then said, "His show's good but, it ain't as good as that other magic show that's now on at the brand-new resort that's just opened opposite!"

"Oh, really?" said Eric, thinking, can his day get any worse.

The driver indicated left, then turned and went along West Flamingo Road. "Yeah, my wife and I went to see the opening show a few nights back. It was super-cool! I've never seen anything so spectacular! We were right at the front, and I still can't work out where that white tiger appeared from!"

The magician staring in the rival magic show was an American named Chet Stevenson. He was a flashy type of guy, not particularly good looking, of medium build with longish dark hair, and had a great big bald patch, who was about ten or more years Eric's senior.

The cab driver went on to explain everything he saw in the show without missing a detail, and Eric slid down in his seat and just listened, nodding, and faintly smiling occasionally.

"Here we are," said the driver as he pulled over by the curb outside the entrance to the gated community apartments where Eric lived. And if they hadn't of arrived when they did, the cab driver would've still carried on talking about the fantastic rival magic show.

"Keep the change!" said Eric as he handed over his last crumpled-up $20.00 bill. "I'll only blow it at the casino's anyway!" If Eric hadn't of felt so low: for a bit of fun, he would usually have pretended to pluck the money out of thin air. But not on this occasion – and especially not after hearing how good the other magician was.

"Thank you!" replied the driver, smiling at the generous tip. "I get the impression it wasn't your lucky night?"

"No," Eric just replied, despondently.

"Gambling is for suckers, man – didn't anyone ever tell you dat?" said the driver as if speaking from experience … Hey, by the way, I never did catch your name?"

"The Ama—" Eric started to say. "Eric – just plain Eric," he finished saying as he stepped out into the balmy night and shut the cab door.

Eric punched in the code to open the gates, struggling for a moment to remember the last digit.

"OPEN SESEME!" he called out, which sounds the same whether you're drunk or not.

"HEY, QUIET DOWN THERE!" someone shouted from a nearby upstairs window.

"Sorry!" he replied in an exaggerated whispered voice as he meandered along the shrub lined path leading to his apartment.

As soon as he got inside, he poured himself a generous measure of JD straight up, then plonked himself down on the sofa and switched on the TV. Then after flicking from one annoying advertising or Evangelical preaching channel to another, he decided to switch it off and just sat there quietly, with only Jack Daniels as company, feeling dejected.

"It ain't as good as that other magic show!" and *"I've never seen anything so spectacular!"* he kept repeating in his head, tormenting himself by reciting what the cab driver had said.

He wished now that he'd have gone and joined all the others at the new resort. Then he wouldn't have blown all his money on the blackjack tables, and, he would have been able to go and see if the other magic show was as good as people say it is.

And after castigating himself for being such a fool for losing all that money, he closed his eyes and drifted off to sleep, slumped where he was.

He once said, he would never become like his father, who was a gambler and an alcoholic, but his addictive personality seemed to be leading him down that same sorrowful path.

He hadn't seen his father, Peter Richardson, in a long time. The last time he saw him was when he was still at school, age twelve. One weekend, sometime in June, he took the National Express Coach from Ramsgate to Sheffield all by himself, without telling anyone. And what he saw when he got there, you would've thought would have put anyone off gambling and drinking for life!

He was terribly upset at the time: he'd only recently found out from his mum that his dad had tried to contact them several times since the pair of them split up about eight months prior. Plus, to make matters worse, unbeknownst to him, his father had once even paid a visit to their flat and watched him perform in the school Christmas talent show. And subsequently when he confronted her about it, she tried to deny it at first, but eventually owned up and admitted it.

Eric knew the reason why his mum hadn't told him was to protect him but was outraged that she had kept it a secret from him all that time. And partly as a way of protest, and because he felt the need to go and see his father, he made the decision one day to visit him. He didn't want to upset or worry his mum, but he knew if he had told her about his plans, she wouldn't have let him go.

And so, early on a dismal rainy day, one weekend, sometime in September, there he was, sat by himself on a coach bound for his hometown, staring out of the window at the bleak sky.

Meanwhile his mum had awoken to find her son nowhere to be seen. And as the day went on, she became more and more worried as to his whereabouts. She tried phoning him, but he had switched his phone off. She phoned the parents of all his friends and they didn't know either. Then went out looking for him to no avail.

As he boarded another coach at the bustling coach station in London, he could hear several Sheffield accents, which made him feel more at ease, reminding him of home – his real home. He performed a few cards tricks on the coach for the strangers sat near to him, which helped to pass the time on the long journey.

"You're young to be travelling on your own, aren't ya?" asked a woman travelling with her husband and son to visit their relatives in Sheffield. Eric just smiled. "How old are you?"

"Sixteen," answered Eric, trying to speak in a more grown-up, deeper voice. The couple looked at each other as if to say, "Yeah, right. Who are you kidding?"

"I'm Shane," said the husband.

"And I'm Angela," she said. "And the lad wearing the earphones is our son, Jake. Nice to meet ya … What's your name?"

"… I'm Eric. I'm going to see my dad … I take the coach up to see him every weekend."

"Oh, that's nice. So, where's your mu—?" she said before being cut off.

"I'm hoping he's going to take me to see the Blades play at home!" he said excitedly.

She quickly got the impression that his parents had split up and decided she wouldn't ask him about it in case it upset him. "Well, I hope so for you." …

In the one tense conversation Eric had with his mum about his dad, she didn't say a lot, as it upset her too much to talk about him and she didn't want to re-open old wounds. She told him that his father was getting help with his drinking problem and trying to sort his life out.

The coach arrived at the Archway Centre Station in Sheffield City Centre early-afternoon, where Eric said goodbye to the friendly people he had met.

"Are you *sure* you don't need any help?" they asked.

"I'm sure," Eric replied.

"Well, take care of yourself. Tarra!" the family called out as Eric wondered off by himself in the direction of the bus stop.

At first, he was a bit disorientated, but was soon travelling on a Stagecoach bus to the area where he once lived, north of the city. He couldn't wait to see his dad.

Once off the bus, he quickly weaved his way along roads, streets, avenues, and lanes, until he finally arrived at the beginning of Merlin Way. The houses even form a circular shape, like King Arthur's table, with a small green in the middle with trees all around it.

Memories – some good, some bad – immediately came flooding back to him. This was the place he grew up; where he used to play outside with the neighbours children, ride his bike, and where he used to kick a ball around with his dad.

His heart started beating faster and faster the nearer he got to his old house. He was both excited and nervous all at the same time – even a little scared.

"Twenty-four … twenty-six … twenty-eight," Eric started counted to himself as he got close. He suddenly stopped in front of his old house and just stared, perplexed. He was trying to compute what his eyes were clearly seeing and what his brain was still trying to fathom out. "This must be a mistake?" he thought. "This can't be!" He was staring at a signpost sticking out from amongst the weeds of the overgrown front lawn, reading: "For

Sale". The house looked empty and derelict.

Just then, a passerby walked past.

"Excuse, please. Do you live around here?" asked Eric.

"Aye," said the elderly man.

"Would ya happen to know where the man who lived here has moved to?"

The man could see the boy looked concerned. "No, I don't, I'm afraid," answered the man. "All I know is, he lost his job, and when he got behind with his mortgage repayments, the property was repossessed and had to move out. What a commotion that was: the police had to be called to assist with the eviction – and to be honest, the whole neighbourhood was glad to see the back of 'im! He was often drunk and would make a lot of noise and get angry and aggressive towards the other residents." He then shook his head and went on to say, "It's tragic really! First his wife and son left him, then he got into debt, and *God* knows *where* he's ended up!"

Eric just stood there and listened with tearful eyes. Though, he tried his best to hold them back.

"Why, did ya know him?" asked the man.

"… I used to," Eric just replied after a

moment of reflection. He immediately turned and ran as fast as he could back the way he came, tears now running down his little face. It was no longer the magical place he once knew!

Both his grandparents on his father's side had passed away a few years ago and he had lost touch with the other family members. And so, with a heavy heart, he got on a bus again and headed back to the city centre with no hope of finding his father.

When he arrived, he decided to have a quick look around, and walked through the busy shopping area of Fargate to see if anything had changed since he was last there and get a snack before catching an earlier than planned coach back to Ramsgate.

After having a bite to eat, Eric made his way back through the busy pedestrianised street on his way to the coach station. As he was about to pass the entrance to a closed down empty shop premises, he saw a dirty, scruffy-looking, unshaven man with long straggly unkempt hair, sat huddled in the corner of the doorway with his head down, clutching onto can of beer.

The desperate-looking homeless man looked up and said, "Change, please." Eric reached into his pocket for some small change to give the poor beggar. And as Eric got nearer to hand him the change, he was immediately aware of an awful smell: the man was sitting in a puddle of his own urine.

"*Dad?* Dad is that you?" suddenly asked Eric. Eric didn't want to believe what he was seeing and involuntarily shook his head. "It's me, your son!"

The man at first seemed to recognise him, but quickly covered his face as if in shame. Then hurriedly got up and brushed past him, saying, "No, you're mistaken! Go away! Leave me alone!" and ran off into the crowd. Eric called after him, but he was gone. That was the last Eric saw of his father.

After a very upsetting and traumatic day, Eric finally arrived back at the flat in Ramsgate later that evening, where his mum had been desperately waiting for him to come home. She immediately hugged and kissed him. He told her where he had been and what he had seen, and after mildly telling him off and telling him never do that again, they both had a long much needed talk and cleared the air between them.

It had been a rude awakening for both. Lies can sometimes hurt, but the truth can sometimes hurt even more!

CHAPTER FIVE

THE RIVAL MAGIC SHOW

Eric woke up late the next morning in his Las Vegas apartment sporting a hangover. He slowly sat up on his sofa, thinking, "Never again." Mind you, that's what he said the last time, and the time before that. But a little later, as his brain gradually began piecing together the unpleasant and sorrowful events of the day before, while sipping on strong black coffee, he knew he had to put an end to his irresponsible behaviour.

Somehow, he had to break those bad habits of his and get himself back on track, if he were to make a good life for Emily and him. There seemed to be a pattern forming: the more money he lost gambling, the more he drank. The trouble was: in the city that never sleeps, there were temptations every which way you turned.

A good fry-up, and a few more strong cups of black coffee later, he put on his Ray-Ban sunglasses and headed out the door. Several voice messages from Gloria earlier that morning informed him that the resort's air conditioning was now functioning again, and there was a matinee show that afternoon. And judging by the way she sounded, she too was suffering from a hangover.

He arrived backstage and headed straight for his dressing room to prepare for the show, looking much the worse for wear. Ruben hurriedly minced passed him from behind with his tightly squeezed buttocks on display through his tight, shimmering, lycra leggings. "You're cutting it a bit fine, aren't choo darling?" he said haughtily as he continued walking and talking with his back towards Eric. "Hurry up or the show will have to carry on without choo!"

"Alright – don't get your G-string in a twist!" replied Eric. Eric then laughed to himself, thinking, "It'll be a very short show without me!"

Ruben always walked fast and talked even faster. He was from Manhattan, New York, and although he minced when he walked, he never minced his words. Ruben was someone Eric quickly learned not to trust, as he had made it quite clear that he didn't like Eric – and on more than one occasion had caused trouble and tried to have him fired. Indeed, the cast all had to tread carefully with him, as he had the ear of the show producer, who was his boyfriend and did the hiring and the firing. And if Ruben had his way, it would be an all-dancing show.

Suddenly, there was a knock, knock on Eric's door, which immediately startled him. *"Who's there?"* he called out nervously, fearing it could be the mobsters again.

"It's only me!" called back Gloria from the other side of the door.

"Oh, hiya Gloria," said Eric as he unlocked and opened the door, feeling extremely relieved it was only her.

"You're jumpy, aren't you!" she said as she poked her head into dressing room. "Where did you get to last night?"

"Don't ask – let's just say I didn't make it that

far."

"Oh dear," she said, knowing full well what that meant.

"You've got to quit gambling!"

"I know, I know!" he replied. "Anyroad, sounds like you had a good time last night."

"Yeah, you missed a great night, honey."

"Did you go and watch the rival magic show?" asked Eric, curious.

"… No, it was full!" just said Gloria, shaking her head. Then added, "But some of the others did, including Ruben and his producer boyfriend," she answered. She then spoke in a much quieter voice. "… After the show, while I was at the bar, I overheard Ruben saying to him –" She then paused to look left and right along the corridor. "… Saying, he thought their magic show was *much* better than yours and advised the director that he should replace you with another magician!"

Eric laughed. "Now why doesn't that surprise me?"

"I think, he's got it in for you – you should be careful!" warned Gloria.

Suddenly they could hear two loud claps. "There's no time to be chatting – hurry up and join the others on ssstage!" called out Ruben, not looking happy – which was nothing unusual.

"Thanks for letting me know, Gloria. Let's chat later," said Eric, hurrying to finish getting ready as he slung his Merlin robe on and quickly fastened it up.

"Sure, honey," quickly replied Gloria, and rushed to join the other dancers.

Eric quickly closed the door and locked it again. But no sooner had he sat down at his dressing table, there was another knock, knock at the door – only this time, much louder.

There was a momentary uneasy silence. "Eric are you in there?" called out Jim, which made Eric jump. He then got up again and let Jim in.

"Hi Jim, how are you doin'?" asked Eric with his beard half hanging off.

"Better than you are by the look of it," answered Jim, bluntly. "I shan't ask where you got to last night, but you missed a good night."

"Yeah, so I just heard."

"The new magic show was *awesome!* But to be honest, apart from their showroom having a lot more seating capacity, a much bigger stage, far more up-to-date state of the art lighting, and the show having more dancers, more spectacular illusions, and white tigers, it was no different than your show! The magician performed a lot of the same tricks that you do, and he even closed the show with the same illusion as you do – only instead of the magician being impaled – it's one of the white tigers!"

"*Oh, right!*" said Eric, slightly shocked. "… *Wow! Amazing!*" Then thinking, "I bet animal rights activists would have something to say about that!"

"*Stuffed*, of course!" then remarked Jim. Eric just raised his eyes brows. "… We were lucky to get a seat because it was a full house, and they were even turning people away at the door!"

"Yeah?" said Eric as he straightened his beard, now feeling even more inferior and depressed, and wishing Jim hadn't told him.

"Yeah, and apparently, it's been full ever since it opened last week!"

"Well, alright, Jim, I better finish getting ready. See ya later," said Eric as he ushered him out of the door …

The show got underway, once again playing to only a half-full house, and Eric went and hid in his opening illusion cabinet, relieved that the air conditioning was once again working. And, after the compère finally finished talking, The Amazing Fartzini made his appearance as Merlin and got on with the rest of his act.

His magic act still consisted of some of the magic tricks he performed when he first started: "Air-bourne Glass", "Six Card Repeat", "The Ring in the Nest of Boxes", "The Siberian Chain Escape", and so on. Which, over the years, he honed to perfection. The show also contained several large-scale illusions, including his finale, the "Impalement Illusion".

In this jaw-dropping illusion, The Amazing Fartzini first pulls a sword out of a stone-like prop structure, in keeping with the Arthurian *Sword in the Stone* theme of the Excalibur Resort. Then after a bit more theatrical dramatics, the sword is put back in place the other way around, with the point of the sword projecting uppermost. His assistants then raise him and balance him by the small of his back on the tip of the sword, where he remains suspended. They then spin him quickly around, and to the utter shock and horror of the audience, his body suddenly drops sharply downwards, giving the impression of being impaled by the tip of the sword. Then just as dramatically, he appears to levitate himself off the sword, and the invincible magician is helped down by his assistants to a rousing round of applause.

Well, that's what's supposed to happen anyway. For some reason, on this occasion, when it came to the moment when he was supposed to fall downwards onto the tip of the sword, nothing happened; he just remained there motionless, suspended in midair for what seemed like an eternity. Eventually, Eric had to stage whisper to his assistants to unhook him and get him down.

Then after taking a quicker than usual bow, he and his assistants exited the stage to an embarrassing lukewarm response, puzzled as to what could have gone wrong.

Then as soon as the stage was cleared, the dancers, who were already waiting in the wings, came bounding on stage to close the show with their energetic and spectacular finale number.

"I don't understand it, Gloria?" said Eric as he came off the stage, disappointed. "The mechanism normally *never* fails!" Gloria just shrugged her shoulders as if to say, if you don't understand it, then I certainly don't.

Gloria joined Eric in his dressing room for a much-needed chat. Eric closed the door and locked it just in case anyone might be eavesdropping – and of course in case the mobsters should suddenly show up again.

"When I get the chance, I will examine the Impalement Illusion to find out why it failed to operate," said Eric as both sat down and made themselves comfortable. "I even checked it before the show!"

"D'ya think someone has tampered with it?" said Gloria, raising her eyebrows.

"Who knows?" he replied, shrugging his shoulders. "I doubt it – but if someone did tamper with it, they will have a lot to answer for – that could be extremely dangerous!"

"Well, I told ya already that Ruben's got it in for ya," then said his assistant. "That *snake* was in the wings all the while we were on stage and would've had plenty of time to tamper with it. I wouldn't mind betting he had something to do with it!"

Just then, they heard the compère announce the end of the show; and soon after, the dancers come stampeding down the stage steps and along the corridor.

"Well done girls!" called out Ruben purposely out loud as he passed Eric's dressing room. "Who needs a *magic act* anyway, right girls?"

A few of the troublesome dancers made loud whooping noises. "Ya got dat right!" said Rhonda. "Amen to that!" said Candy.

Gloria jokingly made an "Arrrrgh!" sound, while making a downwards clawing action, which made Eric laugh. "Take no notice, honey – they're just a bunch of silly, small-minded people who are just jealous that you have your own show, and they don't, that's all!"

"Listen, I've got something far more serious to worry about than them right now," said Eric, solemnly.

"What? You mean, someone tampering –"

"No, something *much* worse!"

Eric leaned forward and explained. "Yesterday after you left, the Mafia paid me a visit – I thought they were gonna *kill* me!"

"Oh my *God!*" exclaimed Gloria, looking as if her eyes were about to pop out of her head. "Are you *serious?*"

"Deadly!" said Eric.

"Gambling debts, I bet," she said, knowing already how he liked to gamble. Eric nodded. "What sort of money d'ya owe them?"

"The sort of money I haven't got!" he replied as he got up to pour himself a whisky, only to find the bottle he had stashed away in a drawer was as empty as his wallet.

"Drinking won't solve your problems," said Gloria, giving him a stern look.

"No, ya right," agreed Eric. "… They've given me just a week to pay back $50,000." Eric plonked himself back down on his chair again.

"A week! $50.000.00!" shrieked Gloria.

"Shh! Keep ya voice down!" said Eric just in case someone was eavesdropping.

"Boy, you are in serious trouble!"

"Yeah, well, I should have paid the loan off by now, but out of the kindness of their hearts they've extended it," he disclosed. "… It all started off as just a small loan to tide me over until I got paid, but when that wasn't forthcoming, I borrowed more and more money to try and win back what I'd lost gambling so I could pay off the escalating debt. And before I knew it; it just spiralled out of control – I had no idea I was dealing with the Mafia!"

"So, obvious question, what are ya gonna do?" asked Gloria.

"I need to speak with my manager and get him to cough up the money he owes me," said Eric.

"While you're at it, can you ask him to pay us dancers the money he owes us as well?"

"I can pull a sword out of a stone, but not *blood!*" quipped Eric.

Gloria chuckled, knowing exactly what he meant, as it was always difficult to get Mr Goldberg to part with any money. And he was invariably late paying his artistes.

"*If,* you can get him to cough up the money in time, will you have enough to pay the Mafia back then?"

Eric nodded. "Yeah, just about, I think. And if I can't get the money to them in time, somewhere, if I can find them, I have some rare and collectible 'Superman' comics and a first edition *Harry Potter and the Philosophers Stone* book I could offer them instead!"

Gloria's head sharply moved backwards, and her eyebrows shot upwards in disbelief, speechless. "Oh yeah, *that'll* work!" finally came out of her mouth.

"*What?* They're worth a lot of money, I'll have you know. And if they are not interested – well, they can only kill me once!"

"Oh, *don't* say that – think positive! Anyway, honey, I better be going, I've got loads of stuff to do. You take care now. *Laters!*" she said, blowing him a kiss. "Give Goldberg a ring asap – and *stay* away from the casinos!"

"I will – see ya," Eric replied as she was leaving. "Remember to keep it quiet!"

Shortly afterwards, when there was no one around backstage, Eric went to investigate why the Impalement Illusion had malfunctioned – they still had two shows to perform that evening.

It didn't take him long to find out the truth. Gloria's suspicions were correct. Someone *had* tampered with the mechanism to prevent it from operating. And whoever that someone was must have done it deliberately – because wires don't cut themselves!

Fortunately, Eric soon had the illusion working again ready for the evening shows, much to his relief.

"I wonder why someone would do that?" he thought to himself as he headed back to his dressing room. "Someone with a grudge or a motive to prevent me from performing here – *that's* who!" Eric's suspicions immediately turned to Ruben.

All that week, Eric continued performing his show to demoralising half-full houses, keeping extra vigilant to ensure that no one tampered with his magic props – especially keeping a close eye on Ruben. He also continued to keep his dressing room door locked, nervously half expecting Tony One Shoe and his heavies to turn up earlier than expected, banging on the door demanding his money. And everywhere he went, he would look over his shoulder, worried they might be following him, and pounce on him at any moment.

Every day he tried ringing his manager, unable to speak to him, with the same poor old excuse from his secretary that he was in an important meeting and to try again another day.

I mean, Eric couldn't simply tell his manager that he needed the money to pay back the Mafia – it wouldn't exactly show him in a good light. And no entertainment management would want to employ someone who was involved with the Mafia – it would give them a bad reputation.

On Friday afternoon, before the matinee show, Eric was in the corridor, when the new dancer from the UK came by.

"Oh, hi! I'm Sasha, by the way," she said, smiling broadly and holding her dainty hand out to be shaken. "Nice to meet you." She was a natural blonde and very attractive.

"I'm Eric – nice to meet ya too," he replied, shaking her hand, and smiling back.

"I *know* who you are! I think you're a *really* good magician!"

"Oh, ta!" he replied, now smiling even more. "It's nice to hear a British accent for a change – whereabouts are you from then?"

"Chelsea, London," she answered in her well-spoken voice as they both continued making eye contact with one another and smiling.

"So, how's it going?" asked Eric, making himself comfortable, leaning against the wall.

"… Okay, I suppose," she answered. "Ruben can be a bit *shouty* at times."

"Yeah, I know what ya mean, Sasha," said Eric. "Don't let him bother ya – if ya have any trouble from him, come and see me, and I'll sort him out for ya."

"Oh, you're so sweet," said Sasha, blinking her eyelids. "I can detect a slight northern accent, can't I?"

"I'm originally from Sheffield but moved down to Ramsgate when I was little."

"Ramsgate? Where's that?"

"It's very near to Margate – you must have

heard of Margate"

"Yes, my parents used to take my sister and me there on the train so we could go to the beach – I have very fond childhood memories of visiting Margate."

Just then, Gloria came walking by, and seeing the two of them chatting cosily together, gave them a blank look and just carried on walking straight passed them on her way to her dressing room.

"Hiya Gloria!" Eric called out to no answer, thinking, "What's gotten into her?"

Eric and Sasha just carried on laughing and joking and rekindling happy memories of back home. Eric liked Sasha, and immediately felt comfortable with her.

A little later, he removed his pack of cards from his pocket and offered to show her a card trick. "Oh, I *love* card tricks!" she exclaimed excitedly.

"Take a card, Sasha – any card you like," said Eric as he offered her a selection from the spread. "Now, please remember the card and sign your name across the face of it." Eric gave her a pen and looked away while she did this. "… Now put the card back somewhere in the middle of the pack." Once she had done that,

Eric shuffled the cards until they were thoroughly mixed-up. He next wrapped the pack securely together with an elastic band. Sasha looked on curious as to what Eric would do next. "Now watch!" he said. He then tossed the pack of cards upwards into the air, causing it to spin quickly. Both their eyes following it as it made its ascent. The fifty-two cards thudded against the high corridor ceiling, and to Sasha's utter astonishment, as they bounced off, her chosen and signed card remained stuck to it!

"*Wow!* That was amazing!" she exclaimed, impressed.

"Thanks!" he said, smiling. And judging by the number of other playing cards left stuck up there, he'd performed this trick quite a few times before.

Ten minutes later when Gloria came out of her dressing room, Eric and Sasha were still chatting. As she approached them, she gave Sasha the daggers.

"Have you spoken to your *girlfriend*, Emily, today, Eric?" asked Gloria, not waiting for an answer as she made her way to the stage.

"I think she likes you, Eric," then said Sasha, smiling and raising her eyebrows. "I don't think she likes me talking to you, though."

"No, I doubt that's true!" said Eric. "She's alright once you get to know her."

"Yeah, you're probably right."

More and more dancers then started coming out of their dressing room to go to the stage for Rubens pre-show warm-up session. As Candy and Rhonda walked past Eric and Sasha, Candy made fun of them, saying something rude in a posh British accent. Upon which, Candy and Rhonda burst out laughing.

Eric didn't quite catch what Candy had said but knew her rude and derogatory remark was about them. Upon which, Eric looked directly at Candy and responded by saying, "Candy, your mouth is *bigger* than the Grand Canyon!" Which immediately shut the two troublemakers up. Then it was Eric and Sasha's turn to laugh.

Meanwhile, Gloria was having a quiet word in Ruben's ear. "That new girl from the UK is idly chatting with Eric – I just thought you should know, that's all."

"*Oh,* is she now," said Ruben, displeased. "Well, I'll *sssoon* put a *ssstop* to that!" Ruben immediately pirouetted away from Gloria and went to find Sasha in a huff. "Hurry up girls!"

he said to Candy and Rhonda, clapping his hands together, who were just arriving for the warm-up class.

"You'd better get going or Ruben won't be very happy," said Eric to Sasha.

"Yeah, well, it was nice talking to you," Sasha replied, giving him one last smile before she left.

"Likewise!" said Eric. He then went back into his dressing room and locked the door.

Ruben was waiting for her at the top of the backstage steps with both hands firmly on his hips. "Get up her now!" he shouted angrily at her, instantly managing to change her mood from happy to sad.

As soon as the matinee finished that day, Eric gave his manager another phone call from his dressing room. He should still be able to catch him in his office, he thought. His secretary, whose name was Barbara answered the phone.

"Goldberg Entertainments Inc. *All* your entertainment requirements catered for – how may I help you?" said Barbara, audibly chewing gum down the phone.

"Hi Barbara, it's Eric Fartz here … The Amazing Fartzini."

"… Oh, hi Eric! How are ya – what can I do

for ya today?" she said with the phone propped up against her ear while at the same time doing her nails and watching one of the shopping channels. She knew full well what he was ringing about – the same thing he'd been ringing about everyday that week.

"Can you put me through to Mr Goldberg, please?" asked Eric, now desperate to speak to him and demand the already two months late money that's owed him.

"Just a second," she answered. She put the phone down on her desk, carried on applying pink nail polish to her exceptionally long manicured nails, keeping Eric waiting on the other end until she'd finished.

"… Hi Eric. *Sorry,* but he's extremely busy in an important meeting and won't be back in the office until after the weekend I am afraid. Try him again then."

"Oh yeah? *Sure,* he is – can't you come up with a different excuse for a change?" thought Eric, feeling slightly miffed. But said, "Well, can't you at least give me his cell or home number, please – so I can ring him this evening?"

"No, I'm sorry, but I am not allowed to share private details. Can I take a message for you?"

"Yes, please tell him I called, and that I need to speak to him urgently!" he said to the well-trained secretary.

"Sure! Bye!" She then abruptly put the phone down.

"She would make a good magicians assistant," thought Eric, "because she's good at keeping secrets." They're called *secret*-aries' for a reason!

Eric was fed up with not being paid and continually fobbed off. Then he remembered Mr Goldberg likes to play golf on Saturday mornings at the Bali Hai Golf Club on the Strip. So, he decided that if his manager won't answer his calls, then he would have to go and pay him a visit there!

CHAPTER SIX

BALI HAI GOLF CLUB

The next morning at around 10 am, Eric made his way by taxi over to the five-star Bali Hai Golf Club on the Las Vegas Strip. He hadn't slept much the night before, worrying about paying off his debt, and was feeling anxious about confronting Mr Goldberg over unpaid fees. He was not the easiest of people to discuss things with, especially when it came to money.

And when it comes to artistes obtaining fees owed to them by their managers, it is always a fine line as to how far one is prepared to cross to retrieve it. Eric was fully aware that in this fickle business, called "Show", as the old saying goes: "You're only as good as your last performance!" And his magic show wasn't exactly "smashing it" at the Excalibur any longer, and if he continued to attract less than full houses, the show could be dropped at any time.

So, considering this, he thought it would be best to tread carefully and be discreet when speaking to his manager, adopting a more measured approach, rather than going in with full guns blazing as it were and upset him.

The temperature was already 32 degrees centigrade and rising when Eric got out of the air-conditioned taxi and into the Vegas heat. He was wearing a pale blue Polo shirt, white shorts showing off his tanned legs, a white baseball cap, and his designer sunglasses, looking the part – though, he wasn't a member, and he'd never played golf in his life.

As he approached the club house, he could see groups of golfers already on the fairway. "I expect Mr Goldberg is amongst them," he thought. Mr Goldberg was a keen golfer and took it very seriously. He played off a low handicap and was extremely competitive – often he would play for high stakes.

While travelling from his apartment over to

the golf club, Eric had been thinking about what Mr Goldberg had said to him in his dressing room a couple of days ago about performing the Bullet Catch as his finale. He had to agree that if he were to win the audiences back and compete with the new rival magic show, then he would need something sensational in his show that people would flock to see. And there was no question in his mind that the death-defying Bullet Catch would fit the bill perfectly.

He already knew a certain amount about how it was originally performed but would have to do a lot more research before attempting such a dangerous magic trick stunt.

As Eric walked past the club house reception desk, he flashed one of his winning smiles at the gorgeous young receptionist behind the desk, and winked at her, thinking, "Well, that was easy." But just when he was about to walk through the double doors leading to the fairway, he heard, *"Excuse me sir,* but are you a member?"

Thinking quick on his feet, he spotted a membership card that someone must have accidentally dropped on the floor and picked it up, acting as if he'd just dropped it. "Clumsy me!" he said, smiling again as he walked back to the desk and handed the card over to her.

She smiled back, looked down at the card and said, "Thank you, Mr Nagasaki – have a great day!" and handed him back the card. Eric said thank you, turned sharply and quickly headed for the fairway, desperately trying hard not to laugh.

Once on the edge of the magnificent fairway, with its beautiful surroundings of exotic foliage, towering palm trees, water features, pure white sand, and spectacular views of the famed Strip on one side and the Nevada mountains as a backdrop on the other, Eric spotted an empty golf cart.

It would have taken him a long time to catch up with Mr Goldberg, so he quickly jumped in it and drove off.

"Nē, anata wa kurutta otoko koko ni modotte kite!" shouted an angry group of Japanese men standing nearby, shaking their fists at him. Which, basically translated into English means: "Hey, come back here you nutter!" Eric didn't notice them as he tore his way bumpily down the fairway at top speed with his mind solely focused on finding Mr Goldberg.

Narrowly avoiding a bunker and hitting a

palm tree, Eric spotted a group of golfers up ahead on the par three course, and one of them looked as if it could be him – his huge frame was hard to miss. And so, with golf balls whizzing past him, he put the pedal to the metal and continued after him in hot pursuit. He had swiftly abandoned the softly, softly approach, thinking that that has got him nowhere in the past.

Mr Goldberg was just about to tee off on the eighteenth hole. With him, were three other wealthy businessmen-looking types, all intently watching him about to make his final tee shot.

Suddenly, coming from behind them out of nowhere was a golf cart hurtling through the air towards them with the driver screaming, "MR GOLDBERG! MR GOLDBERG!"

Mr Goldberg vigorously swung his club and badly mishit the ball, embarrassingly losing it off to one side in the nearby rough.

"Who on *earth* is that madman?" said one of the businessmen turning quickly around to see who it was.

Eric slammed on the breaks, bringing the golf cart to an abrupt halt on the seventeenth green, and got out and quickly walked over to where Mr Goldberg and the others were standing.

Still amused at seeing Mr Goldberg's disastrous tee shot, a tall, slim, well-tanned man, whom the other's seemed to be trying to impress, said, "Whoever he is, he's certainly got *balls!*" All his associates laughed, though inwardly Mr Goldberg wasn't amused. His name was Mr Constantino and he was one of the richest and most powerful men in Las Vegas, owning several of the resorts, including the golf course.

"Mr Goldberg I need to talk with you now!"

"Go away and stop bothering me, can't you see I am trying to play a game of golf!" he replied abruptly, heavily perspiring, and clearly annoyed by Eric's audacious interruption.

"I am sorry to interrupt you gentlemen, but Mr Goldberg still owes me money, and I can't wait any longer!" said Eric assertively.

"This is an outrage!" bleated Mr Goldberg.

"Tut, tut, John. Have you not been paying the artistes on time again?" guessed Mr Constantino in a calm and controlled authoritative voice, raising his eyebrows. He knew full well of his miserly ways.

"Well – well – I was going to pay him today," responded Mr Goldberg sheepishly.

"Well, you had better pay him today. We don't want disgruntled artistes performing in my venues, now do we. You hire the artistes but remember who hires you!"

"And the dancers!" said Eric interjecting, followed by more raising of eyebrows.

"Don't worry young man! The money will be with you and the dancers by the end of the day!" said Mr Constantino assuredly as he placed his ball on the tee. "… Wait a moment – aren't you The Amazing Fartzini who performs at the Excalibur Resort?"

"Yes, pleased to meet you," answered Eric, smiling.

"I believe the Excalibur is still one of mine – I am Mr Constantino, pleased to meet you too. Both then shook hands. "I am a big fan of magic and thoroughly enjoyed your show!" He then swung at his ball, sending it soring high into the air and straight down the fairway to land on the green inches away from the hole.

The other two competitors, who had already teed off landing their balls just short of the green, applauded his sublime shot. Eric joined in with the applause. Mr Goldberg, on the other hand, didn't applaud; he promptly went off to look for his ball in the rough in a huff.

"Oh, take no notice of him," said Mr Constantino, "he doesn't like losing, that's all – he'll soon calm down." Then said happily, "And thanks to you, young man, I am now in the *lead!*"

"Well, I am pleased to have been of help," said Eric, grinning.

"While we are waiting for Scrooge over there, why don't you show us a quick magic trick?" asked Mr Constantino.

"Sure!" said Eric, pleased to do so as he removed a pack of cards from his shorts pocket. "Allow me to introduce you to my fifty-two assistants." He fanned the cards and showed them all to be different. Then holding the cards face-down, said, "Pick a card, Mr Constantino." Having chosen one and memorized it, the card was then returned to the pack, which was thoroughly shuffled. "Now watch closely – I am going to make your card disappear!"

No sooner than he said that he riffled the end of the pack, making a sharp snapping sound. *"It's gone!"* he said. "Look I'll prove it to you. Please hold out your hands palm upwards." Everyone looked on intrigued as Eric slowly dealt the cards face upwards one at a time into

Mr Constantino's hands. Every single card was shown except his, which had indeed disappeared without a trace. Everybody applauded.

'Bravo! That was incredible!" said Mr Constantino, patting Eric on the back, well impressed. He then joked, "Hey, you can't make my wife disappear, can you?" Eric joined in the laughter that followed, thinking, he must have heard that corny old line about a million times before.

"Admit defeat, John!" called out Mr Constantino to Mr Goldberg as the rest of the group headed down the fairway towards the eighteenth hole, leaving Mr Goldberg still thrashing around with his club in the tall grass, determined to find his ball.

"... So *where* did my card go?" asked Mr Constantino still trying to figure it out. There was a pause. "You're not going to tell me, are you?"

"Nope!" said Eric smiling with a glint in his eye. Mr Constantino laughed.

"Ah, don't ya just hate it when magician's say that," said one of the others smiling, also amazed, and wanting to know how he did it.

"Do you play golf, Eric?" asked Mr

Constantino.

"I couldn't even swing a cat – *not* that I would ever try to swing a cat!" Mr Constantino and his associates laughed.

"Well, it's a great game – you should take it up sometime."

"Yeah, maybe I will," said Eric, happily.

As they walked and talked, all his troubles seemed to have disappeared like Mr Constantino's playing card – but that was only to be short lived. The conversation now turned to more serious matters.

"Mr Goldberg and the show producer have informed me that your magic show at the Excalibur is no longer drawing in the crowds like it used to," said Mr Constantino, now looking more serious. Eric just listened while he continued. "Not helped by the fact, I hasten to add, that a new and bigger resort has just opened across the Strip and, from what I hear, also has a *much* more spectacular magic show. But I am a businessman Eric, and if your show doesn't start bringing in the money again soon, I will have no choice but to pull the plug on it and put another show on in its place. Do you understand?"

As Eric was listening, he thought, "I need

that to happen about as much as I need a broken leg – and If I don't make the payment to the Mafia on time, that's what will happen to me!"

"Yes, I understand Mr Constantino," said Eric nodding, trying to stay positive.

"Call me, *Luigi!*"

"I am planning on performing an *extremely* dangerous magic trick stunt the like of which Las Vegas has *never* seen before!" suddenly announced Eric.

"I am liking the sound of it already!" said Mr Constantino. "Come and join us at the club house for lunch and you can tell me more about it."

They reached the green and glancing over his shoulder, Mr Constantino noticed that there was no sign of Mr Goldberg anywhere. "Looks like John has finally given up!" he said with a big grin on his face as victory was now only one foot away from the hole.

So, they decided to carry on playing without him; and after the other two competitors took their shots, it was Mr Constantino's turn. He removed his putting iron from his trolley bag and walked over to where his ball had landed. One of the other competitors lifted the flag out from the hole and stepped aside as Mr Constantino positioned himself – wiggling his bottom as golfers do – to take the easy putt. Eric watched from the perimeter of the green; he had one more surprise in store just waiting to happen.

As expected, the ball landed predictably in the hole, scoring him a birdie, and everybody applauded Mr Constantino as the winner. Then as Mr Constantino reached into the hole to fetch his ball, he felt something else in there. He suddenly started laughing, *"Amazing! Look, it's my playing card!"* Thrilled, he pulled the playing card out and held it up high for everyone to see. Everyone gasped and applauded. He then looked directly at Eric. "How did you do that? This is even more incredible than when you made it disappear!"

"It was a hole in one!" said Eric, grinning. Everyone laughed. It had certainly been a surprise all right.

The other two competitors finished playing for 2nd and 3rd positions and then everyone strolled over to the nearby clubhouse restaurant for some refreshments before lunch.

"Here's my business card, young man," said Mr Constantino, flashing his gleaming, cosmetically whitened teeth as he smiled. "If you need anything, just call me!"

"Thank you, Luigi," Eric replied, smiling back. "I will."

Mr Goldberg was already there at the bar drowning his sorrows, having lost the bet. But he was sportsman enough to congratulate his old buddy on winning. "I couldn't find the darn ball anywhere!" said Mr Goldberg, which caused much laughter. Luigi then told John about the incredible card trick Eric had performed – indeed, he didn't stop talking about it: "… and he didn't even go anywhere near the hole!" …

During lunch they all agreed that closing the show with the infamous Bullet Catch stunt was an excellent idea, and that it should be performed like the way it was originally, so there was a real element of danger and excitement involved. And the existing show would be revamped and built around it. "If the Bullet Catch stunt doesn't bring the people in, I don't know what will!" said Eric. Luigi and John said that they would publicise the new show format to the hilt and arrange for Eric to do interviews on local radio and TV, and a new billboard poster would be designed featuring the stunt. And one of the men who played golf with them, whose name was Bill Bridges, also happened to be the Sheriff of Las Vegas, Clark County, and said he could arrange for a police marksman to shoot the gun.

Mr Constantino agreed that because of the dangers attached with the stunt, Eric's fee would be increased to reflect this – which, of course, made Mr Goldberg happy, because it meant he would get more commission. Plus, it was agreed by all that for the time being, at least until rehearsals were well underway, they would keep it under wraps in case any rival magic show should get wind of it and try and copy the idea.

The truth is, very few magicians would even dare to perform the Bullet Catch. Even the legendary "Houdini" chose not to perform it because it was so dangerous!

CHAPTER SEVEN

SUPERMAN TO THE RESCUE!

As promised, later that day when Eric checked his online bank account, all the money he was owed had finally been credited to him. Which was a big relief to say the least, as now he could pay back the money he owed to the Mafia in full. And all he had to do now was keep away from the casino's – not the easiest thing to do in a place that is full of them.

But despite the constant temptations, he was determined to stop gambling and pay back the loan and finally get the Mafia off his back so he could move on with building a secure and happy future for Emily and himself. Though, keeping quiet about the new show was proving to be even more challenging, and he had to bite his lip a couple of times to stop himself from blurting it all out – especially to his assistant Gloria, who was very keen on magic and was always asking him whether he was going to be adding any new magic tricks to the show. He was excited and wanted to tell everyone about it. He hadn't been this excited – or nervous – about performing magic for some time.

On Monday afternoon after the matinee performance, Eric was sat in his dressing room nervously awaiting the arrival of the Mafia. And even though he now had the cash to pay them back the money he owed them; he was still extremely anxious. He had stashed wads of $50.00 bills, totaling $50,000 in his zippered sports bag.

He had since found out from the compère, Jim, while chatting in a lounge bar late one evening, how Tony One Shoe got his fearsome reputation, and how he dealt with people who didn't pay their debts – Eric had grown quite fond of his body parts and didn't want to lose any for the same reason Tony One Shoe had no doubt.

Jim had lived and performed in Sin City for

many years and knew, or knew of, all the Mafia crime gangs that operated there – once upon a time he even mixed with the likes of the Rat Pack, and Sinatra would introduce him to, let's just say, some rather unsavoury characters he used to hang around with.

As usual between shows, all the other cast and crew members had left to go back to their apartments to relax, leaving Eric all alone pacing quickly back and forth across his dressing room clutching the bag of money, getting more and more anxious by the minute. Even Gloria, who would usually have joined Eric for a chat, had left because she was still in a mood with him.

As the time slowly dragged on, Eric would alternate between pacing back and forth with sitting and moving his legs quickly back and forth – he was starting to feel warn out.

An hour went by and there was still no sign of the mobsters. He'd now given up pacing back and forth in favour of remaining sat in his chair and slowly moving his legs back and forth. Yet another hour went by …

Suddenly the door handle moved back and forth rapidly, and then there was a loud knock, knock on the door. And although he had been expecting the mobsters, it made him jump right out of his chair.

"Who is it?" he nervously said, instantly realising how silly that was when he could plainly hear Italian being spoken in the corridor – something about the pizza tasting 'delizioso'!

"Open the door!" demanded the same husky voice he recognized from the week before. "Hurry up, or we'll knock it down!"

"Okay, okay, I'm coming!" he called out in a jittery voice. Eric started panicking and fumbling in his pocket for the key. He then went to unlock the door and accidentally dropped it on the floor. Suddenly before he had a chance to pick it up, the door smashed open, leaving it hanging off its hinges, and standing in the doorway was Tony One Shoe looking terrifyingly angry and brandishing a chainsaw!

The evil mobster revved the chainsaw. "Don't hurt me, don't hurt me! I have the money here!" quickly shrieked Eric as he stubbled backwards into the room holding the bag of money aloft. But the chainsaw wielding maniac and his henchmen entered the room and surrounded him. 'Tony One Show' raised the rotating chainsaw above Eric, and as it descended towards him, Eric screamed out loud …

Eric suddenly woke up from hearing someone banging loudly on his door and raucous noise in the corridor. He'd had a bad dream.

"Eric! Eric! It's me! – Gloria!" she called out while continuing to bang on the door. "Are you okay in there, honey?"

He slowly and unsteadily got up from the chair he had fallen asleep on, immediately checking to make sure he still had all his limbs and went and unlocked the door. "Oh, hi Gloria – sorry, I must have dozed off."

"You were screaming, and I thought something terrible must have happened to ya!" she said peering her head around the door at him. He then noticed that the door wasn't hanging off of its hinges, the bag of money was still securely tucked under his arm, and most reassuringly of all, the mobsters weren't there.

"No, no, I just had a bad dream, that's all," he replied, rubbing his eyes, still half asleep. "… Come in!"

"No, I can't stop, honey – the next show will be starting in about five minutes!"

"*What!*" said Eric, surprised. "*Oh, 'eck!*"

"You better *hurry up* and get ready," she warned him.

"Right, thanks for telling me, Gloria."

"What's in the bag?" she suddenly asked him curiously.

At first Eric hesitated to answer. "… Oh, it's erm … the money I owe the mafia," he confided in her quietly. The door was still open and there were people rushing to and thro along the corridor, so he had to be careful.

Gloria's eyes opened wide. "Oh, I forgot they were coming to collect it today," she said, looking concerned. "Well, what are you going to do with it?"

"I don't know – I guess I'll have to hide it somewhere in here."

"Yeah, best ya do," she advised. "… Oh, and by the way, I'm sorry if I seemed in a mood the last few days – women's troubles!"

"… Oh! I see. That's alright," said Eric, finally understanding what see meant.

"Anyway, must dash and get into position. See ya!" She blew him a kiss.

"Yeah," Eric replied. He then shut the door and locked it again. Then quickly started getting changed into his Merlin costume.

As he was getting changed, he wondered why

the mobsters hadn't come by to collect their money already. "Perhaps they've been arrested?" he thought. "... *Or tortured! Or Murdered!* Anyhow," he then thought, "it wasn't likely that they would show up now with all these people around as potential witnesses."

But whatever the reason was, he now had a dilemma: he had a show to do in less than five minutes and was still in possession of $50,000 in cash.

So, he did what any other man would do in this situation to stop anyone stealing his money: he draped his dirty, smelly underwear over the top of the bag.

While Eric was on stage, he kept his door locked, and between shows checked that the money was still there. Then as soon as the last show of the day was over, Eric once again unzipped his bag and quickly checked one more time. "Thank goodness for that," he thought. And without delay, he left in a hurry without saying goodbye to anyone. He must have been the first one to leave the premises.

This time he left via the backstage door because he didn't want to be tempted into gambling by going the other way through the casino. He signed out, quickly scribbling something that vaguely looked like his signature, and pushed open the backstage door leading out to the rear of the building and onto the dimly lit street. Then without stopping he quickly made haste, down the short flight of steps and onto the sidewalk.

It was gone 11 pm and dark outside, and who knows who could be lurking around in the shadows ready to jump out and mug him. *"That's him!"* somebody called out. "Mr Fartzini! Mr Fartzini! Can we have your autograph?" called out someone else. "We *loved* your show!" voiced another.

There was a small group of people and one other person standing separate from them, who had been waiting for him to come out. Eric just ignored them and carried on briskly walking along the sidewalk, firmly clutching onto his bag of money.

Normally, Eric would have stopped and have been pleased to sign autographs for his fans, but on this occasion he daren't risk it. Vegas was full of low life's and crazies who wouldn't hesitate to slit your throat for ten bucks – especially at this time of night.

"Dirtbag!" then called out one of his so-called fans. "Your show was *trash!*" then called out the same person from the group who only a moment ago said they loved it. But the lone fan persisted in following him, and the quicker Eric walked, so did they. Eric then heard his name being called out again. It was the sound of a woman's voice.

"I'm sorry, I can't stop!" answered Eric. He quickly looked back over his shoulder, but the person was wearing a hood and their face was completely concealed in shadow. "Maybe I should've gone the other way," he thought as he turned the corner and continued along the side of the building, heading for the taxi's parked at the front. As she continued to follow him, his walking became a jog to get away from the overzealous fan. He then warned her, "Stop following me, or I'll call the police!"

She then warned him, "Leave Las Vegas — your life is in peril!"

"Tell me something I don't know!" he thought.

As Eric approached the corner at the front of the building, he took one more look behind him, but the mystery stranger was gone! "How strange!" he said to himself. And with that thought, jumped into a taxi.

Meanwhile, the new dancer, Sasha, was

knocking on Eric's dressing room door, hoping that he was still in there.

"He's not in there!" an unfriendly and abrupt voice told Sasha as the person approached her. "He's already left!"

Sasha turned her head to the right to face the person. "Hello, Gloria. How are y—"

"Never mind the niceties," said Gloria as she grabbed hold of Sasha's upper arm and pulled her towards her, squeezing it firmly. "Stop flirting with Eric – he's in a serious relationship and he doesn't want a scamp like you destroying it."

"I am *not* flirting with Eric. Now *let* go of my arm – you're *hurting* me!"

"*Don't* lie. I saw ya flashing your eyelids at him earlier!" Gloria then let go of Sasha's arm, leaving red marks against her pale white British skin where Gloria's fingers had been. Sasha then ran down the corridor towards the backstage door, crying.

As Eric put the key in the door to his apartment, he noticed a cigar butt stamped out on the ground near where he stood. "Disgusting!" he thought and kicked it away before entering. He felt tired after another exhausting day and was glad to get back home so he could relax.

He entered the hallway and switched on the light, noticing the door to the lounge was left ajar, which he thought, strange, as it is not something he does as a rule. Then as he walked farther down the hallway to go into the lounge, he was immediately aware of the smell of smoke. He opened the door fully and stepped inside the darkened room. Then as soon as his fingers found the switch on the wall, the light came on, revealing Tony One Shoe sat comfortably in his armchair smoking a cigar, while his four heavies were standing around the room with their arms folded doing a good job at looking mean.

"What took ya so long?" said the Mafia Boss, startling Eric. "Oh, dear! Did we *startle* you?" Eric just stood there, frozen, still clutching onto his bag of money. "Take it easy! We're not gonna hurt choo! We like to surprise people. It's what we do – a bit like you when you perform your magic tricks, am I right?" Eric just nodded nervously in agreement. "… Hey, it's not a bad apartment ya got here – the flowery curtains could do with being changed" His heavies started to laugh.

"How did you get into my apartment?" Eric

then said, realising it was a stupid thing to say to the Mafia of all people.

The Mafia Boss/interior designer ignored his question. "I take it that bag is for me?" he asked instead.

"Well, I was hoping I could keep the bag," Eric replied with a slight quiver to his voice. Tony One Shoe then began to snarl. "You know what – *keep it* – you can have it! I'll buy another one."

Tony One Shoe then gestured with his head to one of his heavies to go and fetch the bag. "They've done this before," thought Eric. "That was impressive!"

The mean-looking heavy snatched the bag from Eric's grasp and handed it to his boss, who placed it on his lap. He then laid his lit cigar precariously on the edge of the armchair and slowly began to unzip the bag and peer inside. His face suddenly grimaced, pulling a face like a squeezed lemon, as he gingerly removed a pair of underpants from within and dropped them onto the floor.

"Sorry, they're *mine!*" explained Eric. "I must have left them in their by mistake."

The crime boss's eyes then lit up and he began to smile at seeing his favorite colour green filling the bags interior. Eric immediately breathed a sigh of relief and began to relax at seeing Tony One Shoe looking happy for a change.

But that feeling didn't last long. As Tony One Shoe removed a wad of $50.00 bills from the top of the pile, he stopped seeing green and started to see red with anger!

"MAMA MIA! IS THIS SOME KINDA JOKE!" he yelled full of rage. He then reached into the bag and started pulling out balls of newspaper used to make it look like the bag is filled with money. "WERE YOU TRYING TO PLAY YOUR TRICKS ON ME?"

"NO!" Eric yelled back shocked.

Two of the heavies then promptly grabbed hold of Eric from either side, and one pulled out a pistol and pointed it at his head. It was no use trying to escape.

"D'ya think I'm *Stupid* or somethin'?" then asked the angry Mafia Boss.

"*No!* I can't understand it, I *checked* the bag before I left the theatre!" proclaimed Eric, now fearing for his life.

"Well, by my reckoning, about half the money is missing!" said Tony One Shoe, not amused. "Either you're lying, or someone has been playing tricks on you and stolen the money."

As he was speaking, Eric's brain was working overtime trying to figure out who could have stolen it. "I kept the door locked the whole time I wasn't there!" he thought to himself. "And as far as I know apart from myself the only other person who has a key is the stage manager."

"… Well, which is it?" demanded to know the infuriated Mafia Boss. "Not that it makes any difference – I'm just curious, that's all – either way you're gonna die."

"*Die!* Wait a minute, aren't you just going cut off one of my body parts?" asked Eric, terrified and shaking.

"No, that was in the *old* days – I don't have time to mess around like that anymore." Tony One Shoe answered coldly.

"It was *stolen* – I *swear* to ya, I had all the money ready to hand over to ya! *Don't* kill me!" pleaded Eric.

"If I let choo live, then someday you might try and kill me. Capeesh?"

Eric nodded his head one way and then the other. "I won't! I promise! Scouts honour!"

"Is this guy for real or what?" said one the

heavies.

"I gave you an extra week to pay up, and my patience has run out. It's too late kid," solemnly said Tony One Shoe.

Eric started to wriggle away from the heavies to no avail. *"Please,* don't kill me! *Please* don't kill me – I can get you the money! Or–or what about a first edition copy of *Harry Potter and the Philosopher's Stone* plus some rare "Superman" comics I have instead?" There was a pause, then Tony One Shoe and all his heavies burst out laughing.

Eric managed to crack half a nervous smile, thinking, "What if they *don't* like comics? I'm going to *die* I know it – I've seen it in the movies. The gangsters *always* laugh just before they put a bullet through your brain!"

"Okay!" said Tony One Shoe, smiling. He loved "Marvel" and "DC" comics. And with that, Eric reluctantly handed over his cherished Harry Potter book and his rare collection of Marvel and DC comics, sad to part with them.

But it wasn't over with the mobsters, because the Mafia Boss reminded Eric in no uncertain terms that he still has to pay the interest incurred from the late payment – amounting to $10,000. Which, Eric had no choice but to agree to pay him within a couple weeks.

The next thing Eric knew was that he found himself waking up a few hours later lying on his lounge floor with a terrible sore head: as a parting gift, one of the heavies had whacked him on the head with the butt of his gun, knocking him out cold.

CHAPTER EIGHT

THE CASE OF THE MISSING MONEY!

It was 3.05 am when Eric woke up on his hard, wooden lounge floor. Thankfully, he was still alive and had no missing body parts – he quickly had a feel around to make sure again, though.

After he nursed the sore lump on his head, he climbed into his much more comfortable bed hoping to go to sleep, but his overactive mind wouldn't allow it – he had too many unanswered questions that needed solving. First and foremost: who stole the money? Secondly: how was he going to get his hands on another $10,000? Thirdly: who was sabotaging his magic act?

"Who would have taken the money? And, more crucially, who could have taken the money?" he kept thinking. "The only person I talked to about the money was Gloria ... but she doesn't have a key! And besides, *Gloria* wouldn't do such a thing – she's a *friend!*" he thought. "... Ah, but *who* did she tell?" He then switched his attention to the stage manager. "He's the only person that has duplicate keys to the dressing rooms. Could he have done it?" he wondered. "– But what about the cleaners – wouldn't they have a key as well?" he pondered. Then told himself, "Get some sleep!"

He couldn't go the police about it. So, it was going to be down to him to carry out his own private investigation to find out who was responsible. He wished his friends Emily, Jack and Gary were here – they would have helped him to get the bottom of it! The one thing he did know was that he had to get the stolen money back, and fast, before the Mafia came looking for him again!

And, after a bit more wondering and pondering, and scratching his sore head, he eventually fell asleep.

It was noon when Eric's bedside landline

phone rang again and finally woke him up.

Eric slowly sat up in bed and spoke into the mouthpiece, still half asleep. "Hi," he managed to get out.

"*Hiya* love! How are you – you sound a bit groggy," said his mum, Ingrid, pleased to have finally got through to him.

"I'm fine," he answered while feeling his sore head, "just a bit" – he yawned – "sleepy, that's all."

"Oh, sorry did I wake you, love?"

"No, I was already up, Mum!" he said, telling a porkie pie.

"Late-night was it?" asked his mum.

"Erm, yes–no!"

"Thought so!"

"Well, nice talking to ya, Mum. I've gotta go now –"

"What? Wait! Hold on a minute, Son," she said, surprised. "I've only just started speaking to ya!"

"Mum, you phone me almost every day!"

"*Hey, have you got somebody there with you?* Er, I hope you're not misbehaving yourself out there!"

"*Mum!* I'm not a child anymore. *I'm* twenty-five years old, and I'm a very self-controlled and responsible adult!"

"I know you are, son. I worry about you, that's all. When are you going to ask Emily to marry you? It's about time you got on your knees and put a ring on her –"

"Mum, I've *gotta* go and get ready for my show!" he explained. "I love ya, *bye!*"

"I love you too. Bye! *Listen,* you be careful – everybody's gun crazy out there! –"

"Mum, I'm putting the phone down now – *bye!*" Eric put the phone down, otherwise his mum would have kept him talking all afternoon – and probably all evening.

Over the years since Ingrid first moved to Ramsgate with her son, following the breakup of her relationship with Eric's father, there had been a few changes in her life: she had given up her job at the local supermarket in Ramsgate in favour of once again being a nurse; she had also given up living with her boyfriend Graham – the supermarket frozen foods department manager – their relationship became a bit frosty; and she no longer lived in the tiny flat at 76b, Hope Close.

Eric bought her a lovely three-bedroom house in Pegwell Bay for them to live in – not dissimilar to the one they all lived in as a family in Sheffield. Having all that space, seemed like living in a palace compared to where she was living – especially now that she was living alone. Of course, since her son had left home, she missed him tremendously but was so proud of what he had achieved and was so busy working at the hospital that she hardly had a moment to feel lonely. She still had her friends from her supermarket days and had made some new friends where she now worked.

Despite a sore head, Eric felt okay to go into work that day. He arrived a little earlier than normal. He thought it best – at least for the time being – to carry on as normal as if nothing had happened. And besides, he couldn't just go around accusing people of stealing when he didn't yet have any evidence to back him up.

Apart from the stage manager and a stagehand, it seemed like he was the first cast member to arrive. He decided that before going to his dressing room, he would set up his magic props he kept in the wings.

"Good afternoon, Dirk," said Eric to the stage manager. Dirk responded in his usual miserable way with just a nod. Mind you, he was up a ladder trying to change a stage floodlight bulb.

Whilst in the wings on stage left, Eric did notice that the stage manager had left his large bunch of keys in plain view at his station. "That's a bit careless," thought Eric, "Anybody could just pick them up." So, while the stage manager and his stagehand were pre-occupied, he did just that. There were a lot of keys attached to the keyring. He immediately searched for his dressing room door key, occasionally looking furtively around to make sure no one was coming. But despite a thorough search, his key was missing. "That's strange," he thought, "maybe somebody *stole* the key and was unable to put it back?"

The stage manager had been high up on Eric's list of suspects, but if *he* had stolen the money, why would he have removed the key from the keyring to open the door – he would have just kept it attached, *surely*, Eric then reasoned.

Eric continued resetting his magic equipment ready for the matinee show that afternoon. He could now hear several of the dancer's voices coming from down by the dressing rooms area. He finished what he was doing and made his way to his dressing room. Along the corridor he noticed Sasha coming towards him. He smiled at her and said hello, but she just ignored him and continued walking past him on her way to the toilets. She looked unhappy and a bit upset. "I wonder what's the matter with her?" he thought as he unlocked his dressing room door.

Shortly afterwards Eric could hear Jim coming along the corridor – he could always tell it was Jim because he would invariably be singing a song on his way to his dressing room – either that or blowing off. Eric thought, I must have a chat with him to find out if he'd seen anything suspicious yesterday evening.

He gave it five minutes or so to let Jim sort himself out, and then went and knocked on his door.

"Come in – it's unlocked!" Jim called out from his comfy armchair.

Eric opened the door. "Hiya Jim – how are ya?" Eric asked him as he walked in.

"Well, howdy, young fella. Oh, I suppose I can't complain. I'm doing just fine – well, apart from my arthritis, which is playing me up at the moment, and *terrible* bouts of wind.

"Too much information," thought Eric. "Oh, dear!" he said. "I'm sorry to hear that."

"Come and sit down and join me for a beer,"

then said Jim as he rubbed his left knee with one hand and opened his small refrigerator, revealing it packed full of beer, with the other."

"Oh, no, I better not just before a show – I'd be dropping everything!" replied Eric jokingly. "Besides, I'm trying to cut right down – thanks anyway."

"Very wise!" said the veteran all-round entertainer as he prised open a bottle of beer and began drinking it. After eventually returning the bottle to an upright position, he then said, "Hey, I hope you didn't think I was deriding your magic show the other day when I was comparing it with the one across the" – his face suddenly scrunched up as if he were in agony, his legs parted widely, and his toes curled tightly inwards, letting out an enormous rip-roaring fart – "*Strip*. Excuse me!"

"No, no, I didn't think that at all!" said Eric, returning his expanded eye sockets and raised eyebrows back to where they were a moment ago, and holding his breath for as long as he could, while at the same time, thinking, "Drinking lots of beer probably won't help with your flatulence problem!"

Jim then closed his legs, uncurled his toes, and continued, "Oh, good … I mean, yeah, sure, the other magic show is more spectacular, but the magician doesn't have your personality and skill!"

Eric quickly gasped for air. "Oh, thanks, Jim!"

"But I expect Gloria's already told you all about the rival magic show!"

"Gloria? I didn't think she'd been to watch the show," said Eric, surprised.

"Yeah, she was sat *right* next to me!"

Eric just continued smiling, while thinking, though, "'Sat *right* next to me?' I'm sure she told me that she didn't go to watch it." He then surmised, "Maybe I heard it wrong?"

Eric then noticed in the wastepaper bin between Jim's feet, there was a rolled-up newspaper. Thinking quickly on his toes, he said pointing to it, "Oh, I haven't read the newspaper yet. Do ya mind if I read it, Jim?"

"Sure!" he replied, starting to pull a weird-looking face again and adopt the same tell, tell position in his chair, indicating a storm was coming. "It's yesterday's" – he started to strain – "mind you."

Eric decided to risk it, and quickly went over and fetched it out of the wastepaper bin – which was filled mostly with empty beer bottles. "That's okay, ta!" said Eric. He then started to move away. Too late! "VRRP!" made the sound of another bout of wind even louder than the first.

When Eric made it back to a reasonably safe distance, and his mind could focus on something else, he noticed that most of the pages of the newspaper were missing. His analytical mind immediately went to work; then remembering that scrunched up balls of newspaper were used to fill out the bag to make it look full of cash, he wondered if Jim might have been the thief.

But then Jim said, "Keep it, I found it like that lying in the corridor yesterday evening – I was only interested in reading about the sport in the rear pages, anyway." Then added, "I wish people would clear up after themselves!"

"Yeah!" just said Eric, nodding in agreement. "… Do you happen to remember, roughly, *when*, you first saw it?"

Jim thought about it a moment and then said, "It would have been sometime during the last show … I think it was when I was on my way back to my dressing room shortly after I introduced your act. *Why?*"

"Oh, no reason," answered Eric. Jim then

suddenly started to grimace again, which was Eric's cue to get out of there. "Well, I better go and get ready – see ya later, Jim!" Eric quickly stepped into the corridor and shut the door behind him just in time before another explosion detonated.

"Hiya, honey!" said Gloria to Eric as the two of them nearly bumped into each other in the corridor.

"Oh, *Hi* Gloria!"

"You're brave – going in there!"

Eric grinned.

Gloria had just arrived. She was all dressed up, wearing expensive new designer clothes and shoes. Eric had certainly never seen her wearing them before.

"New shoes?" asked Eric.

"Jimmy Choo's!" she answered, smiling as she showed them off. "I bought them this morning after church." She regularly attended church and sang in the Gospel choir.

"Looks like you've had a bit of a spending spree!"

"Well, a girl has got to treat herself now and again, honey."

Eric couldn't remember the last time he bought himself some new clobber. And while

Gloria went on describing with great passion and detail what else she'd treated herself to, Eric couldn't help but think, where did she get all that money to afford it, especially knowing what little money dancers make? He also thought that in all the time she's been talking to him, not once has she asked him whether or not he's paid the Mafia back the money he owes them.

"Do you like what I bought?" she then asked excitedly, flashing her eyelids at him, still wrapped up in her narrow-minded world of expensive high-end fashion.

"Yeah," said Eric, forcing a smile and for a split second, wondering whether he has inadvertently paid for it all, then immediately dismissing the idea as ludicrous. And it wasn't his business to pry.

Just then, Sasha, came walking back from the toilets; it looked like she had been crying again – her make-up was smeared, and she looked sad. Eric had his back to her, but as soon as Gloria set her eyes on Sasha walking along the corridor towards them, she said in a loud voice, "Thank you honey!" and wrapped her arms around Eric and gave him a long and tender hug.

"Oh, 'eck!" thought Eric. "That's a bit OTT!"

As Sasha, walked past, Gloria smiled gloatingly at her, as if to say, he's *my* man – stay away from him! Or perhaps it was more, if *I* can't have him, then *neither* will *you!*

Eric eventually managed to squeeze himself away from Gloria's clutches, saying, "Well, we'd better get ready for the show now Gloria!"

Then as he was heading towards his dressing room, she called out to him, *"Eric!"* He stopped and turned his head towards her. And keeping her voice down, then asked, "Have you paid the" – she mouthed 'Mafia' – "back the money yet?"

Eric just nodded and then carried on walking. He reached his dressing room, with lots of unanswered questions still buzzing around in his head, unlocked the door and walked in. To Eric, she appeared to genuinely not know about the money being stolen – either that or she was an amazingly good actress.

Eric sat at his dressing room table, feeling none the wiser as to who stole his money. There were a lot of people around last evening: Ruben, Jim, Dirk, and his stage crew, not to mention twelve dancers. But he thought that if he could find the missing key, he would find the culprit. He then heard the familiar hand clapping that preceded Ruben's annoying shouty voice. "Hurry up girls!" he hollowed. "Into your placccesss now!"

After all the noise made by the dancers had subsided in the corridor; dressed in his Merlin costume, Eric left his dressing room and headed for the security office next to the backstage rear door entrance.

There, a member of the security team named Tom greeted him. Tom was an elderly gentleman with a beard nearly as long as the one Eric was wearing, whose job it was to make sure everybody signed in and out of the building -- unless your name happened to be Tony One Shoe and you were a member of the Mafia that is.

"Hi, Eric, you're not going out now, are you?" questioned Tom, as the show was due to start very soon.

"No, no," Eric replied, partly lowering his elasticated beard to do so.

"I can't do that with my beard!" said Tom, chuckling to himself as he tugged on it.

"I just wanted to ask you, Tom, if you had seen anyone acting suspiciously backstage yesterday evening during the last show?"

Eric knew that he had to be careful not to say too much; the last thing he wanted to do was get the in-house security team involved because then it might all come out about his dealings with the Mafia.

Tom thought about it a moment. "No, I can't say that I have," he replied. "Why, is there a problem? Eric hesitated and during that moment of silence Tom continued. "You've not had something stolen as well, have you? Only a few of the other cast members have been complaining that they've had money stolen from out of their dressing rooms recently."

This was new to Eric, and the first he'd heard about it. He hesitated for a moment and just said, "Yes, I've also had money stolen." Then asked, "Has any progress been made in catching the thief?"

"Not so far, but now that security is aware of it, rest assured we will be doing our best to catch the person, or persons, responsible!"

"Thanks!" said Eric, allowing his elasticated beard to pop back into place. He then turned and started to head back to his dressing room.

"Oh, Eric!" called out Tom. "I almost forgot

again. Last evening, after you'd left, somebody handed this letter in for you."

Eric went back to collect it, thanking Tom as he did. He noticed the envelope was addressed to "The Amazing Fartzini". "Do you remember what they looked like?" asked Eric, curious.

"To be honest, she was in and out of here very quickly and I didn't get a proper look at her –"

"Sorry to interrupt. So, it was a 'she', you say."

"Yeah, youngish looking, probably in her mid-twenties – it was hard to tell because she was wearing her hood."

Eric immediately remembered the woman that was following him last night, and who tried to warn him that he was in danger. Just then the show music started. "Okay, thanks, Tom. I better get going!"

Eric rushed back to his dressing room and immediately opened the letter. In large, capitalized letters, it read: "LEAVE LAS VEGAS WHILE YOU STILL CAN!"

CHAPTER NINE

ERIC GETS A LOVELY SURPRISE!

Throughout his performance that afternoon, Eric couldn't stop thinking about the message he received and tantalizingly wondered who the mystery woman who wrote it was. Was it genuine? Could it be a prank? Or a crazed stalker? All these types of questions kept bombarding him. And after the show when he was sitting alone in his dressing room, drinking an iced tea with milk, he thought, he's already got enough to concern himself about, let alone have to worry about this as well. He wondered if the stark warning was related to the Mafia. But then he thought they would have killed him already by now if they wanted him dead.

It also crossed his mind that it could be someone who had a grudge against him and was trying to scare him so he would leave Las Vegas – a rival magician, or some other type of entertainer for instance. Showbusiness was a cutthroat business and nothing would surprise him. There was certainly plenty of other entertainers that would love to have their name up in lights instead of his. Something else to add to the list of mysteries to be solved, he concluded.

Just then his phone alerted him to an incoming skype call. It was his girlfriend in England, Emily.

"*Hiya!* How's things?" she said smiling. She was wearing a beautiful floral dress and it looked like she'd had her hair styled differently since he last saw her.

"*Hiya* darling! I'm doing fine, thanks." He wasn't doing fine, but he wasn't going to tell her that. "How about you?"

"I'm grand!"

"You look gorgeous!" he said, smiling widely. "You've had your hair done, haven't you?"

"Ah, you noticed!" she said, pleased to bits. "It's *so* lovely to see ya!"

"You, too!"

"How's your family?" then asked Eric.

"Ah, just as mad as usual," she answered. Eric laughed. "How's ya mum?"

"I spoke with her earlier today, and she seemed fine. No different from how she normally is – overthinking things and worrying about nothing, you know. I think she gets a bit lonely living in the house all by herself; but she's extremely busy at work, as always, which helps to take her mind off things."

"I must pop round and see her soon," said Emily.

"Yeah, that would be nice – she'd like that a lot."

"So, how's the show going?" then asked Emily.

"Good – well to be honest, ever since the rival magic show opened, our audience numbers have dropped dramatically!"

"Oh, that's not good!" she responded, concerned.

"I've not had the chance to go and watch the show yet, but from what I hear, the American magician, Chet Stevenson, has been performing a lot of the same tricks and illusions as me. Even using the same patter lines!”

"*Really!*" said Emily, surprised. "What *copying* your act?"

"*Yeah*, can you believe it?" said Eric. "I wouldn't mind betting that he's been to see my show a few times – either that or someone's been secretly feeding him information about my act. It's too much of a coincidence!"

Eric didn't tell her that someone had also been sabotaging his magic props because he didn't want to worry her. And he certainly wouldn't tell her about his involvement with the Mafia. But he did tell her briefly about his new magic show that is planned – omitting the dangerous part where he attempts to catch a bullet between his teeth.

"Well, that sounds exciting. Hopefully, that will win back your audiences soon!"

"Anyroad, Em, how's it going at the stables?" asked Eric.

Emily loved horses, and for the past few years, she has been working at the local stables caring for them.

"I'm still enjoying it as much as ever – you know how much I love horses," she replied. She then laughed. "D'ya remember that time when we were kids when you first tried to mount my horse and fell *right* over the other side of it!"

Eric joined in with the laughter. "How could I forget – I had bruises for about a *week* afterwards!"

She laughed again. "I remember you told your mum that you accidentally fell off of the back of Jack's bike."

"Yeah – well she would have only worried, and I didn't want her to stop me visiting you at the Travellers site."

"Ah, we had so much fun when we were kids – I *really* miss those times!" she said with great fondness.

"Yeah, me too!" said Eric, while thinking, "Except when David Smythe was still alive and used to bully me!"

The amount of bullying Eric received when he was young was enough to scar anyone for life – if one allows it.

Trying to get the picture of the bully out of his head, Eric asked. *"Hey,* have you heard from Jack or Gary lately?"

"No, not for a while," she replied.

"Me neither," said Eric. "Once you leave school, it's easy to drift apart from your school friends, isn't it?"

Emily agreed, then said, "As far as I know, Jack is still teaching PE at a secondary school in Maidstone – but *who knows* what Gary's now doing since he got fired from B&Q."

"I didn't know he was fired!" said Eric.

Yeah, he got fired for accidentally dropping a tin of paint on top of the supervisors head while shelf-stacking up a ladder."

"*Surely,* that's not a good enough reason to fire someone though, is it?" said Eric.

"*Three times!*"

Eric couldn't help but burst out laughing, shortly joined by Emily. "Yeah, that sounds like Gary!"

"I think he's still got anger issues. *Anyway,* there's something I am *dying* to tell you!" said Emily, all excited.

"You're *pregnant?*" said Eric. Just then Eric heard a noise by his dressing room door. "Sorry, just a minute Em – I'll be *right* back! Eric left tablet device screen propped up on his dressing-table and quickly went to see if there was anyone there. He opened the door, but there was no one about, though he did hear the dancers dressing room door shut.

"Sorry, Em, I thought there might have been someone at the door," he said as he returned to the screen.

"No, I'm *not* pregnant!" said Emily, finally answering his question. "I was going to say that I have booked some time off from work to come out and see you in a couple of weeks! I was going to surprise by just turning up, but I just couldn't wait any longer to tell you. I can't wait to see what it is like living in Las Vegas!"

"Oh, 'eck!" thought Eric, starting to panic. "Oh, well, it's a lovely surprise, anyroad!" he said. "I'll pay for everything!" Then thinking, "What with, scatterbrain!"

"Thanks! I'll send you the flight details by text. I can't *wait* to see you!"

"I can't wait to see you, either!" he replied. "Well, I better start getting ready for the next show. Speak to you soon darling. *Bye!*"

"Okay, *bye* my love!" They blow each other kisses and the screen went black.

Eric was very pleased and excited that Emily was coming out to see him – they had never been this long apart before. But he also felt anxious about it because he didn't want her to find out about the trouble that he had gotten himself in.

A few days passed by, and Eric was still none the wiser as to who stole the money. He asked his assistant, Gloria, if she had seen anything suspicious that evening, but she said she hadn't. And the same answer was given to him by the other cast members and backstage crew he had asked. And when he made up a story about losing his key and asked Dirk, the stage manager, if he would open his dressing room door for him; to his surprise, the duplicate key, which he could have sworn was missing, was once again back on his keyring. Eric was hoping that Dirk would've given him an explanation as to why the key was missing and maybe shed some light on the mystery – but alas not. (Soon afterwards, Eric pretended that he had found his key to save Dirk the trouble of having another one cut.) Detective Eric was getting nowhere fast, and time was running out. He couldn't see the Mafia letting him off lightly another time.

The shows were being well received, and it appeared that whoever it was sabotaging his act had stopped. But on Thursday evening, during the last show, when all the press and media were there to review the show, it couldn't have gone much worse for Eric.

Eric made his appearance, as usual, dressed as the wizard Merlin; when no sooner had he stepped forwards and bowed to the audience with his long white beard touching the stage: a woman on the front row stands up and starts screaming hysterically at the top of her voice. Then starts bawling her eyes out as she is lead out by the hotel security.

Meanwhile, the show came to an abrupt halt, leaving the rest of the audience, including the press, none the wiser. Then to make matters worse: when the show did finally start again, it soon became apparent that someone had purposely tipped a load of rubbish, including rotten smelly eggs and fish guts into one of the stage illusions. The two assistants, understandably, then refused to step inside – and Laura had to run off stage to be sick.

The show was starting to look like a farce and people started walking out. And those that remained were howling themselves with laughter. And to top it all, due to the delay earlier and the venues tight schedule, the show had to be cut short, and they had to miss out the finale illusion.

It turns out that the hysterical woman on the front row suffered from severe Pogonophobia, which is a fear of beards. Though, Eric suspected that she was a plant, paid to disrupt his act on purpose.

Eric stormed off the stage, furious. "I can't believe what has just happened!" he shouted out. "The hysterical woman must have been a *plant*, I know it!"

"You don't know that!" said Gloria, trying to calm him down. "I had an auntie once who was frightened of moustaches!"

"It's too much of a coincidence that of all the nights the press is in, someone turns up frightened of *beards!* You can't tell me that she wasn't aware that Merlin had a beard – *everyone* knows that! And you can't tell me either that someone mistook my stage illusion for a trash can!" His assistants just listened …

Meanwhile, the dancers were on stage doing their best to save the show again. And Ruben grinned as he listened to Eric's rant close by in the wings.

"… Can you *imagine* what those reporters will write about my show after this disastrous performance!" continued Eric. "I'm going to speak with the show producer!"

The show producer Benjamin was in the auditorium not looking at all pleased when Eric approached him. Eric told him that his act was being maliciously sabotaged and explained what had happened. Benjamin was shocked to hear it and was a lot more sympathetic and supportive than Eric thought he would be. He told Eric that he would deal with it and try to get to the bottom of it.

The next day, Mr Constantino called a meeting in the morning, which included: Eric and his manager, John; the show producer, Benjamin; the choreographer, Ruben; and the stage manager, Dirk, to inform those who were not already aware of the new show and to discuss the planning of it going forward.

Ruben sat through the whole meeting stony-faced, occasionally giving Eric the daggers. And as soon as it was over, strutted out of the room, looking most displeased. He was not going to get an all-dancing extravaganza that he so much wanted after all.

It was intended that the new show would be a big production, and Mr Constantino didn't mind splashing the cash to make that happen. He certainly didn't want to be outdone by another casino resort.

After a long meeting, everyone agreed that the new show would be open in approximately one month. Eric thought that this was too soon but knew that Mr Constantino was keen to bring the business back to the resort's showroom ASAP, and feeling pressurised, reluctantly agreed.

It would mean that he would have to step up his research into finding out how the original method of presenting the Bullet Catch was done; and lots and lots of rehearsals as well as all the shows he was already doing three times a day! One consolation, Eric thought, was that it also meant less time to be tempted to gamble and drink.

As it happened, he'd heard of an elderly, extremely knowledgeable magician, named Robert Maloney, living somewhere in the Vegas area, who he thought might be able to advise him with performing the stunt.

CHAPTER TEN

ROBERT MALONEY

Eric came out of the meeting feeling pleased, and with a new sense of vigour. Rehearsals were due to start as early as next week, and in the meantime, Eric was keen to find out where the magician Robert Maloney lived.

Eric knew little about him. Only that he was a well-known magician in his day and performed regularly in Vegas, until one day at the height of his success, he just gave it all up and retired from performing magic. He found it hard to get people to talk about him, as whenever he tried, people didn't seem to want to for some reason – they would suddenly change the subject or make some excuse that they had to go somewhere.

So, Eric thought it would be a good idea to have a chat with his manager and see if he could tell him more about this mystery magician.

"John!" Eric called out as he ran to catch up with him and followed him into the lift (or elevator as it's called in the US); the smell of BO immediately hitting him.

"You've *already* been paid up to date, if that's what you are about to ask!" his manager said immediately.

"I know, thank you. It was something else I wanted to ask you, that's all," said Eric slightly out of breath and keen to find out where the magician now lived.

John pressed the button for the ground floor and the elevator doors began to close. "What is it, then?"

"I'm trying to locate the whereabouts of an old magician that used perform in Vegas, called Robert Maloney," said Eric as the elevator made its decent.

"Robert Maloney! Did you just say Robert Maloney?" repeated his manager, raising his eyebrows.

"Yeah."

"I haven't heard that name in a *long* time – nor do I care to or want *anything* to do with him. And if you have any sense, *neither* would you!" warned his manager as if Eric had just dug up a ghost from the past.

"I heard that he is an extremely knowledgeable magician and might be able to advise me on performing the Bullet Catch."

"Oh, he's extremely knowledgeable alright," said his manager, "but he's also very dangerous!"

"Dangerous!" responded Eric. "In what way?"

"Dangerous enough to get people *killed* – is that dangerous enough for ya?"

"Oh, I see," said Eric, taken aback in horror.

"He was one of those, what is termed today as thrill-seeker types – *a daredevil.* He always wanted to push the limits and would sometimes take chances to satisfy his thirst for an adrenalin rush," explained his manager. "The audiences loved him for it and would flock to come and see his show. But one day he went *too* far and accidentally killed his newlywed wife – who was also his glamorous assistant and whom he loved dearly – while performing a new death-defying stage illusion he'd invented involving an industrial wood shredder! It was in *all* the papers at the time. Though, some, accused him of jealousy and murder, when it came to light that his wife was having an affair with another magician. His lawyer managed to get him the lighter sentence of second-degree manslaughter, serving only six months jail time. But he was a broken man after that and vowed never to perform magic again."

"Tragic!" said Eric sympathetically, shaking his head.

"You can *say* that again – I lost a *lot* of commission when he packed up performing!"

Eric just looked at him, stunned by his last callous remark.

"The last I heard, he was living by himself in a run-down RV trailer park, north of the city, up on the Indian reservation."

"Thanks!" said Eric.

"But even if ya do manage to track him down, I doubt very much that he'll talk to ya. He *hates* magicians after what happened. If you take my advice, you'll stay *well* clear of him!"

The elevator doors opened and the two went their separate ways.

Despite his managers advice, Eric was

undeterred and decided he would try and meet this daredevil the very next day. And before he went back to the Excalibur to prepare for the matinee show later that day, he bought a detailed map of Las Vegas and the surrounding areas and hired a low budget rent-a-car. It was a white Chevrolet Aveo – the American equivalent to a Ford Fiesta.

He hadn't much need for a car before, as it was so easy to get about without one in Las Vegas; and he didn't get a lot of time to go sightseeing – he hadn't even been to see the Grand Canyon. And although the journey wasn't very far, he thought it would be convenient to hire one (especially if he needed to make a quick getaway), and useful for when Emily arrived in a couple of weeks so that they could see the sights together.

Later that afternoon, while in his dressing room, Eric heard a knock at his door. He had continued to keep his door locked just in case the Mafia or anyone else with ill intent towards him should turn up – he wasn't taking any chances, especially after he received the warning letter.

"*Who* is it?" he called out.

"It's *only* me, Gloria."

"Okay, hold on," he replied, and went over and unlocked the door.

She looked at him puzzled as she invited herself inside. "Hi honey, I thought you said that you'd paid the Mafia back the money you owed them?" said Gloria, implying why did he still feel the need to lock his door.

Eric didn't answer, just let her come in and closed the door immediately behind her. Eric then spoke quietly.

"I didn't want to tell ya in the corridor the other day in case anyone overheard, but I had about half the money stolen!" he said resting back against his dressing table, frowning and looking forlorn.

"*Stolen!*" repeated Gloria, sounding shocked.

"Yeah, it was stolen on the same day I was supposed to hand over the money! Somebody must have broken into my dressing room sometime during the last performance."

"Oh dear!" said Gloria.

"And later that evening when I got back to my apartment, the Mafia were there already waiting for me –"

"Oh, my *God!*" she said, putting her hand over her mouth. "What happened?"

"Well, d'ya remember I told you that I had a

rare collection of Superman comics and a first edition Harry Potter book?" Gloria nodded. "Well, fortunately for me, the Mafia Boss is also a big Marvel and Harry Potter fan, and I traded them instead," he explained.

"*Wow!*" just said Gloria, flabbergasted.

"But I hadn't taken into account that I would still have to pay them the interest accrued for the delay in payment, and I still owe them $10,000."

"Did they hurt you?" asked Gloria, looking concerned.

"No, not really," answered Eric.

"What d'ya mean, *not really?*"

"Well, as they were leaving, one of the heavies whacked me over the head with the butt of his pistol and knocked me out."

"Oh, you *poor* thing!" she said, and gave him a loving hug, planting her fulsome chest firmly up against his much less than fulsome one.

"I'm alright now, Gloria," he said. "It's just a bit sore still, that's all."

"You need to be more careful who you mix with, especially now you're gonna be a father!"

Eric slipped away from her grasp. *Father? Father?* I never said I was gonna be a *father!*" Eric replied, shocked; thinking, where on earth had she heard that?

Gloria hesitated for a moment. "You must have told me," she said. "Probably the other day when we were chatting – you must have just forgotten! Maybe being hit on the head has caused you to forget? *Anyway,* I've got to go and get ready!" she responded and made her way hastily to the door.

"Yeah, maybe? Okay, see ya on the stage," said Eric, still perplexed by what she said.

Then Eric remembered his conversation with Emily. "Had Gloria misheard his conversation with Emily?" he wondered. "In which case, had she been snooping?"

It was after the matinee show that the show producer called everybody involved together for a meeting in the showroom. The first thing he addressed was the sabotaging of magic props Eric had reported. Benjamin spoke in a stern manner, warning everyone that if the culprit is found, they will face immediate dismissal and prosecution charges. "I won't tolerate it in my theatre!" he told them.

Everyone acted surprised to hear it, trying their best to look innocent – even if they were. Then, before moving on to announce that there was going to be a new magic show,

Benjamin said, "If anyone knows anything about this, then please come forward."

The show producer then announced that there was going to be a new magic show to a mixture of raised eyebrows, smiles and frowns. Though to several of the dancers, this was already secondhand knowledge no thanks to Ruben spouting his big mouth off.

It is true to say that not everyone was pleased to hear the news. Some of the dancers were pleased that they were going to learn a couple of new routines and perform something different for a change. While others, including Candy, Rhonda and Samantha were less impressed because it meant they would have to come in extra early to rehearse. And when the meeting was over and everyone was leaving, Candy remarked: *"The Bullet Catch?* What, he's *actually* gonna catch a bullet between his *teeth?"* Ruben then chirped in saying: *"I* wanna fire the gun! *Pleassse* let *me* fire the gun!" causing Candy, Rhonda and Samantha cruelly to laugh. The stage manager, who was nearby, then coldly added: *"Join* the cue!" causing more laughter.

Meanwhile, Eric, who had remained sat in the showroom, heard these unkind comments. Though, none of it surprised him coming from them – they had always been unfriendly towards him. But what did surprise him was when Gloria came rushing over to him looking annoyed and spoke to him angrily.

"How come ya never told me about this *new* show of yours then?" she spurted out, clearly upset. "I *thought* we were *friends* and friends always tell each other everything!"

"We *are* friends, Gloria," answered Eric. "Why are you getting so upset over that for? I was told by the management to keep quiet about it!"

"*Huh!* Well, how come half the *darn* cast knew about it already then!" she said, before storming off.

Her bad mood didn't change for the rest of the day, either. And throughout the magic shows that evening, she never smiled once. Eric even apologized and tried reasoning with her, but that didn't work.

Eric got home after a stressful day at work listening to silly tittle-tattle and people moaning – which was nothing unusual – and immediately opened the map and started to plan his route for the following day. His mind was now only focused on tracking down Robert Maloney.

CHAPTER ELEVEN

ERIC TALKS TO THE DARE-DEVIL

Eric knew that the chances of finding Robert Maloney were slim, let alone persuading him to give him advice on performing the infamous Bullet Catch. But he also knew that he needed his expert advice if he were to perform this crazy magic trick stunt successfully.

Ever since being a kid, Eric never liked waking up early. He is what you call a "night owl" – though not always wise. And despite being advised not to go and adopting the more cautious motto: "If in doubt, leave it out!" he decided to opt for a more adventurous one: "Nothing ventured, nothing gained!" and set off bright and early in the morning on his quest to find the daredevil magician.

The morning sunlight had replaced the neon lights, and as Eric drove north along South Las Vegas Boulevard on his way out of the city, passing one tall building after another, he thought about what he would say to Mr Maloney. He got as far as: "Good morning, Mr Maloney. My name is Eric." But that was it, and soon gave up when nothing resembling anything remotely persuasive as to why Mr Maloney should help him presented itself to him. He decided that he would just have to improvise. Then warned himself: "Whatever you do, *don't* mention anything about his wife's tragic accident!"

Eric wasn't used to driving on the right-hand side of the road, and after several beeps and expletives from impatient, hot-headed, and caffeine-fueled drivers in their big American fuel-guzzling cars, he soon got the hang of it.

Once he got more onto the open roads, he started to enjoy himself. The car windows were down, allowing the cool mountain summer breeze to join him. The radio was on, playing a familiar tune he found himself singing along to. The tall buildings were replaced by tall cactus plants, and he was soon surrounded by beautiful countryside with magnificent mountains as a backdrop. It was so nice just to get out of the city for a change, he thought.

Eric could see a sign for the Indian reservation just up ahead, so knew that he must be close. In his vivid imagination, he expected to see "Wild Indians" galloping around on horseback, wearing traditional costumes with headdresses and war paint and so on, and wigwams scattered all around, but he saw nothing like that.

The Indian reservation belongs to the Paiute tribe and is located between the eastern slopes of Mount Charleston in the Spring Mountains and the western fringes of the Sheep Range, covering an area of 3,850 acres.

Farther ahead, Eric pulled into a gas station to ask for directions and was directed to an RV trailer park close by. "I hope it's the right one," Eric thought as he got back into his car.

The park was off the beaten track, but it didn't take him long to find it, thanks to the good instructions he was given. As Eric pulled up to park his car at the entrance to the site, dust billowed up all around him. He quickly shut the windows and got out and locked it.

Then brushed himself down as he walked over to the reception office. As he scanned the area, he remembered Mr Goldberg saying the place was run-down, and this place certainly matched the description all right. Eric could only see five RV's parked up on the grounds, and by the look of their condition they had probably been left static for a long time – they were all discoloured and rusty, and some had flat tyres while others didn't have any at all. Most had their curtains still closed.

He then discovered that the reception office was closed. He peered through the window, but it looked desolate. There was no sign of life anywhere, except a skinny-looking dog that came wandering buy, probably looking for scraps.

It was gone 9 am, which was when the sign said it would be open. Eric decided he would wait in his car in case someone should show up and get out of the uncompromising heat of the sun. "I need a cowboy hat or a sombrero," he thought.

Then, as he was walking across the carpark towards his car, out of the corner of his eye, he noticed someone pulling their curtain aside in the trailer home nearest to him. He stopped and turned to look. The curtain fell back in place, and a few moments later the door to the RV opened and an old skinny woman with long grey straggly hair appeared.

"*What* d'ya want?" she said abruptly, standing at the doorway with her arms folded, looking at him up and down suspiciously.

"Oh, hi, I'm looking for a man named Robert Maloney – I understand he lives here," replied Eric, feeling slightly ill at ease. Eric thought, "She's probably got a shotgun hung up above the door."

The old lady paused a moment. "Are you a reporter or a detective?" she said inquisitively with a nervous twitch.

Eric smiled. "No, Mam, I'm not," he answered politely. "My name is Eric Fartz, and I'm a fellow magician. I just wanted to meet him and have a chat, that's all," he explained, removing his shades, and then putting them immediately back on again to stop himself squinting. Even though it was still morning time, the sun was bright in the sky.

"You'll find him in the last trailer along," she said, seeming more relaxed.

"Thank you!" said Eric. He then started to walk in the direction of his trailer.

"*Say!* You're from *Australia*, aren't choo?" the elderly woman suddenly called out.

"*Yeah!*" answered Eric nodding his head to save himself time explaining he was from England.

"*Thought* so!" she said. "Well, *good luck* – the last magician that came knocking on his door, he pistol-whipped!" She then started cackling like an old witch and promptly went back inside.

"*Yikes!*" thought Eric (instead of 'Oh, 'eck!').

As he passed each trailer, curtains parted open, and more curious faces peered out from within. It felt like the longest walk he'd ever made, even though it was only less than forty metres away. And the nearer he got the faster his heart started beating.

When Eric reached Mr Maloney's trailer, he just stood there staring at it for a moment. His inner voice was telling him to turn back, get in his car, and get the hell out of there. He was glad he had his trainers on in case he had to dodge out of the way of bullets and make a run for it.

Too late! The door to Mr Maloney's trailer suddenly burst open and standing there glaring at him, was an unkempt, gaunt-looking old man, whose old, tattered jeans would most certainly fall to his ankles if it weren't for his tightened belt holding them up. His white vest was holey and looked like his clothes hadn't been washed in a while – and neither had he by the look of him.

"*Who* are you – *what* d'ya want?" the man hollowed in a curt, unfriendly manner.

"Mr Maloney?" asked Eric nervously while reminding himself not to mention the accident. The man didn't answer. "Good morning –"

"What's *good* about it?" he then miserably replied.

"I'm Eric Fartz, known as The Amazing Fartzini!" he said to no response. The old man clearly hadn't heard of him, which Eric was a little bit disappointed about, though, it wasn't surprising since he was a recluse. Eric then added, *"A Magician!"*

Upon hearing he was a magician, the old man yelled, *"Clear off!"* and immediately slammed the door shut.

Eric climbed up the three-tiered steps and knocked on the door, but it remained shut. "Mr Maloney, I've not come here to talk about your wife's tragic acci—" He stopped himself from finishing the word, thinking, "You *idiot,* now

you've gone and *blown* it!" Then continued. "—
I just wanted to ask for your advice, that's all!"

"I told ya to *clear off,* didn't I?" the voice
behind the door shouted angrily. "Now *go* away
before I call the *cops!*"

Eric just stood there for a moment
contemplating what to do. The barrel of an
old-fashioned musket then appeared from out
of a small open window, pointing directly at
him, and made his mind up for him. Eric
quickly turned and jumped off the steps.

"I've not come here to cause you any
trouble," Eric called out. "I just wanted to ask
for some advice on performing 'The Bullet
Catch', but if you don't want to help me, that's
fine!" Eric then started to walk away.

After a moment or two, the trailer door
swung open. *"Hold* on, *wait!"* Mr Maloney
called out to Eric. 'The Bullet Catch' you say?"

Eric stopped in his tracks and turned around
to face him. "Yeah," he replied in anticipation
for what the man would say next.

"Well, why *didn't* ya say so *beforehand?"* said
the old magician, standing in the doorway now
minus the gun. He even had a faint smile
cracked across his face – probably for the first
time in years. *"C'mon* back – *I'm* all ears!"

"*Thank you* Mr Maloney — I won't take up much of your time, I *promise!*" said Eric as he walked back towards him, pleased as punch.

"Call me Robert. Please excuse my gruffness a moment ago," said the old magician, whose smile had grown slightly wider. "What did ya say ya name was again?"

"Eric — pleased to meet you, Robert!" said Eric excitedly and in awe of the famous, or some would say, infamous magician.

"Likewise, Eric. You sound like you're from England!"

"*Yeah, I am!*" he replied, slightly taken aback that someone got it right for a change.

"… So, go on then, tell me what it is ya wanna know!"

"Well, I am going to be presenting a new show at the Excalibur very soon featuring The Bullet Catch. And so, I would appreciate your advice on which type of musket is best to use, and which method you would recommend for retrieving the bullet, and —" explained Eric very excitedly at breakneck speed.

"*Hold* on, *hold* on! *Slow* down, *slow* down! I tell ya what, why don't cha come into my palace and we can talk about it out of the sun."

Eric followed the daredevil magician into his trailer. It was dark and dingy and full of clutter, though, there were no signs of any magic paraphernalia anywhere. And it smelt like the bottom of a parrot's cage – which wasn't surprising when Eric spotted a large green feathered parrot sitting on a perch in the far corner, minus a cage.

"*Clear* off! *Clear* off!" shrieked the agitated parrot.

"*Henry!* Don't be *rude* to our guest!" said the old magician to his pet.

"He can *talk!*" said Eric, smiling.

"You can say that again – *too* much, sometimes!"

"*Clear* off, or I'll pistol whip ya!" then shrieked the bird.

"Be *quiet!*" said his owner, giving him a certain look.

Eric laughed.

"Just ignore him – Henry can be annoying sometimes, but he keeps me company in my old age."

"Have you had breakfast Mr Malo – Robert I mean?"

The old magician shook his head. "No – as you can probably tell, I don't eat much," he replied.

"Well, I noticed there's a diner not far from here, and I don't know about you, but I'm starving!"

"Ok, sure, if you're paying?"

"It will be my pleasure," Eric replied. He then noticed the old-fashioned musket that was pointed at him earlier, perched across the arm of the sofa, next to the window.

Robert saw him staring at it. "That's an antique muzzle-loading flintlock musket!" he announced. He then explained, "It was handed down to me by my father, who was also a magician and a good friend of the famous magician Chung Ling Soo! And I don't know how true it is, but my father told me that it once belonged to the great magician himself, and it was bequeathed to him when he died!"

"*Wow!* Does it still fire?" asked Eric, curious.

"Yep! You betcha! I've maintained it ever since it was presented to me," Robert answered. Eric's eyebrows went up slightly, feeling uneased. "It's about the only magic apparatus I kept after I packed up performing magic ..."

Robert put on a crinkled old shirt, then sat while he pulled on his cowboy boots, and on the way out picked up his tatty white Stetson hat.

"*Bye*, Henry!" Eric called out.

"*Clear* off!" the parrot replied.

Eric drove them both to the local diner, which was busy and noisy. The two magicians sat opposite each other in one of the booths and ordered some breakfast. Eric ordered crispy bacon, eggs and hash browns, and Robert ordered sausages and pancakes with Maple Syrup, and both also ordered toast and coffee.

After the young waitress had taken their orders and filled their mugs with coffee, Eric showed her a quick magic trick. It was the old trick where the magician pretends to bend a teaspoon in half, and after making a few magical gestures, restores it.

"That was *amazing!* I thought you'd damaged it!" she remarked, laughing.

"Nicely done!" said the old magician as the waitress left to give their orders in.

"Thanks!" said Eric, pleased to get the veteran magician's approval.

"That trick is even older than I am!" he said jokingly. "But as simple as it is, it is very effective."

Eric agreed. "Yes, it is. It was one of the first tricks that I ever learnt."

"Probably, one of mine, too," Robert commented, smiling vacantly for a moment as he reminisced back to a much happier time in his life. He then gave Eric a tip on performing it. "If you hide a dime in your hand, you can make it look to the audience that the tip of the handle is still in view while you're bending it."

"That's a *great* idea!" said Eric, pleased for his advice. "Thanks!"

One could clearly see the wise old magician was pleased to be helping the much younger magician, whom he could see had something about him that many other magicians didn't have.

"So, you were telling me that you are going to perform the Bullet Catch," he then reminded Eric, looking serious again. Eric nodded. "You do know this trick has claimed the lives of many magicians, don't cha?"

Eric nodded, then said, "I have done a fair amount of research into it already, and I want to perform it in the way that the great master magicians like Chung Ling Soo originally performed it, so as to create a real sense of danger and excitement."

The daredevil magician's eyes lit up, flaring a burning passion up inside him that he hadn't experienced in a long, long time.

"I remember my father telling me stories of when he watched Chung Ling Soo perform the stunt, and the great excitement it caused among the audience. My father also told me that to create excitement, it wasn't enough just to perform dangerous magic tricks: he told me the most important thing the magician must have is –" The wise old magician paused a moment, and Eric leaned in closer as he waited to hear what great wisdom he was about to give, completely transfixed. "COFFEE!" he suddenly called out to one of the waitresses carrying the coffee jug, completely sidetracked.

"Coffee?" Eric said to himself, bewildered, until he saw the waitress coming over with it.

Once she refilled their mugs and was about to leave, the old magician said to the waitress, "Will the food take long, only I am *so* hungry I could eat my knife!"

"Eat your *knife!"* she replied aghast, not knowing whether he was joking or not.

"Yeah, they're *delicious!"* he replied.

He gave Eric a knowing wink from across the table. It was an old magic trick that he was about to do, which Eric already knew. He picked the knife up from the table by sliding it off the table with both hands, tipped his head back, and brought it up to his wide-open mouth as if he was about to swallow it. He then hesitated and lowered his hands and placed the knife back onto the table, saying, "Oh, I forgot to add some salt." Upon saying that, he picked up the saltshaker and proceeded to sprinkle the knife with salt. Then, without hesitation, he picked it up again, and to the shock and horror of the waitress, acted as if he pushed it down his throat and swallowed it! The waitress instantly let out a big scream. Robert and Eric both laughed. Then when she saw that the strange man was perfectly all right, and realised that it was just another magic trick, she relaxed and began to join in with the laughter.

"You scared the living daylights out of me then!" she said as she was leaving, laughing, and shaking her head still.

When the waitress had left, the old magician then subtly reached into his lap, picked up the knife, and placed it back into its place on the table, smiling the widest he'd smiled for a long time.

Eric thought it was nice to see the old

magician enjoying performing magic again. He could see that he hadn't lost his touch. He complimented him on the performance of the trick and then after a moment, said, "You were saying?"

The old magician took a sip of coffee. "Oh yes, *sorry,* I couldn't resist showing the waitress a trick just then," he said with a twinkle in his eye, suddenly remembering. Eric leaned in closer to listen again. "My father told me that the most important thing a magician must have is –"

"BACON AND EGGS AND SAUSAGES AND PANCAKES!" suddenly screamed the waitress, holding one plate in each hand and making Eric jump.

"OVER HERE!" called out the old magician. The waitress promptly came over and set their plates down in front of them and promptly left again, still slightly in shock and wondering what else the two magicians might do. Well, no sooner had she set the plates down, Robert started gulping down his food, not saying a word – he couldn't get it into his mouth quick enough!

"And I thought I was hungry!" said Eric to himself. He didn't want to disturb the hungry old magician eating, so tucked into his food without speaking as well …

"*Passion!*" suddenly announced the old magician as soon as he had made all his breakfast disappear.

"'*Passion*'?" said Eric, just as he was about to put a slice of buttered toast into his mouth, bewildered again.

"Yes, '*passion*' is the most important thing the magician must have!"

"*Oh, yes!*" said Eric, remembering. "I thought you were going to say showmanship."

"Well, of course, a magician must have showmanship. But, before a magician can be a showman, he must first have '*passion*'!"

"Right!" said Eric, listening intently.

"You can't fake it – it's something that comes from deep down inside you, and it's *got* to be real! All the great magicians had passion!"

Just then, the waitress came back over. "Can I get you, Gentlemen, anything else?" she asked as she started to clear away the plates.

"I'm full, thanks," Eric replied. "What about you Robert?" Eric couldn't help but notice that he kept looking at the sumptuous apple pie displayed on the counter.

"Why, thank you, Eric. I'll take a piece of that

delicious-looking apple pie with two scoops of vanilla ice cream, please Mam?" he said gratefully.

"Sure!" she answered, looking at him a bit surprised at what he was ordering at breakfast time – though, nothing would surprise her after seeing him swallow a knife. Eric couldn't help but smile, finding it amusing.

Robert enjoyed eating his apple pie and ice cream. "I've not eaten apple pie and ice cream for ages!" he said, lapping it up. And as soon as he had polished it all down, he spent the rest of the morning advising Eric on the best type of gun and method to use to accomplish the Bullet Catch, while continuing to drink endless refills of coffee.

"… But where would I acquire such a trick musket – I've *never* seen it advertised in a magic shop catalogue, *or* online?" asked Eric.

"Well, you won't," answered Robert. "They are not made anymore. The only way you would be able acquire one would be to go to a professional magic prop's builder, but I doubt whether you would be able to have it made in time!"

Eric looked dismayed. It was the one thing – and most important thing – that he had overlooked in his haste to perform the crowd-pulling stunt.

After a moment of silence, "Look, I tell ya what, Eric. I will happily give you my gimmicked musket if you promise to look after it – I can't see me ever using it again," kindly said the old magician, pleased to help the young magician with whom he had become taken with. That "passion" for performing magic he was referring to earlier he saw Eric had in abundance.

"*Really!* Oh, that's enormously kind of you, thank you *so* much – I promise I will look after it!" replied Eric, delighted.

And so, after Eric payed for the meals and left the waitress a generous tip, they both left the diner and headed back to the RV trailer park. In the trailer, Robert presented Eric with the gimmicked musket and ramrod – it even came with the original carry case – and then explained the secret workings of it more thoroughly. As it was a flintlock muzzle-loading musket, he also provided him with an ample supply of gunpowder and lead musket balls.

They then went out the back onto open ground, and Robert taught Eric how to load and fire the weapon. As Eric soon found out, muskets were not all that accurate. But after several failed attempts at the target, he did manage to hit it, much to his joy and satisfaction.

Eric had spent a wonderful morning in the company of the daredevil magician, but it was now time to make his way back home. Eric thanked Robert once again and said goodbye to him and Henry. To which Henry immediately replied: "Clear off!" making Eric laugh. Before Eric left, Robert reminded him: "Remember, safety must come first, and as well as regularly maintaining the gun, it is also most important to make sure that you trust whoever it is that will be firing it – your life may depend on it! Never forget that although you're a magician in name, you are merely but a mortal by birth!"

As Eric walked back to his car with his head filled with ideas and his arms full of weaponry, curtains inside the other trailers parted open once again, and the reception office was still closed. He got in his car, and drove off, disappearing in a cloud of dust!

CHAPTER TWELVE

THE ENEMY WITHIN!

Eric arrived back to his apartment – which seemed like a luxury 5-star apartment compared to where he had just been – early afternoon. He put the antique musket and explosives away somewhere safe, and quickly got ready to go and amaze people during the matinee show.

Meanwhile, at the newly built rival resort, Eric's rival magician, Chet Stevenson, was discussing his rival magician, The Amazing Fartzini's, rival magic show.

"The Bullet Catch!" said Chet alarmed to hear it. "You're *kidding* me! Well, why didn't ya tell me this beforehand?"

"Because *I've* only just found out myself, so don't *blame* me!" said the curvy-shaped female standing opposite him in his dressing room.

"Are you positively sure that you heard it correctly?" questioned Chet, who was becoming more and more agitated by it.

"*Yeah!* I'm positive. The rehearsals start on Monday, and he's also gonna be publicising the new show on all the local news channels and just about everywhere else –"

"*Darn* it!" he shouted, thumping his fist down hard onto the dressing table in a rage.

"*Calm* down! Calm down!" she said to her angry and jealous boyfriend as she turned up the sexy R&B Slow Jam music track that was playing.

He sat down. "I can't have him get one over on me, d'ya understand. *I'm* the best magician in Vegas, not him!"

"*Of course,* you are! *Of course,* you are!" she told him, moving seductively behind him, and massaging his shoulders to help soothe him – and his ego – as the crucifix on her necklace danced about on his bald patch as if it were a dance floor while gyrating her hips to the beat. "Look, I've not let ya down so far, have I?"

"No," he just replied, starting to relax.

"*Remember*, I was the one who informed you about all his secret methods, and what new tricks he was going to be including in his show! And, risked being prosecuted for sabotaging his magic props! *Not* to mention the $10,000. I stole from out of the that fool Eric's dressing room (she failed to mention the other $15,000 she had stolen from him), along with all the other money and jewelry I stole from the other dressing rooms, *which* I didn't hear ya complaining about then!"

"Listen, I do appreciate what you are doin' for me."

"*Us!* What I am doin' for *us!*" she made clear.

"Of course, *us!*" he replied, smiling.

She started to chuckle. "Mind you I thought I was gonna have kittens the other day when I saw Eric holding the remains of the newspaper that I used to fill out the bag of money!" Both chuckled.

"By the way, how did you get into Eric's dressing room. I thought you said ever since he was in trouble from the Mafia, he kept it locked?"

"He does," she replied. Then explained as she continued massaging him and stroking his mane. "It was easy – Dirk, the stage manager fancies me – mind you, I think he fancies all the dancers – and he's always asking me out for a drink. So, I flashed my eyelids at him –"

"*Oh*, did ya now!" said Chet, looking displeased.

She then carried on. "– and, between shows that evening he took me to a small bar close by – a real sleazy joint – and a little later when he started to get a bit frisky –"

"*Frisky?*" said Chet interrupting again.

"Well, I didn't go with him for fun – *urgh!* He's *disgusting!* He's in his fifties! Now will you *shut up* and listen …? When he started to get a bit intimate with me, I picked his pocket and stole his bunch of keys. Then when he went to buy me another drink, I just removed Eric's dressing room key, labelled conveniently number one, and hid it in my handbag. There's so many keys attached to his keyring; he wasn't gonna notice just one missing!"

"Well, how did ya get the bunch of keys back to him without him realizing they were missing?" he then asked.

"Oh, I just left them on his seat and when he returned, I told him his keys must have dropped out of his pocket." She laughed.

"Crafty! You ought to be a magician!" said

Chet grinning. "You'd be really good at it!"

"Anyway, I then made my excuses and disappeared outta there faster than you can make those white tigers vanish! The trouble is, he now keeps making eyes at me even more!" They both laughed.

"But then how did ya get the key back on the keyring?" he then asked, even more curious.

"The next day, I saw the stage manager's bunch of keys just lying around in the wings, and so when he was distracted, I secretly slipped the key back on the keyring. *Easy!*"

"Well, as long as nothing else happened."

"Are you *jealous?*" she asked.

"No, course, not! I have twenty-five thousand reasons not to be jealous!" he said smiling widely.

"Yeah, and don't cha forget it!"

He reached up and held her hand tenderly. "I'm sorry, I didn't mean to take my frustrations out on you earlier, darlin'," he told her, tilting his head back to look up at her. "But the sooner he leaves Vegas and goes back to jolly old England the better!"

"Don't choo worry, I'll make sure that he doesn't get to perform the Bullet Catch trick. We can't have any rival magicians stepping on our toes, now can we?" she said smiling connivingly. He then smiled back at her in the same way.

"That's my darlin'," said Chet, now feeling much happier. He then got up and they both hugged one another and kissed passionately.

After a short while, she pulled her lips away from his. "… Hey, I've gotta go and get ready for the matinee show!" she said suddenly, realising the time.

"Okay, yeah, go and wreak some more havoc at the Excalibur." He then started laughing.

"What are ya laughing about?" said his girlfriend.

"I was just picturing that actress we hired, screaming and make a scene at his show because she was frightened of *beards!*" Both laughed out loud together. "And *what* was it you told him again?"

"I told him my auntie was scared of moustaches!" They both burst out laughing again.

"I also thought it was funny when you sabotaged the Impalement Illusion, and he got stuck on the tip of the sword in midair!"

"I think the funniest moment was when I secretly tipped a load of trash into his 'Sub

Trunk Illusion'," she then said, laughing at the thought of it. "It stank the whole showroom out! The other assistant had to rush off and puke up in the wings! As soon as the show was over, I made the excuse that I had to leave straight away because my mother had become very ill. And I just left the two of 'em to clean it all up!"

"Now that was wicked!" said Chet.

"Yeah, I know," she agreed, smirking, "but you were the one who wanted me to disrupt his show, and it certainly did that alright!" she said laughing again.

"Well, just be careful that choo don't get caught!"

"Of course, but it was funny, you've got to admit."

"Yeah!" admitted Chet, grinning.

"Anyway, see ya tonight!"

"*Oh,* before ya go! I've bought you a present!" announced her boyfriend. He reached into his coat pocket, which was hanging up on the back of the door and pulled out a small jewellery box and gave it to her. She opened it, and to her delight, inside were a pair of diamond earrings.

"Oh, they're *beautiful!*" she said, thrilled to

bits. *"Thank you!"*

"I thought you'd like 'em!"

She then kissed him quickly on the cheek and said, "I must go! Bye, honey!"

"See ya, Gloria!"

Eric arrived at the resort and parked his car in the Excalibur staff car park at the rear. Then made his way over to the stage door rear entrance, where he was greeted by the security doorman, Tom.

As he was signing in, Tom said, "Oh, I've got another letter for you. Just a minute." Tom then got up from his chair and went and fetched it from a pigeonhole shelf compartment located at the rear of the office. Eric immediately thought, while Tom's back is turned, anybody could just walk in without being noticed, which was concerning. After a little bit of searching, he found it and handed it to Eric, smiling through his thick beard as he said, "Another letter from one of your many fans I expect!"

Eric laughed and said, "Thanks, Tom!"

Eric took the letter with him to his dressing room, sat down at his dressing table, where there was more lighting, and ripped open the envelope. Upon opening it, he immediately noticed it was the same handwriting as the previous warning message he received. Only this time the message was longer. It read:

Dear Mr Fartz,

Please excuse my scribbly writing, but I am writing this letter in haste. You don't know me, but my abusive and controlling ex-partner is hellbent on killing you! And I am risking my own life by trying to warn you!

Despite my previous warnings to you, it appears that you haven't heeded my advice and continue to remain in Las Vegas still. I deplore you to leave now before it is too late. I promise you that the threat is not a hoax, but very real!

Meet me in the lobby at the Desert Sands Motel, Freemont Street in Downtown Las Vegas tonight at 11.30 pm sharp, and I will explain everything then. I shall be in disguise wearing a long blonde wig, and a red dress and matching red handbag. Don't worry if you can't find me, I will introduce myself to you, anyway.

Yours sincerely,

Once again, there was no signature or clue as to who wrote it, or more worryingly, *who* it was intent on killing him. "The only way to find out is if I meet this mystery woman in person," thought Eric. "But what if the person I meet is the actual killer trying to lure me to my death!" he then suddenly thought. "I'll just have to be careful – because if there is someone out there wanting to kill me, I need to have them arrested!"

Eric folded the letter, put it back into its envelope, and left it on his dressing room table, while he went to set up his magic apparatus and check it was all working correctly, and that no one had tampered with it. On the way there, he met Ruben coming the other way, who as usual had his nose in the air and tried to blank him, but Eric had had enough of his trouble making and decided to have word with him.

"I heard what you were saying about me yesterday behind my back," Eric said to him assertively. "*Listen,* if you've got something to say about me, then *say* it to my face, d'ya understand!"

"I don't know what you're talking about,

darling!" Ruben replied curtly with both hands on his hips in defiance.

"Oh, yes you do – don't try and pretend otherwise." Ruben started to walk away ignoring him. "Hey, *don't* turn your back on me when I'm talking ya! That's *rude!*"

Ruben then flapped his right hand limply in the air, acting dismissively, saying, *"Whatever!"*

Then just as he was about to enter the dancers dressing room, Eric quickly called out, "Look, if you are gonna try and cause trouble for me, then I will speak to Mr Constantino about not having dancers in the show at all!"

Well, as soon as Eric said that, Ruben stopped, turned to face Eric, smiled and said grovelingly, "I was only *joking* Eric! There's no need to speak to Mr Constantino. I promissse you won't get any trouble from me or any of my dancers!" As soon as Ruben heard the name Mr Constantino, he changed his attitude completely.

Eric nodded and said, "Good!" He then turned and headed for the stage once again, thinking, "Yeah, right, I'll believe that when I see it!"

"I've already choreographed a *fabulous* opening routine, darling!" Ruben called out to

Eric before going into the dressing room and immediately dropping his well-choreographed fake smile.

After setting up his magic apparatus, Eric made his way back down to his dressing room to put on his makeup and get dressed into his stage costume. When he got there, he discovered his door was unlocked. "That's strange," he thought. "I could have sworn I'd locked it?"

No sooner had he entered the room and closed the door, he heard a knock, knock on the door, which, ever since the Mafia showed up that time has always made him feel wary.

"It's only *me*, honey!" called out Gloria, sounding chirpy compared to how she last was the day before when she left him in a huff.

Eric quickly folded the envelope in half and shoved it in his rear jeans pocket. Then went and opened the door and let her in. She was already dressed in her skimpy stage costume and wearing her new diamond earrings.

"Hiya Gloria, come in," said Eric, not knowing where to look. Then in a slight flummox, said, "They're a lovely pair – of *earrings* I mean!"

Gloria grinned. "Why, thank you, honey!"

In that awkward moment, they then both tried to speak at the same time, but Eric let Gloria continue.

"… I was about to say that I apologise for the way I was with you yesterday," she said. "It's just that I was tired and a bit miffed that I only found out about the new show then." Before Eric had a chance to speak, she then quickly said, *"Let's* hug it out!" and immediately wrapped her arms around him in an overfamiliar way. Eric didn't know where to put his hands!

Truth be known, she had always had a mad crush on Eric ever since she first laid eyes on him, and if he hadn't already been in a serious relationship, she would've dumped Chet in a heartbeat to be with him. And although she would never show it in public, she felt not only very jealous towards his girlfriend, Emily – or any other girl that flashed her eyelids at him – but also very bitter and resentful towards Eric because she knew that he preferred someone else and could never have him.

Chet was also very jealous, bitter, and resentful towards Eric, but for a different reason: he knew what a naturally gifted magician Eric was, and would give his right arm to be as good as Eric (though, that wouldn't be very sensible given that he is a magician).

And, all the while Eric remained in Las Vegas, he was a constant reminder to them both that in their narcissistic kingdom, they were inferior – which they hated. As to whom out of the two of them wore the crown for being the most egotistical and vain and prepared to go to whatever lengths it takes to reign supreme is hard to tell.

Once Gloria had let go of him, and Eric could breathe again, he said, "Don't worry, Gloria, it's fine! And I'm sorry that I didn't let ya know sooner."

"Well, as long as you let me know straight away in future, I'll forgive ya," she told him with a smile.

"I *promise!*" he said grinning back at her.

Changing the subject, she then said to him, "It was terrible that somebody threw a load of disgusting trash into your Sub trunk Illusion." After a moment's pause, she then asked, "Has anyone mentioned if they saw anyone do it yet?"

"No," he just replied, shaking his head, much to her relief.

"Well, *hopefully* the culprit will soon be caught!"

"*Yeah,* let's hope so," Eric replied, sighing.

He had enough inner demons to deal with as it was, let alone an unknown enemy within the theatre. Not to mention the Mafia was still on his back. Oh, and someone who may be trying to kill him!

"I'm thinking of laying a trap," then said Eric.

"*A trap?*" said Gloria inquisitively.

"Yeah, I could hide tiny cameras inside each of the stage illusions – then we'll not only know *who* the culprit is, but well have *proof* as well!" he answered buoyantly. "… In fact, that's *just* what I'm gonna do!"

Her face dropped slightly, but then she quickly recovered her smile and said in a slightly strained way, "What a *good* idea!"

Then smiling wider, she said, "Oh, it feels *so* good that we are on talking terms again." She then went to kiss him on the lips, but he moved sharply to the side, leaving her kissing the air instead. Both pretended it never happened to save any embarrassment, though secretly she felt like he'd stuck a knife in her heart by rejecting her advances again.

Eric cleared his throat. "Well, we'd both better get ready for the show!" he said as he went and sat down at his dressing table.

"Yeah!" she just replied, inwardly upset, and feeling hurt, as she went to open the door to leave.

"… *Oh,* by the way. How's your poor sick Mum?" asked Eric caringly.

She stopped and turned around to face him. "My sick *Mum?*" she answered, as if she didn't understand what he meant. She then suddenly remembered the excuse she had told him. "Oh, she's fine now, thanks – just indigestion, that was all."

"Oh, that's good to h—" Eric began to say, but she had already left.

CHAPTER THIRTEEN

A GRIM DISCOVERY!

Thankfully the shows that day were performed without any hitches, and as soon as the last show was over, Eric quickly got changed and headed out onto the Strip where he flagged down a taxi going in the direction of Downtown. He thought it would be quicker to take a taxi rather than to drive, and just in case his inner demons got the better of him and he decided to have a drink – or two – or three. His heart was racing fast. He got in the taxi and pulled out the letter to check that he had remembered the name of the motel correctly. "Desert Sands Motel, Freemont Street, please!" he said to the driver. As soon as he said it, the driver raised his eyebrows as if to say, why would you want to go there. "Okay, sir," is what he said. Where Eric had asked to go was a seedy part of town renowned for drug dealing and prostitution, and not considered to be safe after dark.

The driver reached Downtown Vegas. "Just pull over here, please!" said Eric. He thought it wiser not to go directly to the motel and instead got out at the bustling central area of Downtown Vegas, not far from the Golden Nugget Casino where Freemont Street goes through, favouring to walk so he'd be less conspicuous.

It was very crowded and noisy with lots of people enjoying a night out. Eric glanced down at his watch; it was 11.08 pm. The letter stated to meet him at the motel at 11.30 pm. So, he weaved his way quickly through the crowds heading east along Freemont Street so as not to be late. The farther he walked along the street the quieter it got. He could see undesirables hanging about on street corners on either side. Lady's of the night called over to him touting for business. He could also hear several police sirens nearby. He just kept walking and looking purposefully straight ahead. It couldn't be far now. He looked at his watch again, and it was now 11.20 pm.

As he got nearer, he could see the flashing lights of emergency service vehicles farther up ahead and was suddenly aware of a lot of commotion. People around him were rushing over to the scene to find out what was going on. He quickened his pace and could soon see the motel sign on his left, but as he approached the motel, he discovered that he couldn't go any further because the police had corned off the area and were telling people to move back. Eric squeezed his way through a group of onlookers to the front and spotted three police cars and an ambulance parked up directly outside the motel entrance. There was also a TV news reporter there.

"I wonder what's happened?" he thought. He quickly glanced at his watch again, and it was now 11.28 pm. "Oh, no!" he then thought. "I'm going to be late!" He then called out to one of the police officers nearby. *"Excuse* me please, officer! What's happened?"

"There's been a homicide, so please keep back!" he answered somberly.

"Oh, that's terrible!" thought Eric. A few minutes later, two ambulance men escorted by several police officers came out of the motel entrance wheeling someone in a body bag. Everyone looked on aghast. The ambulance men stopped at the rear of the ambulance while one of the detectives partially unzipped the body bag to show the victims corpse to one of his colleagues waiting outside. From where Eric was standing, he had a clear view. He was shocked to see that the victim was a young-looking woman with blonde hair, whom he could just about glimpse was wearing a red dress. She fitted the description in the letter perfectly. "Maybe it's not her and it's just a coincidence!" he thought. But what made him convinced that it was her was when one of the detectives removed a wig she was wearing and put it into a clear forensics bag already containing a small red handbag. The detective then quickly zipped the body bag back up, and the poor woman, whoever she was, was loaded into the back of the ambulance.

Eric stumbled backwards slightly, still in shock. He turned and quickly made his way back along Freemont Street. He didn't want to wait around any longer in case the killer was still around and may come after him next. His heart was pounding with fear. He looked for a taxi, but there were none in sight. By now most people were gathered at the crime scene, so the street was now almost deserted up ahead. Every sudden noise made him jumpy.

As Eric continued to walk at a quick pace, he couldn't help thinking, "If *only* I'd have got there sooner, then perhaps I could have met the mystery woman, and she could have told me the name of her brutal ex-partner. I should have taken the taxi all the way there – maybe then I could have even saved her life!"

Maybe Eric was being paranoid, but he couldn't help but feel that someone was following him. He quickly looked behind him, but there was no one there. "Calm down!" he told himself.

Just up ahead he could see a small group of young thuggish looking guys wearing hoods, behaving like they were up to no good, so he decided to cross the road. They then spotted him and started crossing the road towards him. One of them had an unlit cigarette in his mouth.

"Hey man, what's ya rush?" he said, as his cigarette moved about in the corner of his mouth. "Have ya got a light?"

"No, sorry, I don't smoke," just said Eric and

carried on walking. But before he knew it, his path became blocked, and he was surrounded by five of them all snarling at him like a pack of hungry wolves. Suddenly Eric then felt himself being dragged and pushed backwards towards a wall. His back thumped up against it.

One of them quickly pulled out a knife and held it to his throat. "Gimme ya money, or I'll *kill* ya!" he demanded threateningly through gritted teeth. Eric just froze for a moment.

"Hurry up!" said another impatiently. Looking quickly back and forth over his shoulder.

"Alright! Alright! Just give me some space!" said Eric, whose senses were now fully heightened. The pack stepped back a bit. Then Eric reached into his trouser pocket and pulled out his wallet. "Can ya break a fifty?" said Eric, straight-faced as he pulled out a fifty dollar note from his wallet.

"What?" said the alpha male of the pack, still brandishing the knife, taken aback by Eric unusual request. The others all started laughing at Eric's nerve, and then he too also saw the funny side of it and joined in with the laughter. This was Eric's chance to get away from them, but the jollity didn't last long, though. The leader of the pack said angrily, "Gimme dat!"

and went to snatch it out of Eric's hand. But before he could, Eric used his magic skills and transformed the bill into a pack of fifty-two playing cards far out numbering them! Everyone was flabbergasted and couldn't believe what they had just witnessed right under their noses. Eric immediately bent the pack sharply inwards, and then sprung the cards into the face of the knife wielder, surprising him, and causing him flinch and stumble backwards. Eric seized the moment, and pushed his way passed him and another thug and ran.

"After him!" called out the pack leader. They gave chase along the sidewalk. Eric still had a few cards left in his hand and twisted his torso around as he ran and spun cards at them to slow them down. He was an expert at "Card Throwing" and landed one of them on target giving one of the thugs a papercut.

But the thugs weren't about to give up that easy and kept chasing him. Fortunately for Eric, just as a couple of them were gaining on him, a police car was gaining on them from behind with its lights flashing and its siren blaring. The pack then stopped chasing him and quickly sprang off in different directions, down alleyways, and adjoining streets.

Eric looked over his shoulder, and when he saw that he was no longer being chased, he stopped running. He immediately bent over, resting his hands on his knees to get his breath back. The police car screeched to a halt alongside Eric, accidentally breaching the curb and hitting a fire hydrant, and two young chubby police officers quickly jumped out aiming their handguns at him.

"HANDS WHERE WE CAN SEE 'EM!" screamed one of the officers. "ON THE GROUND!" screamed the other. Then the next thing Eric knew was, one of them was pinning him face-down on the ground, while the other was putting handcuffs on him behind his back. Eric tried to plead his innocence and explain that he had just been mugged and was running away from the gang, but they told him to remain silent, assuring him that they take down his statement in a short while. They then lifted him to an upright position and told him to lean up against the car, facing away from them. One of them then kicked his legs wide apart and began frisking him while asking if he was carrying any hidden weapons or in possession of any drugs.

"They must suspect I'm a gang member!" thought Eric, still feeling shaken up by his previous ordeal, let alone now this. And even though he was no longer being hounded and harassed by the criminals, it didn't feel much different now – except that the police were wearing uniforms. Meanwhile, the real criminals were getting away. He was annoyed but kept silent and did as he was ordered.

Once the cop had finished patting him down from the rear, he turned Eric around and began patting him down at the front. "… He's clear!" said one of them to the other.

"It's just a precaution, sir," said the other, returning his gun to his holster.

The cop that had been searching him then went to turn him around to remove the handcuffs, but to the officer's utter surprise, Eric saved him the trouble and brought the pair of unlocked handcuffs around to the front and handed them over to him. "Are you looking for these?" he said, grinning slightly.

"*What? Wait!* Hold on a minute! How d'ya get out of –?" said the flummoxed cop.

"You must have forgotten to tighten 'em!" said the other cop.

"*Oh* no I didn't!" replied his partner.

"*Oh* yes you did!" then responded the other one. "You *must* have done."

Eric thought, "What is this – *a pantomime?*"

"I can assure you that I *definitely* did not!" then stated the other cop again in his defence …

This squabbling back and forth went on for a little while, which Eric found highly amusing. He just stood there leaning against the police car with his arms folded. The cop who put Eric in the cuffs then asked *him,* "I did put the cuffs on ya tightly, didn't I sir?" Eric just nodded, trying not to laugh. "See!" said the cop to his partner.

Eric's amusement didn't last long, though.

"I am afraid we're gonna have to issue you with an on the spot fine of $50.00 for littering the sidewalk with playing cards, sir!" then said one of the officers.

Eric couldn't believe his rotten luck but thought there was no use disputing it and making a fuss. And so, instead of handing over the $50.00 bill to the criminals, he ended up reluctantly handing it over to the police instead.

The rookie cops finally got round to taking down Eric's details.

"What is your full name, sir?" asked one of

the cops.

"Eric Fartz,"

A large grin started to appear and grow and grow on the police officer's faces.

"Would ya repeat that, please sir?" said the same officer.

"Eric Fart—" Both officers suddenly burst out laughing. "I thought that's what ya said!"

It reminded Eric of being back at school again, but he kept his cool and just smiled, thinking, "I've heard it all before," and didn't let it bother him – he had the last laugh because he was the one with his name up in lights.

"… Sorry about that, Mr *Fartz!*" Both officers started laughing again. "… Please continue." …

Eventually the two officers managed to control themselves and took down the rest of Eric's details. Then Eric finally gave them his statement of the alleged crime. He told them about the attempted mugging, describing the gang as best he could. And when they inquired what he was doing there in the first place, he explained about the warning messages and that he had arranged to meet the murder victim at the Desert Sands Motel.

He showed them the letter, and the

policemen decided it would be best if Eric was taken to the police station to make a further statement and to help the police with their investigation.

"Did they catch the killer?" asked Eric hopeful.

"No, I'm afraid not, sir. The perpetrator is still at large. And whoever it was is one *sick* individual!" said one of them.

"It's a grim state of affairs!" said the other, shaking his head.

"Yeah, the poor woman!" said Eric, looking sorrowful"

"I was referring to our *squad car* – look at the *whopping* big *dent* in it!" he immediately responded by saying.

And so, after the policemen finally finished lamenting about their damaged police car, Eric got a free ride to the Las Vegas Police Department Headquarters on the Strip.

CHAPTER FOURTEEN

THE LAS VEGAS METROPOLITAN POLICE DEPARTMENT HEADQUARTERS

The police deputies escorted Eric into the Las Vegas Metropolitan Police Department Headquarters, or LVMPD for short, on Las Vegas Boulevard South. It was a large building, and right next to the Bali Hai Golf Course Eric noticed.

On the way there in the police car, Eric struck up quite a conversation with the two deputies, even talking to each other on a first-name basis – one of the deputies was called Bob, and the other was called Eddie. And as soon as Eric mentioned he was the magician, known as The Amazing Fartzini, and was staring at the Excalibur, the officers were keen and excited to talk to him. They asked him lots of questions about magic, such as: "How do magicians do that trick where they saw a woman in half and then put her back together again?" And: "How'd they levitate someone?" (of course, Eric didn't tell them). Eric even agreed, after having his arm twisted (not literally!) to show them a couple of quick magic tricks before entering the main building – he would have shown them a card trick, but his cards had performed their final trick and were now all littered along Freemont Street. Despite doing magic tricks for them, he never got his fifty dollars back, though.

When they entered the building, it was a hectic scene of lots of people shouting and hollering, with police officers moving about here and there – some escorting handcuffed criminals and drunken and disorderly individuals to their rent-free rooms for the night.

The two rookie deputies brought Eric in front of the desk sergeant. He was a straight-faced, middle-aged, overweight guy with a large moustache named Jessie (that's him, not his moustache), who as well as the spare tyres around his waist also seemed to be carrying the weight of the world on his shoulders.

"Well, if it isn't 'Tweedledee' and 'Tweedledum'!" he said to the two deputies. "And who have you two clowns brought along to see me this time?"

"This is Eric … Fartz," said Bob. Both the deputies looked at each other with creased-up contorted faces, desperately wanting to laugh, but a stern look from the sergeant immediately put a stop to that.

Now more serious looking, both the deputies then briefly briefed the sergeant and handed him their notes.

"… He's a *magician*, Jessie!" said Bob, or it may have been Eddie. I can't remember, but anyway, before they left to go and patrol the streets once more, the pair of them continued to express their excitement about meeting The Amazing Fartzini to the desk sergeant. "He's staring at the Excalibur!" said one of them. And "You should see his magic tricks – they're *awesome!*" said the other. Both acting like little children – which was worrying.

The sergeant waved goodbye to the rookie deputies, immediately shaking his head in disbelief, while thinking, "The force must be desperate for numbers!" and said to the tired looking, slightly bedraggled figure standing in front of him, "I'd love to watch your magic tricks Eric, but right now I'd be more impressed if you could make all the criminals here disappear!"

Eric chuckled. "But if I did that," he replied, "you'd be out of a job!"

"That's true," said the sergeant, cracking the faintest of smiles – though, it was unclear as he could have just been passing wind. He then quickly scanned over the deputy's poorly scribbled notes. "I understand that you've reported a crime – an attempted mugging, correct?"

"Yes, officer."

"Well, rest assured, we will investigate this thoroughly, sir!" he reassured Eric. He then clarified Eric's details – where he was currently living and working, and his contact details and so on. "Now I understand that you may have some evidence involving a homicide that took place at the Desert Sands Motel late last evening?"

"Er, yes, officer," Eric replied. He then reached into his trouser pocket, feeling nervous and fumbling slightly, and removed the folded letter and handed it to the sergeant as possible evidence in the case. And then went on to explain about the mysterious warning messages he received and told him that he had intended to meet the mystery woman at the motel that same evening, where she was going to reveal the identity of the person threatening to kill him. But, of course, when he arrived, it was too late.

"I see, sir," kept saying the sergeant as he listened closely and took down Eric's statement in more detail. "… Well, thank you for your statement, sir. Now are you sure that's everything?"

"Yes, I believe so," replied Eric.

"Well, that'll be all for now –"

"Will I receive police protection – I mean, someone is clearly out to kill me, officer?"

"Well, based solely on a letter, without knowing who this someone is, and having no real proof of their intentions, that will not be possible, I'm afraid. This letter could be a hoax for all we know. Being a celebrity in Vegas does, unfortunately, attract hoaxers. But, *of course,* if someone is attacking you, don't hesitate to call us, okay."

"Well, that's reassuring!" thought Eric, cynically. He nodded, saying, "Right!"

"We may need to ask you further questions about this case sir, so please don't leave the country in the next few weeks or so while the investigation is still ongoing," said the sergeant in a more serious tone.

Eric suddenly thought, "Oh, 'eck, do they think I'm a suspect?" Then asked, "What, d'ya think *I'm* a suspect?"

"Well, at this stage, sir, we can't rule anything out –"

"The Amazing Fartzini! I thought that was you!" said a loud booming voice, walking towards him from the other side of the desk. It was the Sheriff Bill Bridges – the same person Eric had met on the Bali Hai Golf course recently. With him was detective Mark Hitchcock, who was heading the murder case investigation. Hitchcock was a very serious looking gentleman – but then, murder was a very serious business.

At first Eric wasn't sure where he had seen the Sheriff's face before. Then he remembered. "Oh, hi, Bill." It had been a long day, and he was feeling shattered.

"Committed a crime, have ya?" then said the Sheriff jokingly.

"Yeah, I've been caught for murdering

someone!" replied Eric, going along with his joke. Though, immediately thinking, that perhaps that wasn't the best thing to say about under the circumstances.

Bill laughed. Though, the detective and the desk sergeant didn't.

"… I still can't figure out how you got that playing card into the 18th hole!" said Bill, shaking his head in amazed disbelief still. "It was amazing!"

"Oh, thanks!" said Eric straining to smile. "It was an enjoyable morning."

"Oh, while I remember. I've arranged for a retired police marksman to come and shoot you," said Bill loudly to Eric so he could be heard over the increasing noise.

The noisy police department suddenly went quiet for a moment.

"Did ya *hear* that!" protested a handcuffed drunken and disorderly man being escorted passed the main desk. "That's police brutality!"

"Oh good!" replied Eric.

"Good?" exclaimed the drunkard, before being taken to a cell.

"Rehearsals start at 10 am on Monday, is that right?" asked Bill.

"Yeah, that's right," reaffirmed Eric.

"His name is Rick Poplowski. You can't miss him – he wears dark glasses and carries a white stick!" wickedly joked the Sheriff. Eric looked worried before the Sheriff added, "Just kidding!" Eric half smiled, feeling relieved.

Just then, the desk sergeant called his boss the Sheriff and the detective over to one side and handed them Eric's statement. Then quietly spoke to them with a sombre looking facial expression – which to be honest, didn't appear any different to how he usually looks.

As the Sheriff and the detective listened, they occasionally looked back and forth at Eric, looking concerned.

Meanwhile, also looking concerned, Gloria, rang the bell to her boyfriend, Chet's, plush apartment suite in the newly built casino resort where he performed. (By the way, the very same newly built casino resort that Chet's dad owned.)

"Hi – what's the matter, darling?" asked Chet, seeing that she looked bothered about something as he welcomed her in.

"Oh, nothing," she replied, shaking her head. Though, her demeanour was telling him something to the contrary. She moved briskly past him, heading for the bathroom.

"Is that *blood* on your dress?" asked Chet, now concerned himself. He followed her. Then as she turned to go into the bathroom, he noticed bloodied scratch marks on the right-side of her neck. "Why have you got scratch marks on your neck?" She shut the door and locked it. Then turned on the shower. *"Gloria! Are ya listening to me?"* he then called out from the other side of the door. "What's happened?"

"Nothing to worry about, honey!" she called out. "I went for a drink after the show and got into a silly quarrel, which led to a scrap with one of the dancers, that's all."

"Well, as long as you're *okay!*"

"Yes, I'll be fine. Now, please don't ask me anymore about it!"

"Okay, okay," answered Chet, and left her in piece.

Back at the police department headquarters, the Sheriff, the detective, and the desk sergeant had finished talking with one another. The Sheriff then went back over to Eric and thanked him for giving his statement and handing over the letter. And just before he said goodbye, he tried to reassure Eric that although the police resources wouldn't stretch to providing him with police 24 hr. protection, at least the retired officer, Mr Poplowski, would be on hand during the rehearsals.

Eric left the police department headquarters, and since he now had no money left on him, had no choice but to walk the reasonably short distance back along the Strip to the Excalibur where he'd parked his car.

A little later, partners in crime, Chet, and Gloria, sat down on his plush leather sofa together with a large glass of bubbly each. And, after some small talk, Gloria turned the conversation around to Eric's magic show.

"I think I'm gonna have to lay off sabotaging Eric's magic act," she told him, sounding disappointed.

"Oh yeah, why's that?" asked Chet.

"Well, today Eric mentioned that he is gonna install hidden cameras inside each of his stage illusions."

"Smart! But I'm sure that there must be somethin' we can do to disrupt his show instead," he replied. "… He didn't mention anything about putting cameras in any of his smaller magic apparatus, though, did he?"

"No," Gloria confirmed.

"Well, you could target his smaller magic apparatus instead," said Chet starting to grin.

"I know what would stop him performing magic for a while."

"What?" asked Gloria, curious.

"Hide a small mouse trap inside the last box of his Ring in Nest of Boxes trick – so when he puts his hand in to remove the spectator's finger ring, he'll set the trap off – you can't perform magic with broken fingers!" said Chet laughing.

"Now, who's being wicked!" said Gloria, also grinning. Her wicked grin soon morphed into a wicked laugh.

"You could make the spectator's finger ring really disappear – then he'll get the blame for it!

"She laughed again. "Yeah, that would be funny!"

"Cheers!" said Chet. The two of them then clinked glasses. He then advised. "But give it another week or so before you do anything, when he least expects it."

"Yeah!" she agreed, thinking, "I'll teach him to spurn me!"

Eric finally stepped into his apartment at around 2.30 am. He quickly grabbed the remote, switched on the TV, and flicked it on to the local news channel in case there was a report about the homicide. He was so tired he could hardly keep his eyes open. Then after a short while, on came the female reporter he saw earlier at the scene. The grim footage being shown was the moment when the medics brought the victim's body out of the motel.

Bleary-eyed, he stared intently at the screen. The camera shot then moved away from the reporter and briefly over to the crowd that had gathered nearby. There he was! Eric could see himself at the front speaking to the policeman. Then as he quickly glanced over the crowd, his head suddenly shot back in surprised shock. "No, it *can't* be!" he thought. The feeling of dread suddenly consuming him. "That's *impossible* – he's *dead!*" The camera shot then quickly moved back to the reporter. For a moment he thought he'd caught a brief glimpse of someone at the back of the crowd he recognised from his past. Although, this man looked much older than he would have been, with lots of wrinkles and lines, and it was hard to tell because it was dark, and he now had a beard.

He must have been mistaken, he told himself. And besides, there are only so many different shapes of faces that it is easy to mistake someone's identity, he reasoned. "Why am I even thinking this?" he suddenly thought to himself, shaking his head. "He's *dead!*" he repeated to reassure himself. "And dead men don't walk!" But it was a face he could never forget. And even in his death, this ghost from the past continued to haunt him. He quickly shrugged it off, thinking he must be imagining it, and continued to listen to the reporter: "At this stage, the identity of the deceased is yet unknown," she told the viewers, "but the murder victim is believed to have been in her mid-twenties, and to have died at the scene. Police are warning the public to stay vigilant as the murderer is still at large –!"

Wearily, Eric switched off the TV. His tired aching feet then led him to his bedroom. There, he didn't even bother to get undressed, just flopped onto his bed and fell straight to sleep. What an exhausting and eventful day it had been!

CHAPTER FIFTEEN

REHEARSALS GET UNDERWAY

It was noon before Eric woke up the next day. So, it was just as well the rehearsals weren't until the following day. His immediate thoughts were for the poor murder victim. Flashbacks from the night before kept reminding him about it. Did her murderer discover that she was trying to warn me? Her last letter expressed that she was risking her life by warning me. Now he still doesn't know the identity of the killer. "Maybe I should leave Las Vegas?" thought Eric. "Just get on a plane and leave the US for good. A one-way ticket back to the UK!"

Then he remembered what the desk sergeant

politely warned him the night before: 'Don't leave the country in the next few weeks or so while the investigation is still ongoing! *"Or so? That could be months! Or maybe years!"* thought Eric, immediately worried and concerned. "It's bad enough having to watch my back from the Mafia, let alone now a crazed killer!"

He tried to shut it out of his mind, but all throughout that day, his mind was consumed with worry. If he wasn't worrying about the threat of being killed by a madman on the loose, he was worrying about how he was going to find the $10,000 he still owed the Mafia. For the last several days, he had been so pre-occupied thinking about other things, that he had completely overlooked it. And, thought, "If the killer doesn't get me first, the Mafia will!"

Monday morning, Eric carefully packed the musket, gunpowder, and lead bullets, that could loosely be called his 'magic apparatus' and loaded it into the back of his car. He then drove over to the Excalibur hoping that he didn't get stopped by the police. "That would take some explaining," he thought as he drove more carefully than he's ever driven in his life.

"At least I would have a weapon to defend myself if the killer strikes!" he then thought. "Though, a musket is no match for a modern gun. By the time I've loaded it, I would be dead!"

It had been arranged that the musket and ammunition would be stored safely backstage in the stage manager's office in a locked steel cabinet, along with the other stage pyrotechnics. And the only person who would have a key was the stage manager himself and the resort security department. It was insisted upon that the only people allowed to handle the musket was Eric; the marksman, Rick Poplowski; the stage manager, Dirk Rollinson; and the resort security team.

When Eric arrived, the resort security was already there waiting and immediately escorted him backstage so the weaponry could be stored away safely until required. And this procedure of having an armed security guard present every time the weapon and ammunition was transported back and forth to the stage was to be strictly adhered to.

As arranged, at 10 am everyone involved in the new show, called 'The Amazing Fartzini Dodges Death' (another dodgy name made up by the show producer), met in the showroom to start rehearsals.

The show producer Benjamin was sat right at the front in the centre. Next to him was the resort owner, Mr Constantino, keen to show his support, and his assistant, Carolyn. Most of the showgirls were already on the stage warming up, dressed in their lycra leotards and leggings. Ruben could be heard somewhere backstage shouting to the remaining dancers to hurry up and join the others. Jim the compère was still in his dressing room, restocking his fridge. The stage manager was busy running around instructing his assistants with what to do. One of the stage crew was up a tall ladder changing the stage lighting gels, while others were moving the new scenery into place. The sound and light techs were busy at the back of the room re-programming the lighting and adjusting the sound levels as the overture played. Eric, who had been backstage securing the weaponry safely away until it was needed, walked out onto the stage, weaved past the dancers, and went and said hello to Mr Constantino and his assistant, and Benjamin. All three were drinking coffee.

"Good morning Eric!" said Mr Constantino

chirpily, followed by the other two.

"Good morning!" Eric replied, smiling. "How are ya?"

"Fine!" they replied.

"But we're not the one's who have to catch a bullet between our teeth!" expressed Mr Constantino, joking.

Eric chuckled. "Oh, don't worry about *me* – I'm used to dodging bullets!" he quipped back. Then thought, "And *knives!*" How very nearly true that was!

Just then the other dancers came on stage, dragging their heels slightly in protest for having to give up part of their mornings. Namely: Candy, Rhonda, and Samantha, followed by Ruben hurrying them along at the rear.

The stage producer got up from his seat. "Why is it taking so long?" he called out.

"Nearly finished!" called out the stage manager.

"Right, into posssitionsss girls!" then screeched Ruben, clapping his hands, annoyed.

"Is everybody here?" asked the producer.

"No, we're just waiting for Mr Poplowski," answered Eric.

"Mr *who?*" said Benjamin, with a blank look.

"Mr Poplowski, the ex-police marksman," explained Eric.

"*Oh,* yes! Well, we can't hang around – we'll get underway with the opening number. Are you ready now Dirk?"

"Yeah, we're ready!" he called back, with his thumb pointing towards the Gods as he swiftly made his way over to his station in the wings and put on his cans.

The showgirls opening music started and Ruben, who was standing downstage at the front, put them through their paces as he taught them the new routine. He also had lycra leggings on – his leggings were *so* skin-tight that when he bent over, you could see him perform the disappearing G-string trick!

"*Ssstop!*" and "From the top!" he kept calling out. Plus a few other things in between *far* too rude to mention in this story. His frustrations showed as he wanted to make a good impression in front of the show producer, and especially Mr Constantino.

Being professional dancers, it didn't take long before the routine started taking shape. Though to Eric, apart from the music, it didn't look much different from the previous opening routine – the same moves but in a different order. Benjamin and Mr Constantino, however, seemed to be enjoying watching it.

"You wait till you see the new costumes, Luigi!" said Benjamin – who was on a first name basis with Mr Constantino – smiling with excitement.

"I can't wait!" he answered, smiling back just as enthusiastically.

Just then an elderly man came striding down the centre aisle, looking slightly lost.

The producer, who just happened to look over his shoulder, spotted him. *"Excuse* me, sir!" he called out. "We're *closed* for rehearsals!"

"Hi, there! *I'm* Mr Poplowski!" he called out as he continued walking. Mr Poplowski was a very tall, slender man with a bushy moustache.

Benjamin and Eric stood up and greeted him at the bottom of the aisle. "Ah, Mr Poplowski. Sorry for the confusion, we are expecting you," said Benjamin.

"Sorry I'm a little late, only I went to the Luxor next door instead," explained Mr Poplowski. "For some reason I had it in my head that I was to meet there."

"Well, you're in the right place now," said Benjamin. He then introduced the others, and they shook hands.

"I'm a good friend of Bill Bridges, who hired you," said Mr Constantino as he shook his hand.

"Oh, yes, Bill's told me about you," Mr Poplowski replied.

"I understand you're a retired police officer," then said Eric.

"Yes, sir! I'm proud to say I spent forty-five years of my life serving as a police officer," he answered. "And I'd still be doing it now if I could."

"Well, the country owes servicemen like yourself a great deal of gratitude, sir," then said Mr Constantino. "And I'm glad that you've agreed to be a part of the show."

"I'm afraid I'm not much of a showman though. Showbusiness is about as different as you can get from what I did."

"Well, that's quite alright, Mr Popoff …" started to say the producer, struggling to remember his name. Eric found it amusing but refrained from showing it.

"Poplowski," said Mr Poplowski, reminding him, "but just call me Rick."

"I was just gonna say, don't cha worry about that, Rick – we'll leave all the showmanship up to The Amazing Fartzini," said Benjamin, relieved he didn't have to try and repeat his surname again. "We prefer that you're *not* a showman because we want the performance to look as real and authentic as possible. We just need you to point the gun and fire on command."

"Well, as a trained marksman, that I can do!" stated Rick smiling as he said it.

Meanwhile, the showgirls were getting to grips with the new routine, the stage crew were adjusting the sound and light controls, and Jim was – in his own little world.

A little later, Eric took Mr Poplowski privately over to one side to explain about the Bullet Catch stunt – the type of gun and ammunition that was going to be used and so on, and what he wanted him to do."

"*Oh,* so I'm not actually gonna be firing a real bullet at cha?" said the marksman, slightly disappointed.

"Correct! Just a blank," replied Eric. "But if it is performed well, the illusion will be perfect!"

"Well, it's been a while since I've fired one of these things – not since my reenactment days – but I'll give it my best shot – ha, best *shot!* D'ya get it?"

"Yeah, very funny," said Eric, forcing himself to chuckle out of politeness – secretly thinking what a terrible corny joke.

"So, if as you say the signed bullet is loaded into the muzzle and rammed home; how d'ya end up getting the same bullet in ya mouth then?" asked the still investigative ex-policeman.

"Ah, well that part will remain a secret!" said Eric resolutely with a smile.

"Fair enough!" Mr Popolowski replied, quickly realising that he wasn't going to get the answer no matter how many times he asked. And Mr Poplowski didn't push it any further either – he was glad of the extra money that he would be getting in his retirement living in Las Vegas.

Eric only told those involved in the stunt what they needed to know and kept the method of how he ended up with the same signed bullet wedged between his teeth a closely guarded secret. He wouldn't even tell his so-called friend Gloria – which was probably just as well.

"As you know, Rick, when firing a blank cartridge, there will still be a certain amount of propellant shot out of the chamber – so I must be standing a safe distance from you to avoid injury!" said Eric matter-of-factly. It was something that the old magician, Bill Maloney, warned Eric about.

Mr Poplowski nodded. *"Absolutely!* Even without a bullet, the ignited gunpowder and wadding can travel several feet and cause serious injury!" he said, agreeing.

"And this is something we have to ascertain during the rehearsal today," added Eric.

In terms of the new show, Eric only needed to rehearse the Bullet Catch stunt, as the other magic tricks and stage illusions he intended to perform were already well-rehearsed.

When Ruben and the exhausted dancers eventually left the stage to go and take a break, Eric and Rick made their way up onto the stage. More lighting flooded the stage as they both walked across its huge, blackened boards to centre stage. The stage manager and the show producer then joined them, and Dirk and Rick greeted one another for the first time. Dirk seemed quite friendly for a change, thought Eric. And after discussing what Eric wanted in terms of staging, Dirk, along with an armed member of security, then went and fetched the musket and ammunition.

"Ah, that looks a beauty!" said Mr Poplowski, excited upon seeing the antique musket for the first time. He took it in his hands and gave it a good looking over. "I can see it has been well maintained."

Eric nodded and said, "Yeah, it was given to me by another magician called Bill Maloney." As soon as Eric mentioned his name, Mr Poplowski's eyebrows shot straight up.

When everyone else had vacated the stage, the marksman loaded the musket with a blank cartridge – while those who remained in the wings stuck their fingers firmly in their ears – and fired it across the stage to test where it would be safe for Eric to stand during the performance. It made a loud retort and smoke filled the air, making some of the cast jump – especially those in the dressing rooms not expecting it. And after several trial shots and fingers going in and out of ears, the stage management concluded that twelve paces would be sufficient to maintain Eric's safety.

For the rest of the morning and into the afternoon, Eric rehearsed the Bullet Catch routine repeatedly; only taking a short break for lunch. As in the traditional way of presenting the stunt, once the compère has made his introductory remarks and built up the suspense, the idea was that The Amazing Fartzini walks out on stage and stands in position on stage right. The marksman then walks out, dressed as the Grim Reaper and wearing a deathly skeleton mask (which was the producer's idea, thinking it would add to the drama – much to Mr Poplowski's dismay), and stands opposite the magician about twelve metres away on stage left. Then one of his assistants goes down into the audience and has a volunteer on the front row sign or mark the bullet to alleviate any suspicion of using duplicates. The signed bullet is then brought back upon the stage to where the marksman is standing, keeping it in clear view the whole time, and loads it into the muzzle of the musket. Then using the ramrod, the assistant rams the bullet down the barrel of the already primed gun. Meanwhile, dramatic music is playing to further add to the drama. The assistant then fetches a china dinner plate and hands it to The Amazing Fartzini to hold in front of his face as his only means of protection, to supposedly help slow down the velocity of the bullet for when he miraculously catches it between his teeth. The assistant then promptly leaves the stage, leaving only The Amazing Fartzini and the marksman remaining there. The music stops, and a solitary drumroll is then heard. The marksman raises the musket, cocks the hammer, and takes aim. And after a tense build-up, the drum roll stops. Eric gives the command to fire. The marksman fires. The plate smashes to pieces. And a split-second later The Amazing Fartzini stumbles backwards and then dramatically falls to the ground … He then slowly gets up and shows the bullet is now between his teeth, which to the astonishment of the audience proves to be the very same signed bullet! – at least that's what is supposed to happen!

Well, after a few stops and starts, the madcap stunt routine started to take shape. And certainly, astonished the few remaining cast and crew members watching from the wings and auditorium – and despite Mr Poplowski watching as close as he could, he still couldn't fathom out how Eric ended up with the bullet in his mouth. And after what proved to be a successful first day of rehearsals with no accidents or injuries, the gun and ammunition were locked safely away once again.

CHAPTER SIXTEEN

ERIC SETS A TRAP!

Pleased with how the rehearsals were going, Eric performed all the shows that week with great gusto, and couldn't wait to start presenting the new show. Even Ruben seemed pleased – and that's saying something. The cast had grown tired of performing the same old show day in day out, week after week for the last six months. It had become too monotonous. So, a change was good.

The resort's PR team arranged for Eric to do local TV and radio interviews all that week to promote the new show, and he was even booked to appear on a well-known prime time national TV chat show in a couple of weeks. He phoned his mum and Emily immediately to tell them the exciting news. The huge new illuminated billboard advertising the new show was also erected later that week. At the top of it in huge bold letters it read: "The Amazing Fartzini Dodges Death!" and underneath was a picture of him, not smiling cheesily as in the old billboard, but looking solemn and mysterious, holding a china plate with the barrel of a musket pointing right at him. And the promoters plastered posters and handed out leaflets all along the Vegas Strip.

Everything was happening so fast: a new contract had been signed; the rehearsals were underway; the new billboard had been erected, and the show was being heavily promoted. There was now no going back – even if Eric wanted to.

But also, on top of all that, Eric had been busy setting a trap to try and catch the culprit who was sabotaging his act. In fact, he was so busy rehearsing, promoting, and setting a trap that week, not to mention still performing the current show, that he completely forgot that he now only had until Saturday to pay back the $10,000 he still owed to the Mafia. It was now

Thursday, and if wasn't for a phone call from the Mafia that afternoon reminding him, he would have probably forgotten all about it. The gruff sounding mobster told Eric to meet them at noon on Saturday in the food court at the Showcase Shopping Mall on the Strip. And just before he ended the call, warned Eric that if he didn't pay up all the money he owed, this time, they would make *him* disappear!

Eric was in his usual haunt – his dressing room – having just performed the matinee show, wondering where on earth he was going to get that sort of money in time now. His bank account showed $0.00 balance, and his credit cards weren't far off being maxed out!

He knew it would be a waste of time asking his manager, Mr Goldberg, for an advance. But then he remembered Mr Constantino giving him his business card and telling him to contact him if he needed anything. "Well, I wonder if *he* would give me an advance," he then thought? He did say *'anything'*, and *'anything'* must include money!"

Eric hesitated at first, then opened his sorrowful looking thin wallet, where he kept Mr Constantino's business card tucked away, and gingerly removed it. Then quickly put it back, thinking that maybe it wasn't such a good idea. He then quickly removed it again and immediately began dialing the number in case he changed his mind again.

He felt a bit embarrassed asking for money, but desperate times call for desperate measures. The ring tone continued monotonously. Then he heard Mr Constantino's commanding voice. But it was only his pre-recorded voice asking the caller to leave a message.

"Oh, 'eck!" thought Eric. And after some quick deliberation decided to end the call. He didn't want to leave a message asking for money. He then said to himself, "I knew it was gonna be difficult to get hold of him."

Earlier in the week, Eric had been to an electronics store in one of the vast shopping malls, and being as inconspicuous and secretive as he could, bought spy surveillance equipment. Eric learnt how to use the equipment, and after rehearsals on Tuesday, when everyone apart from himself and Gloria had gone to lunch, he put his plan into action. He hid the Wi-Fi spy camera's with DVR in each of his stage illusions while Gloria watched.

Now, I expect you're thinking it was a mistake for Eric to inform Gloria that he was setting a trap, let alone show her where he'd hidden the cameras – foolish in fact. But Eric was a shrewd young man – even though his open and trustworthy nature might suggest otherwise – and at the back of his mind he was becoming more and more suspicious of her. Certain things she'd said or done started to make him feel that way. Only little things, but little things mount up and start to nag at you that something is not quite right – it's like your inner self is knocking at the back door of your mind trying to warn you.

The reason why his suspicions had been at the back of his mind was because he chose to keep them there. He just didn't want to admit to himself that maybe his friend – probably his only friend in Vegas – is the culprit, and just ignored it. Of course, he was hoping that it wasn't Gloria sabotaging his act because he had grown to like and trust her as a friend. And even at this point, he still didn't believe that she would do such a horrid and spiteful thing.

Anyway, unbeknownst to Gloria, a little later when she and nobody else was around. Using Dirk's ladder, Eric quickly set up another hidden camera high up on a lighting rig, which covered the entire backstage area where he kept his magic equipment and would capture anyone meddling with it.

He had also set up an app on his mobile phone so that he could monitor all the camera's views. He switched everything on to check it was all working correctly and was chuffed to see it was. Then quickly put the ladder away and went back to his dressing room – which served as his secret intelligence headquarters.

Eric felt bad about not telling Gloria because it went against his nature, but he knew it had to be done.

Since setting up the spy camera system, Eric took every opportunity he could to check his app but saw no evidence to suggest that anyone was tampering with his magic equipment. People would just pass by it without even showing the slightest bit of interest.

Gloria would quietly ask him every so often if he'd seen anything suspicious yet, and he would answer, no. It was a bit frustrating, as he was hoping that he would've caught the culprit in the act by now. But resided himself to the understanding that he would just have to be more patient and wait for as long as it takes.

Well, Eric didn't have to wait much longer, because after ending the call to Mr Constantino, he decided to have a quick look at the spy camera app, not expecting to see anything suspicious, but what he saw truly surprised him. His head shot forwards, and his eyelids opened wide in sheer disbelief.

"What's she doing?" he asked himself, eyes glued to the slightly fuzzy movement on the grainy screen. It was Gloria, looking around suspiciously as if to make sure nobody was looking, then removing the cover from his table where he kept his smaller magic props. To his astonishment, Gloria – the person he thought was his friend – picked up his Nest of Boxes trick – the same cherished wooden Nest of Boxes he still had from when he first started performing magic – and quickly shoved it into a large plastic Gucci shopping bag. Then just as quickly covered the remaining props on the table again, trying to make everything look the same as before. The spy camera then caught her heading with the bag towards the steps at the rear of the stage. Eric kept watching until she vanished from the screen.

He couldn't believe his eyes. "So, was Gloria, the person who had been sabotaging my act all along?" he asked himself. Still not wanting to believe what his eyes were now telling him. "What on *earth* would she want with the Nest of Boxes trick?" was his next question. "Judging by the way Gloria was acting it certainly didn't look like she was playing a prank on me ... Surely, she wasn't stealing it ... was she?" Panic started to set in. "I *need* that trick for my next show!"

Just then, Eric thought he heard someone walking hurriedly down the steps and along the corridor. Then a thud against his door.

"*Hiya* Gloria!" said Candy's voice, which confirmed it was Gloria. "Been shopping again have ya?"

Gloria just ignored Candy's catty remark as they passed one another and continued walking quickly towards her dressing room. Eric, who by this time had moved towards the door, quietly opened it and peered down the corridor. Gloria had her back to him, carrying the bag as it swayed back and forth down by her side. And judging by the weight and the box-like shape bulging out on both sides, left no doubt as to what was inside. She then turned, causing Eric to sharply retract his head back inside his dressing room, as she disappeared into hers.

Eric went and sat down, feeling in a quandary. He didn't know *what* to do next! Should he go and report her straight away to the resort security? Or should he just wait and see how things develop? After all, despite now having the video evidence, he still couldn't be absolutely certain that her intentions were to steal his magic prop. These were all thoughts racing through his mind.

It started getting nosier backstage as more of the cast and crew arrived and started preparing for the first evening show. There was only about an hour to go before curtain-up, so Eric needed to act fast. And after some quick deliberation, he decided he would opt for the latter option to first check if in the remote chance Gloria admitted that she had the missing prop, and it was all a prank.

Meanwhile, Gloria had since come back out of her dressing room and was now outside at the rear of the building smoking a cigarette while talking to her boyfriend, Chet, on her phone.

"… Oh, well done, darling!" said Chet, sounding pleased, then laughing. "Where did ya put it?"

"I hid it in my dressing room locker for now," Gloria replied, starting to laugh.

"But I thought I told ya to leave it a while before you started meddling with his props again?" Chet said in a jokingly telling off sort of way.

"Yeah, but like ya said, honey, he's only rigged up cameras in his stage illusions," she reminded him with a smirk on her face. "Don't worry – he'll never suspect *I've* got it!"

"Well, I hope not!"

"Anyway, there's some people coming, I'd better go. *Bye* honey!"

"Bye!"

"*Hiya, Gloria!*" called out a couple of the dancers just arriving.

"Oh, *hi* gals!" she called back, realising who it was. She quickly stubbed her cigarette out on the ground and ran to join them. "Wait for me!"

Eric quickly left his dressing room in search of a dark horse – named Gloria. It was time for him to put on the best acting performance he could.

It just so happened that as Eric entered the corridor, Gloria was walking towards her dressing room from the opposite direction, busy chatting with the other dancers. He headed towards her, feeling uneasy, but determined to get to the bottom of it once and for all.

Gloria acted as if she hadn't seen him and was about to follow the other girls into their dressing room.

"Gloria!" Eric called out, sounding distressed.

Without him even saying so, she could tell immediately by the tone of his voice that he had discovered the magic prop was missing. She turned and looked at him, smiling.

"Oh, *hi* honey! Everything okay?"

"No," he replied, "can I talk to ya?"

"Yeah, sure. What ever is the matter?" she said, knowing full well.

That was all Eric had to hear. He now immediately knew that she *had* stolen his magic prop. "Not here – let's talk where it's is quieter."

He started to walk away back towards his dressing room, and she reluctantly followed him.

"Has something happened?" she asked him as they continued to walk past Jim's dressing room. He didn't answer. He then stopped outside his dressing room where there was nobody around.

"The Nest of Boxes is missing, and I think someone may have stolen it?" he said quietly, genuinely upset.

Gloria gasped and feigned shocked surprise. *"Oh, that's awful!"* she said. "What are you gonna do now?"

Eric didn't answer, just shrugged his shoulders, thinking, "How could you do this to me?" He had always been kind and friendly towards Gloria and put his trust in her.

"I don't suppose the spy cameras would've picked up the thieving culprit who did this, would they?" she then remarked, already believing she knew the answer to that – or so she thought.

"No," he just answered. Then after an awkward pause. He then asked. "Have ya see anything suspicious since I re-set the props?"

She paused slightly. "No, I've spent the whole time in my dressing room," she told him. She then remembered that he'd seen her in the corridor. "… apart from when I went outside for a smoke, that is."

Gloria sounded very convincing. Only this time Eric wasn't buying it. He had heard enough of her lies and had to do his level best to contain his anger and keep calm so as not to alert her to the fact that he knew she was the culprit.

"Okay, I'll just have to miss that trick out," he told her, "I'll go and inform the stage manager now. See ya later!"

He then promptly turned one way and headed towards the stage with a look of sorrow on his face, and she turned the other way and headed towards her dressing room with a sly grin on hers. But as soon as he had mounted the steps leading up the stage, he casually glanced over his shoulder and seeing that Gloria had gone into her dressing room, doubled back on himself. And armed with the video evidence, he hastily made his way to the backstage security office.

CHAPTER SEVENTEEN

AN ARRESTING DEVELOPMENT!

Eric quickly approached the security desk. *"Tom!* May I speak to you in private, please?" spoke Eric with urgency in his voice.

"Why, but of course," replied the old security guard. "C'mon through."

"Thanks!" said Eric, removing his mobile phone from his pocket.

"Something troubling ya, young man?" asked Tom, seeing quite clearly that there was.

Eric explained what it was about and showed him and one of his female colleagues, named Mary, the incriminating video evidence. Mary was a fierce-looking, large built woman with more muscles than most men, who always kept her hair up in a tight bun at work – she looked a bit like a sumo wrestler without the nappy.

Tom then immediately radioed the head of security, who after hearing what he had to say, said he'd be on his way as soon as possible.

Stephen Carpenter, the head of resort security was there within minutes. He greeted everyone and watched the video footage.

"I must agree, it does look very suspicious," he said, twiddling the ends of his moustache. Then looked at Eric. "And you say that you saw her carrying the bag containing your magic prop into the dancers dressing room?"

"Yes," Eric replied, "and I'm convinced now that she is the culprit who has been sabotaging my act all along!"

"If she has got light fingers, maybe she is also the one who has been stealing money out the dressing rooms?" said Mary. The others nodded in agreement.

"That may well be so," said the Chief of Security. "Well, there's only one way to find out – we will need to conduct a search of her locker right away and then question her. Mary and Eric, you come with me, and Tom, you get in touch with the show producer. There's no time to explain anything to him, just tell him it's urgent and to come to the dancers dressing room right away!"

"Right away, sir!" replied Tom. Both were ex-policemen and still conducted themselves in the same way.

"Right, follow me!" said the Chief of Security as he led the way to the dancers dressing room, with Mary and Eric right behind him.

They arrived outside the dancers dressing room and both security officers switched on their body cam's. The female officer entered first to make sure that the dancers were decently dressed – if you call just tassels and a G-string dressed, that is! Some of the dancers had already left and were warming up on stage – everyone could hear Ruben's irritating voice bellowing in the distance. And about six of the other girls, including Gloria were still in the dressing room chattering away to one another when Mary walked in – more like barged in.

"EXCUSE ME LADIES, CAN I HAVE YOUR ATTENTION, PLEASE!" Mary called out in an authoritative voice, immediately getting everyone's attention – Mary had worked as a state penitentiary officer before she took on this role. "Don't be too alarmed but we are going to have to conduct a search for suspected stolen property!" There were a few gasps around the room.

Just then the Chief of Security and Eric walked in, arms folded. "Good afternoon ladies, sorry to disturb y'all. This will only take a short while," said the Chief of Security in a slightly less harsh and more diplomatic manner. Gloria's eyes immediately looked at Eric – and she wasn't grinning now. "Gloria," the Chief of Security continued to say, "will you please open your locker so that we can look inside, please. We have reason to believe that you have an item in your possession that doesn't belong to you."

Gloria's face had the look of horror – that look when someone knows that they've been caught red-handed – like a wide-eyed, motionless squirrel that has just been caught, stealing other squirrel's nuts. She then forced a nervous smile. "The *only* thing you'll find in there is my *dirty* underwear!" she joked. Some of the other dancers laughed, and even Mary, who was normally very tight-lipped cracked a smile. Another dancer then called out, "He probably likes investigating women's underwear!" causing more laughter.

"*Now!* Please," insisted the Chief of Security, raising his voice, with no trace of a smile.

"Have you got something to do with this?" said Gloria, directing her question towards Eric. Eric just continued to look towards her locker. Gloria slowly and reluctantly unlocked her locker and opened the door. The locker was crammed full of things. She then said smugly, "You can't *prove* that I stole anything!"

"Oh, *yes* we can – I have video evidence!" stated Eric. Gloria's mouth opened, but nothing came out – instead, she just looked shocked.

"Now kindly remove what is inside so we may make a thorough inspection," demanded the Chief of Security.

Under duress, Gloria did as she was told and removed the bulky designer labelled plastic bag. She then dropped it on the floor on purpose, causing Eric's magic prop to tumble out. "Whoops!" she said with a smirk.

There were audible gasps of shock and surprise. Not because Gloria dropped the bag on the floor, or because Eric's missing magic prop suddenly reappeared. It was because piled up now on view were lots of wads of $50.00 bills! Eric's money she had stolen to be precise

– or what was remaining of it!

"That's my stolen money!" exclaimed Eric, recognising the banding around the bills. He then turned his gaze towards Gloria. "So, it was *you* that stole that *too!"* Gloria kept quiet. "But *why* Gloria?" he then asked her; but again, she remained tight-lipped. She just stood there with her arms folded, looking down towards the floor, too ashamed and embarrassed to look at him straight in the face. Eric then turned his head sharply towards the Chief of Security. "If you check the serial numbers on the bills, you'll find that they match the bills issued to me at the bank!"

"All in good time, all in good time!" replied the Chief of Security. "Now stand aside please, Gloria," he then said as he went over and poked his head inside the locker. Eric, meanwhile, bent down and picked up his magic prop from the floor and checked that there was no damage – and fortunately, there wasn't. The Chief of Security then said solemnly, "This looks like a matter for the police!"

"Oh, *please* don't get the police involved! I *needed* the money to support my baby!" pleaded Gloria trying to get sympathy. She tried to put on the waterworks, but the taps were dry. And, she didn't have a baby – that was a lie!

Like Eric, Gloria was also good at keeping secrets – though, for completely different reasons. And for a good reason: she had a long list of criminal convictions and had even served time – mostly for theft, but also for serious assault.

"I'm afraid it's too late for that, miss!" said the Chief of Security unsympathetically. He was used to dealing with habitual criminals like Gloria and wasn't falling for her plea's for sympathy. He then turned his head towards Mary and just nodded. She knew exactly what to do and immediately contacted the police. He then reached inside the locker and removed an expensive looking gold bracelet and a set of gold earrings.

They're my earrings! shrieked one of the dancers. And *That's my bracelet!* claimed another, followed by a tirade of profanities.

"Now, now, please keep calm ladies!" said the Chief of Security, trying to maintain the peace.

Just then, the show producer entered the room along with two more security guards.

"I got here as soon as could!" said Benjamin, looking flummoxed and slightly out of breath.

The security officers had informed him somewhat as to what had happened.

"It would seem that one of your dancers is not only *light* on her toe's but is also *light-fingered!*" said the ex-detective Chief of Security.

"Oh dear, oh dear! We have a show starting in less than twenty minutes!" exclaimed the producer, panicking.

"Well, I'm afraid you're gonna be one dancer short!" quickly responded the Chief of Security.

It suddenly dawned on Eric that he was going to be a magician's assistant short, too; but thought, he'd be okay with only one assistant for now. He certainly didn't want Gloria to be his assistant any longer – she had caused him a lot of trouble and grief.

By this time, the noise had caused quite a commotion. Jim came out of his dressing room next door to see what all the fuss was about and stood at the dancers dressing room doorway. Ruben, followed by several of the dancers, then came hurtling down the corridor shortly afterwards and crowded around Jim to watch the drama unfolding inside.

"*What'sss* goin' on?" asked Ruben nosily.

"Gloria's, been caught stealing!" answered

Jim.

"I *knew* it wasss her!" said Ruben, raising his eyebrows – well, they would have done if he hadn't already plucked them – and shaking his head and tutting along with the dancers.

Projecting his voice, the show producer said, "Would all the dancers *apart* from Gloria" – he scowled at her as he said her name – "please pick up your headdresses and feathers and quickly make your way up to the stage!" Then after only a slight pause, turned his gaze towards Gloria once more and said angrily "And as for you, Gloria – you're *fired!*"

"What about our stolen belongings?" asked one of the dancers, concerned.

"Don't worry about that," said the Chief of Security, "it will all be securely bagged-up, and you'll get back what belongs to you in due course."

"Right! C'mon girls, we've gotta show to put on!" called out Ruben as he led the procession of noisy showgirls minus one along the corridor towards the stage. The others could hear them gossiping all the way there. Jim followed them and went back to his dressing room.

"Start bagging the stolen goods please,

Mary," said the Chief of Security.

"Yes, sir," answered Mary, who got to work on it right away.

Eric could see that a lot of his money was missing, presumably already spent on expensive designer clothes, jewellery, and nights out, he thought. By his estimate, there was only about $12,000 or so remaining out of the original £25,000 stolen. But with some comfort, he thought at least that will be enough to pay back the money he owes the Mafia – providing he can collect it in time, that is.

Once Mary had emptied Gloria's locker, and the loot was securely sealed into bags, the Chief of Security, then asked the other two security officers to escort Gloria to the backstage security office where she was to be maintained until the police arrived.

As Gloria was unceremoniously led away by an officer on either side of her, holding onto her arms, she had a face like thunder. She'd kept quiet for most of the time, but as she was almost out the door, she twisted her head around to face Eric, and swore something obscene at him, and vowed to get her revenge – this was the ugly side of her, which Eric hadn't seen before.

"I'm sorry that you had to go through all this, Eric," said Benjamin sincerely. "But at least the culprit has been caught, and it's all over with now!"

"Yeah, thanks, Benjamin. It's been a nightmare," replied Eric, somewhat relieved, though still feeling hurt about being betrayed.

"I can *assure* you; she will not be stepping foot on *any* of my stages ever again!"

"Good!" said Eric.

"Do ya intend to press charges?" then asked The Chief of Security.

Eric wasn't sure and needed more time to think about it; and so, just shrugged his shoulders without saying a word. He didn't want it to all come out in court about his involvement with the Mafia – even though it was unwittingly. But at the same time, he thought it was a lot of money to lose if she denied stealing the money.

"I would if I were you," said Benjamin instead. "She's stolen a lot of money from you. Mind you – she'd probably make bail, thanks to her *rich* boyfriend!"

"*Rich boyfriend?*" repeated Eric, looking surprised. It was the first time he'd heard that she had a boyfriend, let alone a rich one – she certainly hadn't given him that impression.

"Yeah, the magician Chet Stevenson. His multi-millionaire papa owns the newly opened casino resort" said Benjamin. "I thought you would have known."

Eric shook his head, mumbling to himself, "That explains a lot!"

"What was that?" asked Benjamin, unable to make out what he was saying.

"*Oh,* nothing!" said Eric still mulling over what he just heard.

"It surprised me too because I always thought that she preferred women – *especially* judging by the way I've seen her act in late-night bars!" then said, Benjamin …

Eric finally got around to making his mind up and answering the Chief of Security's question, confirming that he did wish to prosecute Gloria; and then realizing the time, said "I'd better *hurry up* and finish getting ready for the show. See ya later!"

"Yes, break a leg Eric!" said Benjamin, now panicking less.

"*Eric!*" called out the Chief of Security as Eric started to leave. "The police will need you to make a full statement as soon as the show is over!"

"Yes, of course. Thank you for your help, sir," said Eric, forgetting about that for a moment with his mind now focused on the show.

"Well, that's my job!" he replied with a fleeting smile, pleased to take credit for capturing the offender, even though it was Eric's detective work that had led to her arrest. "Don't forget in future, though, to tell us when you are rigging up spy camera's, will you Eric?"

"Will do, sir," replied Eric, grinning slightly. He then left, still cradling his magic prop; and made haste, sprinting down the corridor to his dressing room to get changed into his costume.

Eric didn't need two assistants for his magic show – having more than one just helped to dress the stage and facilitated a quicker pace to the show. As, while one assistant would remove one stage illusion off stage, another would bring one on stage.

Despite the pre-show panic, the show began on time as usual. And despite having only the one assistant, they still managed to pull off an excellent performance. And he was pleased that he was still able to perform one of his best and favourite magic tricks, The Ring in the Nest of Boxes!

As soon as the matinee show was over, Eric didn't even bother to get changed; he quickly rushed over to the security office to make his statement, where the Chief of Security and the police were already there waiting for him.

CHAPTER EIGHTEEN

PAYBACK TIME!

"**A**h, Mr Fartz!" said Stephen Carpenter, Chief of Security, acknowledging Eric's sudden presence.

"*Hi,* I got here as soon as I could!" said Eric, still panting slightly. He immediately noticed that Gloria wasn't there, thinking, "She's probably been arrested, and taken into police custody."

Eric was right, the police did arrest her, and after being read her rights and handcuffed, she was taken to the LVMPD headquarters and detained in police custody. But it wasn't just her detained in police custody – so was his money and the various other stolen items found.

"How was the show?" asked The Chief of Security.

"… *Oh,* sorry. Good, thanks!" said Eric with a slightly delayed response. He had been distracted wondering where he had seen the tall, casually dressed, unshaven man, standing next to the Chief of Security before? He then noticed the man was wearing a police badge displayed on the waistband of his trousers – or pants as they say in the US – and then suddenly remembered that he was the plainclothes detective he saw the other night at the police headquarters.

"Eric, this is police detective, Mark Hitchcock," said the Chief of Security, introducing him. Eric and Mark shook hands.

"We meet again, Mr Fartz!" said the detective.

"Yeah," replied Eric, with a slightly nervous chuckle.

"Trouble seems to follow you around, doesn't it, Mr Fartz?" then commented the detective with a tone of suspicion attached.

Eric just smiled, thinking, "You only know the half of it!"

"First things first, Mr Fartz. Do you still wish to press charges against a Miss Gloria Henderson for allegedly stealing from you?" asked the detective, needing clarification.

Eric, still slightly unsure, said, "Er, yeah!" thinking he still has time to change his mind.

The detective first took down Eric's details, and then began taking down his statement and asking him questions about the alleged crime, which Eric was becoming used to doing!

"… I understand that as well as one of your magic props, which you have since recovered, you also had a lot of money stolen. Is that correct, Mr Fartz?" the detective asked, with his pencil poised just above his notepad.

"Yes, sir," answered Eric.

"And how much was that in total please, Mr Fartz?"

Eric thought it would be all right to tell him the full amount – providing he didn't mention it was money he owed to the Mafia.

Eric hesitated, then said, "Twenty-five thousand dollars in cash."

As soon as he said the amount, there was a momentary pause and a few surprised gasps and raised eyebrows from among the security team.

"That's a lot of cash for one individual to be carrying around, isn't it Mr Fartz?" questioned the detective.

Eric thought before he spoke for a change. "I suppose you're right, officer … and in hindsight, it was foolish of me."

"Well, mistakes happen! And I guess for rich stars like yourself, $25,000" is a mere drop in the ocean!"

Eric laughed inwardly and smiled outwardly, thinking, "I *wish!*"

To Eric's relief, the detective didn't probe him any further on the matter; so, he didn't need to come out with the excuse he'd already prepared, which was: "I was hoping to buy a new car that day and pay cash so that I could get a discount, but I changed my mind, and because the banks were closed by that time, I kept the money in my dressing room."

Lucky, the detective *didn't* probe him any further: otherwise, Eric might have then had to try and explain what happened to the *other* $25,000 he withdrew from the bank that day as well! The truth is the detective had far more important cases to deal with than this one, and the sooner he got this case dealt with, the sooner he could concentrate on the others. So, he continued asking Eric other questions instead.

"… And you are *positive* that you locked your dressing room door behind you, and that this isn't just some sort of misunderstanding," quizzed the detective, "because if your case does go to court, the prosecutor will need to convince the judge that her motive was to steal if you are to win!"

"Absolutely!" replied Eric with certainty. "She must have stolen the key from the stage manager, who is the only other person who has a key to my dressing –"

"Well, hopefully, it won't come to that, Mr Fartz. We will have to wait and see if the alleged perpetrator comes clean and owns up to it while being interviewed. It appears to be a clear-cut case to me!" said the detective. "The alleged perpetrator was found in possession of the stolen goods And, thanks to the Chief of Security's ingenuity she has also been caught stealing on camera!"

Well, the Chief of Security smiled widely, feeling chuffed to bits at hearing such praise. And Eric just went along with it and smiled, letting him take the credit for it.

"But then, who am I to know," continued the

detective shrugging his shoulders, "I am just a detective that questions people and makes arrests!"

The detective and the Chief of Security then spent a while chatting with one another about life in the police force, while Eric pulled up a chair and just listened.

Deep in conversation, the detective's walkie-talkie interrupted them.

"Excuse me while I take this!" said the detective. He then quickly moved over to the other side of the room, saying, "Roger!"

Eric thought chuckling to himself "Why is the person on the other end of a walkie-talkie always called, 'Roger'?"

After a short while, the detective came back and said, "Good news! The perpetrator has just confessed to the crimes! It turns out that she already has a string of convictions, and due to the overwhelming evidence stacked against her, her defense lawyer advised her to plead guilty."

"So, will I be able to get my money back today?" asked Eric, hopeful.

"I doubt that it will be today but providing what's left of the money can be accounted for, I don't see why you couldn't have it returned to you in the next couple of days!" answered the detective with a smile.

That *was* good news for Eric to hear, and everyone could see the sheer relief on his face. The detective, though, then continued with a "but".

"*But* the perpetrator is denying that she stole $25,000, claiming it was $15,000 instead. And she claims to have already spent about £3,000 of it, and now has no more money left."

Eric couldn't believe it, thinking, "She's still got the nerve to try and steal from me!"

Continuing, the detective said, "Which *means* you would need to go to court to claim the rest of the money you have accused her of stealing – which based on my experience, Mr Fartz, can be a long and drawn-out process. *And* it still doesn't guarantee that you will ever get the rest of the money. So, the question now is, Mr Fartz, do you still wish to press charges?"

Eric remained silent, while he weighed it all up, contemplating what he should do.

The detective then spoke again. "Regardless of whether you seek to press charges or not, her misdemeanor will still go down on her criminal record."

"No!" Eric replied, answering his question

directly, which surprised everyone there. He hated letting Gloria get away with the rest of the money, but as you know, Eric had his reasons not to go to court. And there was enough money remaining to pay back the Mafia the outstanding $10,000 he still owed them, and, once he'd done that, he just wanted to put that foolish and regrettable episode of his life behind him.

And so, that was how it was left. The detective quickly wrapped up the interview and then left. And in the meantime, Eric would just have to wait patiently for his money to be processed before he could get the remainder of it back – and hopefully for his sake, by Saturday.

As the detective was leaving, Eric quickly caught up with him outside.

"*Excuse* me please, Mr Hitchcock!" Eric called out.

The officer stopped and turned. "Yes, Mr Fartz," he replied, clearly in a hurry.

"I can see you're in a hurry, so I won't keep ya long. I forgot to ask if you found the murderer yet?"

"*Which* one!" he fired back cynically, implying the LVMPD was dealing with a lot of murder cases.

"Oh, *sorry!* The young woman murdered recently at the Desert Sands Motel."

The detective shook his head. "No, the killer is still at large," he answered almost casually. Which was not the answer Eric was hoping to hear.

"Okay, thanks!" said Eric as the detective got in his car and sped off.

Meanwhile, Gloria was left stewing in a police cell awaiting her fate, convinced that she would be going to prison for a lengthy sentence this time. And there was no hope of her getting bail: for a start off, she'd had all her money seized; and when the authorities contacted her boyfriend, Chet, on her behalf and asked if he would post bail, he refused, denying he ever knew her.

Gloria had betrayed Eric, and now Chet had betrayed her. Many would argue that she deserved it. But due to Eric's lenience, later that day, she left the police headquarters without charge. She now had no boyfriend, no job, and no money – except for just enough money left in her designer purse to buy a one-way ticket on a Greyhound bus back to her home city of Detroit. So, she let her Jimmy

Choo shoes take her to the bus station, where she waited with lots of other people with long faces, wanting to escape from Sin City.

Another show, and a seemingly never-ending restless night later – mostly spent worrying whether he would get his money back in time to pay the Mafia – the sun eventually came up the following day. And Eric then spent a seemingly never-ending anxious day waiting to hear when he could pick up his money from the LVMPD.

But as luck would have it, the phone call he'd been desperately waiting for all day, came early evening time, and he was able to go and collect his money between shows – $12, 252.00 in cash to be precise. And this time, he wasn't taking any chances and performed his whole act with the money gaffer-taped to his body.

CHAPTER NINETEEN

ERIC MAKES THREE BIG MISTAKES!

It was Saturday morning, and today Eric would make three big mistakes!

At 10.00 am on the dot, having made his excuses not to attend rehearsals, Eric left his apartment firmly clutching onto his new sports bag containing $10,000, a can of Coke, plus some strategically placed underwear concealing it. He then got into his rent-a-car and drove off to the Showcase Shopping Mall to hand over the money to the Mafia.

In the likelihood they should demand he also pays the interest on the interest, which had accrued over the last two weeks, he also had another $2,000 stashed away in various pockets

– he'd got used to the underhanded way they operate by now.

"Once I've handed the money over to them that will be the end of it!" he thought, catching a glimpse of himself appearing apprehensive as he glanced at the dodgy-looking people in the car behind through his rear-view mirror – the thought of being followed not far from his mind. "What if I get carjacked!" he suddenly thought. That would be the last thing he needed right now.

At the junction of West Tropicana Avenue and Las Vegas Blvd, the traffic lights just up ahead were still showing green. So, Eric approached very slowly, causing the drivers behind him to furiously beep their horns at him. Then just as the lights were about to change, he put his foot down on the gas pedal and sped across the junction hoping to lose the car behind him just in case his hunch *was* correct. Maybe it was paranoia, but he wasn't taking any chances.

He'd done it, leaving the little old couple in the car behind him stuck at the lights!

As Eric drove along the Strip in the direction of the shopping mall, he tried to think of more positive thoughts.

"It won't be long now before Em visits me!" he thought, which instantly putting a smile on his face. There was now only one more week to go, and he couldn't wait to see her. He'd been thinking lately that it was about time he proposed to her – his mum kept reminding him every time she rang, so how could he forget. The two of them had been together ever since being childhood sweethearts, and he'd often thought of popping the question, but just never got around to it. He was always too busy performing and trying to make a name for himself in show business and didn't feel the time was right to get married and settle down before. But he did now and wanted it more than anything – far more than the fame and fortune he once pursued with a passion.

Eric pulled into the dimly lit shopping mall's subterranean car park and parked as close to the entrance as he could. He had a quick look round to make sure that there was nobody suspicious-looking lurking around ready to pounce on him. Then got out of the car, grabbing his sports bag from the front passenger seat as he did, and quickly and nervously headed straight for the entrance.

Relieved to be inside among the bright lights

and lots of people, Eric made his way past several shops towards the escalators to take him up to the upper level to the food court. It was now about 10.40 am and he still had plenty of time before he was due to meet the mobsters at 11 am.

Near the escalators, over to the left, a store window glistened and sparkled, catching his eye. It was a jewellery store, with shelves filled with diamonds, emeralds, and rubies displayed in all kinds of gold and platinum settings, beckoning him to come over and take a closer look.

"It wouldn't hurt just to look!" thought Eric. Reminded that if he were going to propose to Emily, he would need to buy her a ring first! Besides, it would give him something to do while he waited for the Mafia to turn up. So, he ventured into this shiny wonderland of a store to take a closer look. (Big mistake number one!)

Just as he entered, unbeknownst of each other's presence, the mobsters approached the bottom of the escalators, with Tony One Shoe up front. He had to be helped onto the escalator by one of the three heavies that were accompanying him.

"Get off me, ya doughnut.!" protested Tony One Shoe indignantly. "I can manage myself!"

"Yeah, of course, Boss! Sorry Boss!" said his heavy, wishing he hadn't tried to help, even though his boss clearly struggled to walk, let alone get onto a moving escalator.

Now although his heavies, or "soldiers" as they are also known in the Mafia, called him "Boss", he wasn't "The Boss". Tony One Shoe was what they call an "Underboss". And his boss wasn't at all happy because Tony One Shoe' wasn't bringing in the amount of revenue "The Family" back in New York expected. There was talk among the Family hierarchy that he was embezzling the money. In other words, he was performing his own kinda magic act and making their money disappear!

Now I don't know if Tony One Shoe was stealing from the Family or not. If he *was*, then that would only result in one thing, if you know what I mean. But one thing I do know is that ever since he got wind that they were suspicious of him, he made sure he collected all the money owed to him on time.

And, on this day Tony One Shoe was feeling particularly anxious and uptight and certainly wasn't in the mood to accept any more excuses from Eric. And while the mobsters were going up the escalator to the food court, Eric was busy looking at a large variety of diamond encrusted engagement rings in a glass counter inside the store.

It was very busy and noisy in the food court. "Take that table over there in the corner!" ordered Tony One Shoe to his heavies, pointing to it.

There was a family already sitting there. But not for long – the mobsters didn't even have to ask them to move, they just gestured to them to skat it, and they did. One of the heavies swiped all the empty paper food and drinks cartons onto the floor, quickly making the table clear.

Tony One Shoe sat down first, looking stern, followed by the others. " 'Slim', get me an espresso!" he ordered, "... and whatever you fellas wanna drink."

"Sure, Boss!" replied Slim. He wasn't really slim, in fact, he was the opposite of slim, but all mobsters have nicknames and that was his. So, Slim went off to get the drinks, and after jumping the cue, quickly came back with them, plus a huge plateful of ring doughnuts for himself – which were his favourites.

"You're *never* gonna eat all of those!" said one of the other heavies.

"Ya wanna bet – just watch me!" replied Slim as he started shoving them down his cakehole (they don't call him a "heavy" for nothing).

"Your head is like a ring doughnut – it's got nothin' in da middle!" said Tony One Shoe, causing the other two heavies to laugh. "Now, keep a look out for that magician fella, ya doughnut!"

Eric was so busy looking at one engagement ring after another that he completely forgot about the time and his other engagement with the Mafia – even though the jewellers had watches and ornate clocks displayed just about everywhere.

After showing Eric several trays of the cheaper range of rings, which he shook his head to each time, the female shop assistant, then brought out another tray containing the most expensive rings they sold. When he could afford it, he wanted to buy Emily something special.

"We also have these beautiful diamond rings, sir, but they are the most expensive!" said the shop assistant, looking at him with her nose in the air as if to say he would never be able to afford them.

The diamonds were so bright and sparkly that they almost blinded him. "Wow! I need to put my sunglasses on!" said Eric jokingly.

And right in the centre of the tray was the most beautiful ring he had ever seen. It had a huge stone set in the centre and was surrounded by smaller stones encircled around it. "Em would love it!" he thought. And whatever the price was, he knew he just had to have it.

"How much is it?" asked Eric.

"$10,000,00, sir," she replied with a cheesy smile. Eric gulped. "It is one of kind, sir! Made by an expert craftsman!"

"I bet!" said Eric, with eyes glistening almost as bright as the diamonds. "Can I take a closer look and check if it is the right size for my girlfriend?"

By this time, the two burly security guards standing by the door were watching Eric intensely like hawks, as was the nervy-looking store manager.

"Erm?" made the sound of the hesitant shop assistant as she looked across to her manager unsure. He nodded his approval, and she removed it from the tray and held it out in front of him.

"Just a minute!" suddenly said Eric. He the reached down to his sports bag, which he'd wedged between his feet, partially unzipped it, and removed a can of Coke. He then promptly prised it open, spraying the shop assistant slightly and making her jump, and quickly pulled off the ring pull. He took a quick sip, and holding the ring pull up, said, "This hole in the ring pull is about the right size!" The shop assistant, along with the manager looked at him strangely. (You see, when Eric and Emily were teenagers, Eric jokingly proposed to her, and put the Coke can ring pull on her left-hand third finger. And so, if both the diametres of the rings matched in size, he would know it would fit.) "Let me just check," he continued saying excitedly. He held the ring pull up against the engagement ring and, to his pleasure, they *were* both the same size diameter. "Perfect!" he announced. "I'll take it!"

Well, the shop assistant and the manager nearly fainted in shocked surprise. Eric promptly plonked his heavy bag onto the counter and immediately started pulling out his underwear and draping it carelessly over the counter followed by bundles of $50.00 bills.

"$10,000, you say?" said Eric as he removed the cash, smiling widely and looking extremely pleased.

"Er, yes sir. Thank you, sir," replied the shop assistant, still in shock – especially from seeing his underwear.

Meanwhile, on the floor above, in the food court, the mobsters looked much less pleased, especially Tony One Shoe. Eric was late – it was now 11.15 am!

"How dare he be late for me!" snarled Tony One Shoe angrily followed by several unrepeatable names he called him. "Wait till I get my hands on him!" he then spat out followed by more expletives. The other mobsters remained silent and just sunk into their shirt collars. They knew better than to interrupt him, especially when he was angry. "I've waited long enough. C'mon let's get outta here!"

"But Boss – I haven't finished all my doughnuts!" unwisely exclaimed Slim.

Tony One Shoe immediately slapped Slim across the head, taking his frustrations out on him.

"Ouch!" hollowed Slim.

"I said let's go – didn't I? That means now! Ya got me?"

"Yeah, sorry Boss!" squealed Slim as he got up from his chair and followed the others to the escalators with a doughnut still stuck half-way out of his mouth.

Eric paid the shop assistant the $10,000 for the engagement ring, and as she placed it neatly back in its black velvet ring box, he stashed away his underwear untidily back in his sports bag. He opted not to have a store gift bag but instead placed the ring box into his rear trouser pocket for safekeeping. Then smiling his head off, exited the scintillating and bewitching store that had allured him into there in the first place, now carrying a much lighter bag as he did.

As he stepped outside the store, it was as if the spell had broken; he suddenly remembered why he was at the shopping mall in the first place. He looked up to the top of the crowded escalators, and there, just about to come down was Tony One Shoe, looking as angry as hell with his heavies.

Suddenly Tony One Shoe's and Eric's eyes met. *"Oh, 'eck!"* Eric said to himself, and immediately made a run for it.

"THERE HE IS!" bellowed Tony One Shoe.

"After him! Don't let him get away!"

"We can't – you're in the way, Boss!" said one of the heavies.

The Mafia Underboss quickly turned sideways and held in his big tummy in as much as he could. "Quick after him, before he gets away!" he yelled. "Mamma mia!"

Two of the heavies managed to squeeze past him, but Slim had no chance, and so stayed where he was finishing off his doughnut. The two slimmer heavies raced after Eric, thudding their way down the moving stairs, uncourteously shoving people aside as they did.

By this time Eric was already out of the main entrance and onto the Strip. The mobsters reached the bottom of the escalators, leaving carnage behind them, and made chase in the direction they had seen him run, "Get outta da way!" they kept shouting; barging past anybody that got in their way and knocking some of shoppers over like skittles. One of the shopping mall security guards took one look at the huge muscle-bound men and decided against chasing after them and walked the other way instead.

The two mobsters reached the main entrance, quickly looked left and right, and spotted Eric running about twenty or so metres away from them heading south along the busy Strip.

"This way!" shouted one of the heavies. They then immediately continued to give chase.

Eric continued running as fast as he could, but the sidewalk was so busy with people walking in both directions that he was continually being slowed down. And when it came to trying to get past people, the mobsters weren't as polite as he was!

Up ahead in the distance, Eric could now see a mass of white heading his way. As he drew nearer, he soon realised that there must be an Elvis Presley convention taking place over the weekend, which explained why there were hundreds of Elvis impersonators all dressed up as the King of Rock 'n' Roll, wearing his famous sparkling white jumpsuit and cape, black wig and gold rimmed sunglasses. He could hear them singing their favourite Elvis songs as they curled up their lips and wildly slung their arms and legs in the air and twitched their bodies about as if they had a wasp trapped inside their jumpsuits.

With the mobsters still hot on his heels and gaining on him fast, Eric immersed himself into the white cloud of Elvis costumes. *"Ouch! Ooh! Ahh!"* voiced Eric as he painfully made his way through them amidst limbs flying everywhere and colliding with him from every which direction.

About halfway through the crowd, and now feeling fatigued, Eric quickly glanced over his shoulder and saw the mobsters were still after him. Thinking quickly, he stopped one of the impersonators about the same size as him and asked if he could buy their costume from them, offering them $100.00. The impersonator shook his head and moved on. Eric then stopped another, but his reply was the same. Eric then realised that he must be offering too little. Now desperate, he stopped another impersonator, who happened to look a bit like Eric – same build and longish blonde hair escaping from the black wig. And this time he offered the guy $500.00. The guy immediately curled his lip up and said, "Uh, huh!", thinking it must be his lucky day. And the two of them quickly dashed across the sidewalk and hid behind a large dumpster, where Eric promptly removed the cash from his pockets and paid the stranger $500.00, and both quickly exchanged clothes. (Big mistake number two!)

As the guy left, now wearing Eric's jeans and orange tee-shirt, he started laughing and boasted, "I only paid $25.00 for that costume! *Sucker!*" But Eric didn't care; all he was concerned with was avoiding being caught by the mobsters.

Eric hurriedly shoved the remaining cash inside his overpriced sparkly white jumpsuit, which had a white cape already attached to it with Velcro, and zipped it up, then put on the black wig and glasses and instantly transformed himself into Elvis. He lifted the dumpster lid and tossed his sports bag inside, thinking, "That's another sports bag I no longer have!" then quickly went and blended in with the remaining karate chopping, leg kicking, hip gyrating Elvis impersonators. Curling up his lip, and imitating the imitators, while at the same time trying to remember the lyrics to "Viva Las Vegas", which all the others around him were singing, he strutted back in the same direction that he just came from.

Suddenly he heard the voice of one of the two mobsters just up ahead. "There he is!" he called out. Eric immediately started to panic thinking that he'd been spotted, but the two mobsters rushed past him and continued in the opposite direction.

"They must have mistaken me for the guy I exchanged clothes with," thought Eric. "Oh, *'eck!*" Eric never stopped to think that the mobsters might chase after him instead. "Poor guy!"

After a little while of energetic Elvis impersonations, he turned his head around and saw that the mobsters were by now far away in the distance. And so, stopped to take a breather and let the rest of the Elvis impersonators pass him. "Being an Elvis impersonator is hard work!" he thought.

He then squatted down for a moment and removed his itchy and uncomfortable nylon wig and gave his head a good itch. (Big mistake number three!)

"There he is!" shouted a hoarse and familiar voice. *"After him!"*

Eric looked up. It was Tony One Shoe and Slim now coming his way!

CHAPTER TWENTY

A WEDDING CHAPEL REUNION

Eric quickly looked around to see what his best escape options were. He didn't want to run back the way he came in case the other two mobsters had decided to double back, and it was too busy to attempt to cross the road. But just a bit farther up was a side street. So, he quickly jumped up, and sprinted towards it with his wig still in his hand.

Tony One Shoe and Slim saw him running and quickened their pace towards him. Eric beat them to the street junction and tore down it running as fast as he could. There wasn't much chance of these two mobsters catching up with him, but he wasn't taking any chances.

This street was less busy, and after whizzing past a couple of fast-food outlets, Eric quickly glanced over his shoulder to check where the mobsters were. By this time, Slim had stopped, though, and was bent over with both hands on his knees, gasping for breath (the tempting smell of freshly cooked hamburgers also probably had something to do with it).

"There's no time to rest – after him before he gets away again!" shouted his angry boss.

Eric, seeing that he was now well ahead of them, slowed down his pace to a trot. He was tired out himself and didn't think he could run much farther in the soaring heat.

A little bit farther up, Eric glanced over his shoulder again to see if they were still coming after him. To his horror, both the mobsters were getting into a black limousine pointing his way. "Tony One Shoe must have called his driver," thought Eric.

Suddenly Eric heard an irritated voice coming from over to his right. "Hey, hurry up – you're *late!*" said a man in a smart suit and tie gesticulating to come towards him.

Eric stopped. "What me?" Eric replied.

"Well, you *are* the Elvis impersonator I hired,

aren't you?" then said the man, getting impatient. The real Elvis impersonator was either late or had decided not to turn up – or maybe he got a better paid gig somewhere else?

Eric looked a bit farther beyond from where the man was standing and noticed that there was a little wedding chapel called 'The O.K Chapel'.

"Do *please* hurry up – there're a wedding couple from the UK already waiting inside for you to marry them!"

'Marry them!" thought Eric.

He quickly glanced back down the street again and saw that the mobsters were now inside the Limo, which was starting to pull away. So, he had no choice but to go along with the charade.

"Yes, *sorry* I'm late!" said Eric, and hurried towards the man, fumbling to put his wig back on as he did.

"Quickly! Follow me around the back!" said the man, whom it was now apparent was the owner of the wedding chapel business …

Wedding chapels are big business in Las Vegas, and one can find them scattered about all over the place. They are extremely popular as it offers couples a quick and easy way to get married. And Elvis weddings are without a doubt the most popular.

With sweat pouring all down his face, and his wig off centre and looking badly lopsided, Eric gingerly entered the chapel through a curtain, and nervously approached the altar.

Standing there in front of him were a loving, very generously proportioned young couple, holding hands, smiling, and staring sweetly into each other's eyes. He had longish black hair, a pencil moustache, and wore a white suit with a matching bow tie; and she was blonde, dressed in a traditional white wedding dress, and looked like she might be expecting. And, sat huddled together on a bench behind, were five small restless children, looking bored out of their brains and shoving one another around.

"*Sing* then!" the business owner whispered loudly from behind the curtain.

"Oh, 'eck!" thought Eric, and started shaking even more nervously.

"Oh, *look*, he's got *all* the moves!" quietly said the bride-to-be to her groom-to-be, mistaking his nervous twitches for Elvis moves.

Eric then began singing "Suspicious Minds", which was hardly an appropriate song for a wedding but was the only Elvis song he vaguely knew. Fortunately for him, he just had the chance to practice singing along to it with the other Elvis impersonators, but unfortunate for anyone listening! He sounded awful!

The wedding couple looked at each other cringing and desperately wanted to laugh but managed to hold it together. The children, on the other hand, were all laughing their heads off. While the business owner didn't find it funny at all, and immediately stuck his fingers in his ears, thinking, "I'm *never* gonna book him again!"

"*Shh!*" said the bride-to-be, turning around to face her children with her finger pressed to her lips.

Eric felt so embarrassed that he didn't even dare look at the wedding couple and sang to the floor instead.

Eric then heard the business owner's grumbling voice behind him again, telling to stop singing – much to his relief – and to get on with the ceremony. Eric immediately stopped singing – much to everybody else's relief – and looked towards the pulpit in front of him. Laid out on it was the script for the marriage ceremony vows.

Eric then smiled at the couple, thinking that

the guy looks very familiar, and following the instructions on the script, asked them to look into each other's eyes and hold hands. He then began reading the script:

"Dearly Beloved, we are gathered here today to witness before family and –" Eric quickly looked up at the congregation again and saw that there *were* no friends present. "… family – the exchange of sacred vows between Gary Evans and Bethany Jenkins."

He then looked at the equally nervous, sweaty big guy, and said, "Please repeat after me," while thinking, "Gary Evans? No, it can't be the Gary Evans I knew from school – can it?" He then looked back down and continued reading from the script: '… I, Gary Evans.'

"I, Gary Evans," the big guy repeated with a bit of a squeaky Welsh accent, turning to look at Eric and thinking he looks and sounds familiar.

Eric paused a moment, staring at him closer, and thinking, "I'm *sure* it's him."

The last time he saw Gary was a few years back, and he had short dyed blonde hair – and wasn't wearing a moustache. And the last time Gary saw Eric, he had short natural blonde hair – and wasn't wearing a black nylon Elvis wig.

"Get on with it!" said the even more agitated voice from behind the curtain.

Eric then continued. "… take thee."

"take thee," said Gary as he looked lovingly back towards his bride-to-be.

"Bethany Jenkins," continued Eric, now convinced it *was* his old school friend and smiling broadly.

Gary then looked back towards the Elvis impersonator and noticed blonde locks of hair creeping out from under his black wig. Beaming his head off, he then screamed, "ERIC FARTZ!"

"Do what?" said Bethany, looking at Gary perplexed.

"Sorry – Bethany Jenkins!" Gary corrected himself by saying, slightly red-faced. "… Carry on Elvis!"

Eric chuckled, and the two old pals couldn't help but grin at one another like they were back at school again. They couldn't believe it.

Eric then continued with the vows. "… to be my bedded – er, wedded wife!"

Gary chuckled. "to be my wedded wife …"

Once Bethany had also said her vows, the Elvis impersonator would then usually sing another song.

"Skip, the singing!" said the fraught sounding voice behind him. "Just get on with the wedding ring exchange vows – we're already running late, and the next wedding party will be here soon!"

Eric quickly read the next line of instructions to himself. "... Do you have the rings?" Eric asked Gary and Bethany.

They both shook their heads. "No, the Best Man has them – he's late!" Bethany informed Eric, now becoming even more anxious.

Suddenly, a tall, slightly disheveled guy in a suit, burst through the rear doors, saying, "Sorry, I'm late!"

The wedding couple instantly turned around. "Oh, *there* you are Jack – *bout* time!" called out Gary, slightly miffed, but very pleased and relieved to see his Best Man.

"I would have asked *you* to be my Best Man, Eric, but I didn't know where you were. And getting married in Vegas was a last-minute decision," Gary said quickly and confidentially to his friend.

"Oh, don't worry, Gary, that's okay! It's great to see ya!" quickly replied Eric also in a whisper.

"... Anyway, *marrying* us is even better!" then

said Gary buoyantly.

Meanwhile, Jack quickly made a run-up along the highly polished wooden aisle and skidded the rest of the way to the altar. The kids thought this was cool and looked like a lot of fun and were about to get up and have a go themselves until their mum told them not to. "… I've always wanted to do that!" said Jack, smiling. He then started to apologise again.

"Nevermind all that, *where're* the rings?" asked Gary, panicking slightly.

Jack quickly patted his pockets in search of the rings, starting to look worried. Then smiling with relief as he reached into his right-side jacket pocket and removed them. "Thank goodness!" he said as he handed the appropriate rings to the bride and groom.

Eric stood there smiling, thinking, "He *still* hasn't recognized me."

"*Hey!* During the taxi ride here, I saw a gigantic picture of *Eric* on a billboard!" quickly commented Jack. "We'll have to go and try and see him later – mind you, he's probably too busy to see us!"

Which, upon hearing, hurt Eric a touch – reminding him about the cost of fame.

Gary looked at Eric and burst out laughing.

"Why are ya laughing?" said Jack, totally unaware that his old schoolmate Eric was standing right opposite him.

"Well, we won't have to go far!" then said Gary.

"Whatcha, pal!" suddenly said the Elvis impersonator in his northern English accent.

Jack immediately jumped backwards in shock at hearing Eric's voice and then recognising his face with the piercing blue eyes and wide smile.

"What the –" started to say Jack.

Bethany cleared her throat twice, interrupting him. "Remember where you are Jack!" she said, frowning at him.

"Oh, yeah, *sorry!"* said Jack forgetting for a moment. *"Eric!* How are ya, mate?"

"Good, thanks!" Eric replied, very pleased to see Jack as well.

"Will you *hurry up* and get on with it!" said the frantic voice behind the curtain again, which everybody heard.

"That was *amazing* Eric! How did you throw your voice like that?" said Jack, grinning. "I never saw your lips move once! He's not only a magician, an Elvis impersonator, but he's *also* a ventriloquist as well!"

Everybody laughed.

"Seriously, though, why are ya dressed up as Elvis?" asked Jack, curious.

"Yeah, why are ya?" also asked Gary.

"It's a long story," answered Eric. "Right now, I'd better hurry up and get you two lovebirds married. We can all catch up later!"

As well as being the Best Man, Jack was also given the job as the official photographer, so started taking photos (well, Gary and Bethany were on a budget).

The others agreed, and addressing Gary Eric then said, "Please repeat after me." He then quickly read out the next part of the script. "With this ring, I thee wed, and with it, I bestow upon thee all the treasures of my mind, heart, and –"

"*Sorry!* Can ya repeat that please, mate – I didn't quite catch all that," asked Gary befuddled.

"Oh, *Gary!*" said Bethany, looking at him and shaking her head. *"Concentrate!"*

Well, after the third go, Gary finally nailed it, and squeezed the ring onto Bethany's left chubby ring finger (it looked like he was trying to screw a nut onto a rusty old bolt), feeling relieved that was all over.

Eric then addressed Bethany and instructed

her to repeat after him: "I will forever wear this ring as a sign of my commitment and the desire of my heart."

Trembling, Bethany got it right the first time without mistakes and squeezed the ring on Gary's even chubbier ring finger.

"It's not *fair!*" said Gary. "Her lines were *easier* than mine!"

"Oh, Gary, be quiet and let him finish!" Bethany told him.

"You can tell who's the boss in their relationship," thought Eric, smiling to himself.

Then while Gary and Bethany were holding hands and looking lovingly into each other's eyes again, Eric announced. "By the powers vested in me, I now pronounce you husband and wife!" Everybody clapped and cheered. "You may now *kiss* the bride!"

Gary leaned in towards her and planted his lips on hers, and both kissed passionately. Which was followed by more applause and cheers.

"*Errgh!*" voiced the children all at once, clearly showing their disapproval. "Can we *go* now?" then said one of them.

Meanwhile, the chapel business owner was outside at the front of the building apologising for running late.

Gary, Beth, and Jack thanked Eric and congratulated him on a job well done – though, Gary had some advice for him.

"I should stick to the magic, though, if I were you!" said Gary grinning.

Eric laughed. "Yeah, I will!" he replied, chuckling.

"Oh, I *missed* all that – go on *give* us a song," then said Jack.

"Trust me, Jack, you *don't* wanna hear him sing!" said Gary, causing everybody to laugh.

"… So, are these all yours then?" Eric then asked Gary, referring to the five children present, who were now noisily running around playing 'Tag' between the empty chairs, much to the annoyance of the female chapel assistant, who was trying to get the bride and groom to sign their marriage certificate amidst the mayhem.

"Gareth, Dylan, and Julie are mine," answered Gary pointing them out. "And Tracy and David" – as soon as he merely mentioned the name 'David', Gary, and Eric both looked at each other with a look of trepidation, knowing what each other was thinking – "are Bethany's from a previous relationship. And we have another one on the way."

Eric thought, "I never knew he had it in him!"

"Kids! Kids!" Gary called out excitedly. "Uncle Eric's a *magician!* Come over here, and he'll show you some magic, won't ya, Eric?"

"Yeah, *sure!*" said Eric, but thinking, what *has* he let himself in for, as by now the children were very boisterous.

"C'mon Gary! We need to sign our marriage certificate." said Bethany, tugging on his jacket sleeve. "The lady is waiting!"

And so, while the happy married couple each signed the wedding certificate, Eric entertained the kids – including Jack, who was still a big kid at heart – with some simple magic tricks. Eric enjoyed watching their little faces light up as he filled them with wonderment performing one magic trick after another until it was time to leave.

As they were about to leave the wedding chapel, the chapel assistant came running after Eric, saying, "Don't forget the money for your performance!"

He thanked her as she unexpectedly handed him $50.00 in cash – he was so pleased to have gotten away from the Mafia that he hadn't even thought about being paid.

"The *drinks* are on Eric!" yelled Gary, followed by loud cheers from his friends.

Eric was having such a good time that he completely forgot about the Mafia who were waiting for him outside!

CHAPTER TWENTY-ONE

SHOWDOWN AT THE O.K CHAPEL!

Later that day, Eric found time between shows to meet up with his friends and join in with the wedding celebrations and to catch up with one another – it had been a long time since they had done that, and everyone was excited to tell each other what they had been up to since they last met.

Gary told Eric that he had started his own business as a painter and decorator, which immediately caused Eric's eyebrows to shoot upwards, and Jack enthused about his job as a PE teacher, and that he was still single, which he was less enthused about.

The Wedding Reception was being held at

the Treasure Island Resort Hotel on the Strip, where the wedding couple and their children were staying. Gary and Bethany had promised to take the kids to Disneyland (which was Gary's idea, of course) and thought that it was about time that they tied the knot (which was Bethany's idea), and so, decided to borrow from the bank of mum and dad do both while they were out there.

The adults were sat around a table together still enjoying the Wedding Breakfast and the children were amusing themselves pretending to be pirates nearby.

"It's a shame that Em isn't here with us!" said Jack.

"Yeah, how is she?" asked Gary.

"Em's fine, thanks. We regularly keep in touch via Skype, and she's coming out here to see me next week," answered Eric with a worried look on his face.

Bethany picked up on this. "Why are you looking so worried and sad?" she asked.

"Yeah, I thought you'd be more cheerful about seeing your girlfriend, mate," said Jack, surprised.

"He's having too much fun out here on his own, I reckon –" said Gary, grinning and winking at Eric, who remained looking a bit solemn.

"*Gary!* Don't say that!" said Bethany telling him off. (Bethany was a few years older than Gary and was the matriarch of the family.)

"Yeah, shut up, Gary!" quickly said Jack. "So, what's bothering ya, mate?" There was a silence. "Surely, you're living the dream out here, aren't ya? I would've thought you'd be happy?"

Eric was reluctant to say at first, because it was a bit embarrassing. But after a moment or two, or three, or four, told them what had happened earlier in the day before their surprise reunion at the chapel.

"… So, those guys dressed in black suits waiting outside the chapel were M–M–M–Mafia?" asked Gary interrupting Eric.

"Yeah, the *same* guys dressed in black that you threatened to beat up if they didn't go away, and *no thanks* to you, nearly got us all *killed!*"

"I still reckon I could have had them!" then said Gary, boasting about taking them all on single-handed again.

"Yeah, *right!*" said Jack sarcastically. "Is that why you ran off then?" Gary didn't respond.

"Jack's right, Gary, it was a foolish thing to do," said Bethany, scolding her newlywed husband again. "And if those nasty men had caught up with you, who knows what they might have done to you and your friends! You don't *think* before you act! You could've *ruined* my wedding day!" To which, Gary slumped down in his chair and supped quietly on his pint of beer while he listened to Eric continuing to tell them about his involvement with the Mafia, and about buying Emily the expensive engagement ring, only to then go and lose it.

"… If *only* I'd have remembered to remove the ring box from my rear trouser pocket when I swapped clothes with the stranger!" said Eric, shaking his head. "Then I would've been able to present it to her and ask her to marry me as planned! It was *such* a beautiful ring; you should have seen it. I'm *never* goin' to get it back – Oh, I'm *such* a fool!"

"You're *not* a fool, Eric!" said Bethany sympathising with him.

"*Yes*, he is!" said Jack, grinning; causing Gary to start laughing.

"Shut up, you two," said Eric, cracking a smile.

"As you say, 'two mobsters were chasing after you', and you were busy focusing on your safety and disguising yourself to avoid being caught!"

"Yeah, I suppose you're right," replied Eric, clearly disappointed though.

"And ya never know, the guy's conscience might get the better of him and he'll return it to you somehow!"

"*Fat chance* of that!" suddenly chirped in Gary. "You've got about as much chance of getting your ring back as *me* becoming a vegetarian!"

"Gary don't be *so* pessimistic – you *always* have to look at things with a glass half empty, don't cha," said Bethany, tutting.

"Speaking of which," answered Gary, looking down at his almost empty pint glass, "get me a top-up, would ya please, sweetness?"

"Don't you *'sweetness'* me!" said his wife, giving him a dirty look. "You get ya own!"

Jack leaned nearer towards Eric and said quietly, "Lookout! The two of them have only just got married, and they're already having a domestic!"

Eric smiled and said to the wedding couple, "Now, now, don't argue on your wedding day!"

Bethany replied, saying, "Oh, this isn't arguing – this is how we normally talk to one another!" Everybody laughed.

Gary then said, "Well, I was only trying to be realistic – I'll tell ya what, if Eric gets his ring back, I'll become a vegetarian! How about that!" Everybody laughed again.

"I'll go and get the next round," then said Eric, thinking, Gary's right.

Now, while Eric's gone to get the drinks, I'll fill you in with all the details of what happened once the wedding party left the O.K Chapel.

Eric and Jack came out of the main entrance first. Eric, armed with handfuls of confetti, courtesy of the establishment; and Jack, with his camera, ready for when the newlyweds made their exit.

Already outside, spread out on the small area of lawn, were the next wedding party waiting to go in – and not looking at all pleased. And through a gap in the much larger crowd, Eric spotted the black limousine; and leaning up against it with their arms folded were the four mean-looking mobsters, plus the driver, who remained inside. "Oh, 'eck!" thought Eric, suddenly remembering why he took shelter in the chapel in the first place.

The married couple stepped out into the blazing hot sunshine wearing their sunglasses, and a couple of the small children who were clinging onto them, with the other older children following closely behind.

"Say *cheeeese!*" said Jack, who suddenly found himself smothered in confetti instead of the bride and groom because Eric had been unattentively looking over his shoulder at the mobsters at the time.

"What are ya *doin'* Eric, you *idiot?* You're *supposed* to throw it over the bride and groom!" exclaimed Jack as he spat out a load of confetti.

"*Sorry!*" said Eric turning his head sharply back around. He still had some confetti stuck to his sweaty palms, so quickly picked off a few flakes and pathetically threw those.

"Who were you looking at?" asked Jack to no answer. He then took some photos minus the confetti.

Once the photographs had been taken, Eric cautiously led the others down the narrow path to the main road.

"Why's he going so slow?" asked Bethany.

"I don't know – he's been acting strange ever since we got out here!" replied Jack.

"*Get a move on,* Eric – I'm *dying* for a drink!"

called out Gary.

"Who are those people staring at us?" then asked Bethany to no reply. "… Ah, Gary, did you book us a surprise limousine?"

"No," bluntly answered Gary.

Eric suddenly stopped about halfway down the path.

"How was da wedding ceremony?" called out Tony One Shoe with an insincere smile, which seemed to continue up the left side of his face due to his scar.

"It was *lovely,* thanks!" answered Bethany, smiling back.

Tony One Shoe then opened the rear passenger door. "Would ya care to come for a ride wid us, Mr Fartz, or should I say, *Elvis?*" said the Mafia Underboss laughing sinisterly at his own wisecrack, immediately followed by laughter from his henchmen.

"What about *us?*" said the Bride, sounding somewhat put out.

"I think I'll give it a miss," casually said Eric, shaking his head.

There was an awkward silence. Then, the Underboss dropped his phoney smile and looked directly at Eric and said menacingly, "It wasn't an option Mr Fartz – now *get* in!" He then reached inside his designer pin-striped jacket and partly removed a pistol to make himself clearer.

In a split second, everyone's mood suddenly changed from being happy and cheerful to fearful. Gary and Bethany quickly huddled all their children close towards them.

"What's wrong, Dada?" asked one of them.

"Hush now darling," softly said Bethany to her child, who then began to cry, while by contrast, joyous church music now rang out in the background

"I think *now's* a good time to tell us what the *hell's* goin' on – don't cha, mate?" said Jack.

"These men are out to harm me!" said Eric staring defiantly at the mobsters without budging an inch.

"No sh—" started to say Jack.

"Jack! Not in front of the children!" quickly said Bethany warning him.

Big Gary remained motionless and quiet, scared as a tiny mouse.

"Go away before I call the boys in blue!" Bethany then warned the men in black.

The mobsters laughed.

"Take it easy! We just'a wanna talk to Mr Fartz, dat's all! We have some unfinished business we need to settle," said Tony One Shoe lighting a cigarette.

"Why didn't ya just say 'the police'?" quickly asked Jack under his breath.

"Because that's all I could think of at the time!" she quickly answered back under her breath.

"Besides, the police out here wear khaki!" advised Jack.

"Oh!" just said, Bethany.

"What are we gonna do?" Jack quietly asked Eric out of the side of his mouth.

Eric remained silent while he continued to weigh up the few options they had during his bottom-clenching standoff with the Mafia.

But the Underboss's patience had now run out. He took a big puff on his cigarette before flicking it away, and staring coldly towards Eric again, angrily began threatening him. "I'll give ya one last chance – either come wid us now or else!" he growled peppered with expletives.

Suddenly, Gary stepped forwards, brushing past Eric with his fists clenched in the air, shouting in his Welsh accent, "OH YEAH, THINK YA HARD DO YA? C'MON THEN IF YA THINK YA HARD ENOUGH YOU PLANKERS!"

Everyone was surprised and taken aback – not least because Gary got his insults mixed up, which his friends would usually have found hilarious if it wasn't for the dire circumstances in which they now found themselves.

"Is he out of his mind?" said Eric.

"Shut up, Gary, or you'll get us all killed!" said Jack. But Gary just carried on calling the mobsters rude names and waving his fists.

"What's a 'planker', Boss?" asked Slim, looking befuddled.

"I dunno? JUST SHUT THE FAT AUSSIE GUY UP AND BRING ME DAT MAGICIAN!" shouted Tony One Shoe to his band of grumpy men, seething with anger.

The three heavies then charged up the slope towards Gary with their arms outstretched towards him.

Gary immediately ran off down the side of the verge telling his wife to take the kids inside the chapel.

"Oh, *'eck!*" thought Eric again.

"What shall we do?" again asked Jack as he clenched his fists in readiness for a fight.

"RUN!" answered Eric straight away this time.

So, Jack and Eric ran, following Gary down

the side of the grass verge to escape from mobsters.

"GET 'EM!" screamed the fuming Underboss. "DON'T LET 'EM GET AWAY!"

So, the three heavies changed their direction and likewise ran down the grass verge and chased after Eric, Jack, and Gary. One of them accidentally slipped backwards on the recently watered, slippery wet grass, landing with a thud. The other two helped him up, which bought the three Brits some time.

"Well, don't just *sit* there! What are ya waiting for? Help me into da car, ya moron!" then rapidly said Tony One Shoe to his driver, full of colourful language again. "Hurry up, before they escape!"

Meanwhile, Eric and his two pals were running as fast as they could back along the same street Eric ran up earlier leading to the Strip, trying hard not to bump into pedestrians coming the other way. Eric and Jack had already caught up with Gary.

"Run faster Gary!" said Jack as he whizzed past him.

"I can't!" shallowly hollowed Gary, who was struggling to get breath – especially in the heat.

"Keep running Gary!" then yelled Eric as he too zoomed past him.

Suddenly, they heard a woman's fearful scream coming from behind them, followed by "He's got a gun!"

"Pop! Pop!" made the sound of the gun as one of the heavies decided to take a couple of pot shots at their evaders. Thankfully both bullets missed; one, ricocheting from off the sidewalk, and the other from off a large signboard a man was carrying which read: "Jesus Saves!"

Eric and Jack quickly looked over their shoulders and saw that two of the heavies were still chasing them, and one of them had a smoking pistol in his hand. The other much larger heavy was now walking way back in the distance.

The busy Strip wasn't that far ahead, and as the chase continued, Eric could see the white mass of Elvis impersonators now coming back the other way across the junction.

"Help! Help!" yelled Eric as he waved his arms frantically about, trying desperately to get their attention as another gunshot rang out.

Upon hearing the gunshot and screams, the army of Elvis impersonators, as if choreographed, sharply turned their heads as one towards the commotion.

"Look!" loudly shouted one of them amid others singing. "One of ours is in trouble!"

Well, no sooner had he said that the masses of Elvis impersonators came pouring down the street running to the aid of their fellow Elvis fan. And at seeing two hundred or more highly spirited Kung Fu fighters coming towards them, punching, and kicking the air, the mobsters immediately stopped chasing Eric, and his pals, and sharply turned around and started running away in the opposite direction.

Jack turned his head round again, and as well as seeing the mobsters running the other way, he also saw to his horror that their mate, Gary, was lying sprawled out motionless with his eyes shut on the sidewalk. "Gary's been shot!" he yelled out to Eric.

Both immediately rushed to his aid fearing the worst. "No! No! This can't be!" screamed Eric as they both approached his lifeless body and knelt down beside him terribly upset. *"Gary! Don't die!"* pleaded Jack tearfully as he began searching unsuccessfully for his pulse. Fearing the worst, each of them then told him that they loved him. Gary's eyes suddenly opened wide, and he sat bolt upright. "AHH!" screamed Eric and Jack in shocked surprise.

"What's that about *love?*" said Gary looking at them both strangely.

"*Nothing!*" Eric and Gary quickly said in unison.

"I got, stitch, and I had to lie down and have a rest," said Gary unmoved by the outpouring of love from his two close friends.

"Oh, *Gary!* We thought you were *dead!*" said Eric, relieved as Jack was that their friend was not dead after all.

"Yeah, mate! Ya scared the living *crap* out of us, ya *wally!*" said Jack shaking his head. All three then burst out laughing.

"Where're the bully boys?" quickly asked Gary.

"Don't worry, they've gone!" said Eric. "*Come on,* let's get you up."

Farther up the street, the black limousine made a sharp U-turn, leaving rubber tyre marks across it, before screeching to an abrupt halt alongside the two fleeing heavies.

The next thing everybody knew was the sound of a police cars siren as it came hurtling around the junction at breakneck speed with its lights flashing – it was Bob and Eddie to the rescue! It sped along the street, passed Eric and his pals – who had by now been swallowed up in the relative safety of the swarm of Elvis impersonators – as the gung-ho rookie cops chased after the criminals. But before getting into the limousine, the two mobsters started shooting at the approaching police car. "Rat-a-tat-tat!" was the sound the bullets made as they hit the cars metal bumper. The driver of the police car responded immediately by doing a handbrake turn, bringing the car screeching to an abrupt stop halfway across the street, where both police officers promptly got out and shielded themselves behind it and returned fire.

Meanwhile, inside the reception area of the OK Chapel, the children asked, "Mummy, what's that noise?"

"Oh, it's just fireworks to celebrate our wedding!" explained their worried and anxious mum to reassure them.

"GET IN!" ordered Tony One Shoe amid the rain of oncoming bullets. The heavies quickly jumped in, and the limousine sped off as they attempted to make their escape.

Once it was safe, Eric quickly made his way back to the shopping mall where he'd left his rent-a-car car parked, and Gary and Jack quickly went and reunited with Bethany and the children.

Eric had arranged to meet up with his friends at the wedding reception later that day. He decided it wasn't safe to go back to his apartment, so went straight over to the Excalibur instead where they had stepped up their security.

"I didn't know you were an Elvis fan!" said Tom as Eric was signing in at the security desk.

"Me neither!" answered Eric, cracking a smile. It had been a stressful and exhausting day to say the least.

It wasn't until Eric got into his dressing room and got out of his Elvis costume that he realised to his dismay the engagement ring was missing. He frantically searched everywhere for it, but it soon dawned on him that he must have foolishly left the ring box in his rear trouser pocket when he exchanged clothes with the stranger. Naturally, Eric was beside himself with anguish, knowing that he couldn't afford to buy another one like it before Emily arrives in one week.

On the bright side, though, Eric and his friends were unharmed, which was something to be thankful for. It could have been a quite different outcome. Eric then smiled and chuckled at the thought of marrying his friends Gary and Bethany dressed as Elvis. "What a bizarre day!" he thought, shaking his head in disbelief. It was most certainly a wedding he and his friends would never forget!

But Eric's mood soon changed back to being sombre again. He thought it was one thing to put his own life in danger, but it was another thing to put the lives of his friends in danger. He was lucky that time, but maybe he wouldn't be so lucky another time. He couldn't keep playing cat and mouse with the Mafia and felt that he now had no other choice but to quit the show and get the hell outta Dodge. Enough was enough he thought and decided he would go straight to the top and tell Mr Constantino himself right there and then that he was quitting, and the reason why.

He fished out Mr Constantino's business card and began dialling his number, determined to get through to him this time, no matter what.

"… Hi, you've reached Mr Constantino Enterprises, how may I help ya?" asked Mr Constantino. "… Hi! *Who's* calling?"

"… Oh, *hi,* Mr Constantino! Sorry, I thought

you were an answering machine at first!" said Eric, surprised that he managed to get through to him the first time. "It's *Eric* – The Amazing Fartzini."

"Gee, thanks! Do I always sound like a robot?" said Mr Constantino chuckling.

"*Oops!*" thought Eric.

"Hi, Eric! How are the rehearsals going? Good, I hope!"

"Yeah, good!" replied Eric, feeling nervous and hesitating slightly.

"Well, what is it? I'm a busy man!"

After an awkward start, Eric told his boss that he wanted to quit the show and went on to explain his reason why. Telling him, he had become caught up with the Mafia, and how it had escalated to the point where his life was now in grave danger – explaining that they tried to shoot him earlier that day.

"… Why didn't ya tell me this before?" asked Mr Constantino after listening to Eric speak. "Then I could have helped ya sooner!" There was a moment of silence. "You'll do no such thing as quit. *Look!* Leave it to me – I will speak to a few people I know and get it sorted by the end of the day! *Capeesh?* And you will never have to worry about that no-good son of a gun

Tony One Shoe again, I promise ya, okay?”

“Okay!” said Eric nodding, even though there was no one else there.

“Now take it easy, relax, and just *keep* focusing on performing a *great* show!”

“Thank you, Mr Constantino!” said Eric just in time before the phone line went dead on him.

And sure enough, when Eric was at the bar later that evening buying a round of drinks for his friends at the wedding Reception, his mobile phone rang. Eric immediately recognised the voice.

“Problem solved! Ya don’t have to worry about Tony One Shoe anymore. By the way – he’s now got a new nickname,” very briefly said Mr Constantino, sounding like a robot.

“Oh, what is it?” asked Eric, curious.

“Tony No More!” The call then ended abruptly before Eric even had a chance to say another word. Reading between the lines, Eric knew what that meant – probably. Was Eric speaking to the “Godfather” himself?”

Eric then went and rejoined his friends. And that’s pretty much all there is to tell that’s worth mentioning so far.

CHAPTER TWENTY-TWO

BACKSTAGE MAYHEM!

After nursing a sore head for most of the day from too much celebrating with his friends the night before, Eric wearily opened his dressing room door to greet them. They had all been to watch his matinee show and came backstage to congratulate him on such a terrific and memorable performance.

During the matinee shows Eric always included a magic trick routine especially for the children, and Gary and Bethany's children loved it!

"You were *amazing!*" screamed the children as they burst into his dressing room and surrounded Eric.

"That's why he's called 'The *Amazing* Fartzini!'" said their mum.

"Show us *more* magic tricks! Show us *more* magic tricks!" the excited children kept requesting.

"Kids! Leave poor Uncle Eric alone. I expect he's worn-out after performing his magic show!" said their mum.

"Cause of the partying the night before more like!" thought Eric. "I can't believe I did a Mooney in front of the bar manager before we were all kicked out!"

Gary and Jack stood opposite each other, leaning up against the doorframe, sunglasses still on, looking much worse for wear.

"That's okay, I don't mind!" said Uncle Eric, smiling. "Come and sit down on the floor, kids, and I'll show ya a magic trick!"

"YEAH!" screamed the kids even louder this time.

"Kids! Kids! There's no need to scream!" said their dad, placing his hand on top his aching head and grimacing in pain.

Just then all the scantily dressed dancers came hurrying past Eric's open dressing room door on their way to their dressing room, which immediately got Gary and Jack's attention. The British dancer, Sasha, turned her head towards Jack, wide-eyed, and gave him a lingering smile, which he immediately reciprocated, thinking, "Cor, she's nice!"

"Eyes front, Gary!" commanded his commander-in-chief – his wife, which he instantly obeyed.

With all the children's eyes fixed firmly on the magician. He made a little sponge rabbit suddenly appear from out of nowhere, then multiplied it into two, then to everyone's further amazement, caused one of the sponge rabbits to disappear from his hand and reappear inside the tightly closed hand of the eldest child, Dylan. All the children were goggle-eyed with their mouths agape in wonderment. He then asked Dylan to hold one of the rabbits in his closed hand again and placed the other one in his pocket. But when the boy opened his hand, the other rabbit had reappeared to join it. And to everyone's sheer amusement and delight, he repeated it – it didn't seem to matter how many times he put the rabbit inside his pocket; it always reappeared next to the other one! And for the finale, instead of just one rabbit magically appearing inside the boy's hand: lots of tiny baby rabbits appeared as well, much to the amazement and delight of the children!

All the children then gave Uncle Eric a big hug.

"Gary's good at doing that trick as well!" commented Jack grinning and causing Gary and Eric to chuckle.

"Hey, I heard that, *Jack!*" said Bethany amid the noise of the excited children. "Behave yourself." Both smiled at each other. She was used to his sense of humour by now.

"Wasn't that *amazing,* kids!" said their mum. *"Yeah!"* was the answer they immediately called back.

"Can we go and eat now?" asked Gary. "I really fancy a big juicy hamburger!"

"Oh, *Gary!* You're always thinking of your stomach!" said his wife shaking her head in disapproval. Jack and Eric just grinned at one another.

"… Well, okay then," said Bethany, "I suppose so, or we'll never hear the end of it!" Gary smiled widely, suddenly feeling a lot better.

"Oh! But I wanna see some *more* magic!" said one of the children followed by the rest of them demanding the same.

"Uncle Eric's got another show to get ready for!" then said their mum.

"Who wants an ice cream?" suddenly called out Gary.

"MEEE!" loudly shrieked the children all at once.

"*Right, c'mon* then, kids! Say goodbye to Uncle Eric!" said their mum as she rounded up her troupe of little soldiers.

"Bye Uncle Eric!" called out all the children at once again.

"Bye Uncle Eric!" called out Jack jokingly. Eric laughed.

"Bye, kids!" said Eric waving to them as they marched out with Jack at the front.

"Quick march! Quick march!" playfully commanded Jack, acting like their Sergeant Major.

Tracy, who was the last in line, and the most talkative out of the children, then stopped at the doorway and said excitedly, "My Mummy and Daddy are taking us to Disneyland tomorrow to see 'Mickey Mouse!'"

"Well, won't that be fun!" said Eric with a big smile. "You, *lucky* things!"

"Well, Gary's not my *real* Daddy." Suddenly blurted out Tracy. "My *real* Daddy is staying in a hotel owned by Her Majesty the Queen, but he's not allowed out because he's been *naughty!*"

"Oh, really!" said Eric glancing up to the little girl's parents, whose smiles briefly disappeared for a moment.

"Come along, Chatterbox," said her mum, smiling.

"Well, see ya later, Eric!" then said his friends.

"Yeah, see ya later!" he replied.

So, while his friends and the children went off to stuff their faces with hamburgers and ice cream, Eric started preparing for the next show.

Eric was still only using the one assistant, which was proving to work out fine after all. The rehearsals were going well. The TV interviews and other means of promoting the new show, also. And with the murderous threat from the Mafia now hopefully gone; and his previous assistant, Gloria, no longer around to sabotage his magic act and steal his idea's – amongst other things. The only other potential danger was from the mystery killer, who had also killed his only hope of identifying who they were – though, as far as he was aware, no attempt of his life had been made thus far. Oh, and of course, not forgetting the daily risk he took by being shot at with an old-fashioned musket. But at least with that, he knew the danger he was facing!

What was pleasing for Eric was that the audience turn out for his shows had increased, and for some of the performances the theatre was full! No doubt a result of all the extra publicity promoting the new show.

There was still a lot of gossip amongst the cast and crew over Gloria getting fired. Eric could hear it in the corridor. He could also hear Ruben and a few of the troublesome dancers making derogatory remarks about him and his loud "British friends". Nothing's changed there, he thought – talk about the pot calling the kettle black!

He thought it was a shame that his friends weren't staying in Vegas longer; he could do with some genuine friends around him right now. But his friends did say that once they have spent some time at the Disneyland resort followed by some sightseeing, they would come back and see him before they flew back to the UK in a couple of weeks. Las Vegas wasn't a place for kids really; Eric got that – a place for grown-up kids, yeah!

"They'll be back in time for the opening night of my new show when Emily will be here also – it'll be like old times!" Eric thought excitedly.

As Eric was preparing for the early evening show, he reminisced about the last time all four friends were together. It was sometime in the summer several years ago when they were all still in their late teens. Emily had suggested that they all go to a music festival, which the others thought would be a fun thing to do. So, Gary borrowed a large four birth tent from his parents, plus everything else one needs when camping, and off they went on their little adventure together. Jack had recently passed his driving test, and once they had all squeezed inside his rusty old Fiat Uno, along with all the camping gear, he drove them to a large field somewhere in East Sussex.

Of course, no music festival would be the same without a muddy field; and no thanks to the continuous downpour of rain, when the group of revellers arrived, it was a muddy bog.

"I'm glad we packed our wellies!" said Emily looking out of her rear side window at lots of other festival-goers struggling to pitch up their tents in the mud and the rain.

And, after a long and frustrating while of sloshing around in the mud and getting soaked while trying to figure out how to erect their tent, they eventually managed it; and after getting some nosh, all four headed off to the main stage area to watch one of the bands. It was already crowded when they got there, but after a bit of jostling, they managed to squeeze their way near to the front.

The band thrashed out a drum and bass number. Everyone was dancing energetically to the pulsating rhythm – jumping up and down, nodding heads, and swinging arms about wildly in the air.

"Hey! Look at that old dude over there giving it large!" yelled Jack, barely being heard above the din.

"Wait a second – isn't that ol' Mr Potter!" then suddenly called out Emily, getting a look at the old man's face as he twisted around. "OMG! It is 'im!"

"No! It *can't* be?" then Eric called out, surprised as the rest of them.

"*Let me see!*" yelled Gary. He put his head between Eric and Emily's head. "It *is* 'im ya know!"

It *was* Mr Potter, their ancient and now

retired history teacher. He was dancing like there was no tomorrow and having great fun with his much younger Filipino wife.

"MR POTTER!" yelled out Jack excitedly, which was immediately repeated by the others all at the same time.

Mr Potter turned his head around. "... OH, HELLO CHILDREN!" he yelled back, smiling widely at them.

"*Blimey,* he's smiling!" said Jack, surprised.

"*CARPE DIEM! CARPE DIEM!*" Mr Potter continued to yell. He then turned back around and carried on dancing and having the time of his life.

"*Wow!* Look at him go!" said Eric impressed, as were the others.

"He's having a *blast!*" said Jack. "I hope I'm as fit as him when I'm his age!"

"*Good* for him!" said Emily.

"*Hey!* Where's Gary?" suddenly asked Eric, spotting Gary was no longer there with them.

"Where d'ya think!" said Jack. They all turned around and there he was heading for the burger bar.

It was there that Gary met Bethany. She had recently split up with her boyfriend with whom she had two children.

"Oh, what fun that was!" thought Eric smiling to himself.

Suddenly there was a loud knock on his dressing room door, which startled him, immediately transcending him away from having a good time with his friends on a muddy field somewhere in East Sussex, back to the present day alone in his dressing room. "Five minutes till showtime Mr Fartzini!" called out the assistant stage manager.

CHAPTER
TWENTY-THREE

GRAVE NEWS FOR ERIC!

The next day, Eric waved goodbye to his friends as they headed off for their Disney Land adventure, in California, wishing that he were going with them. But he had rehearsals to go to that morning and was keen to better his performance of the Bullet Catch in readiness for the opening night, which was now only less than two weeks away.

It was during the rehearsals that morning that he realised just how dangerous performing the Bullet Catch could be. Whilst standing opposite the marksman holding the china dinner plate too close in front of his face, the plate exploded prematurely before he had the chance to position it correctly, sending fragments of sharp china into his cheeks – one just missing his right eye!

Eric didn't feel the impact immediately, but soon after he stumbled backwards, he could feel the pain; and blood was pouring down his face, causing one of the dancers dressing the stage to scream.

The squib, used to detonate the plate electronically, had been packed with too much explosive it would seem, and the trigger-happy stage manager had pressed the firing button too early when Eric was not ready. Dirk, the stage manager, quickly came running on stage with a first aid kit, apologising, and insisting it was an accident while he patched Eric up with some plasters. But was it an accident, or an attempt to stop Eric performing there? – Eric had his doubts.

Ever since Gloria was fired – which Dirk was very upset about and blamed Eric for – he had become even more unfriendly towards him.

Eric had been lucky this time to escape with only a minor injury, but it could have been a lot worse; and despite being injured, he carried on rehearsing like a true showman.

Being injured was the reason why Eric

insisted on continuing to rehearse – so that he could iron out any potential hazards; and, so as not to lose his nerve performing the stunt.

A couple of days went by, and during the morning while Eric was at home in his apartment, his doorbell rang. He promptly checked his CCTV security camera to see who was there – which he'd had set up ever since the Mafia unexpectedly visited him.

It was the LVMPD lead detective, Mark Hitchcock, and his colleague, looking very solemn.

Now minus the plasters, but still with a few nasty-looking cut marks on his cheeks, Eric answered the door, wondering what it could be about this time.

"Morning, Mr Fartz," said the detective in charge.

Eric noted he had omitted the word "good". "Morning," he repeated with a slightly worried look.

"May we come in?" then asked the detective.

"Erm, yes, of course," answered Eric as he opened the door wider for them to enter. "Is something the matter?"

The detectives walked straight in without answering the question, but it was clear that something was the matter. And by the look on their faces, something very serious.

"Go through into the lounge," said Eric pointing them in the right direction.

"Thank you," both said.

Eric closed the front door and followed them in. "Please, take a seat."

"Thank you," said the lead detective, "we won't keep ya long."

"Is it about my previous assistant, Gloria?" asked Eric still slightly nervous.

"No," replied Mark. There was a pause. "I'm afraid we have some grave news. We are here to inform you that the magician, Chet Stevenson, who as you most probably know, performs – or I should say, performed at the new casino resort, has been brutally murdered!"

"Murdered!" repeated Eric, shocked.

"Yes, I'm afraid so!"

"Oh, that's terrible!" exclaimed the fellow magician. Then in quick succession, "When? Where? By Whom?"

Mark removed his notebook, which he still favoured using rather than an electronic device. "... It would appear the murder took place between the hours of three and four this morning. Evidence suggests the killer entered the victim's apartment and gruesomely murdered him while he was still in his bed asleep. I will spare you the gory details, but in all the years I have been dealing with murder cases, this is the *worst* I have ever come across! Very grim, Mr Fartz, very grim!" Eric just listened, still in shock. "… Whoever did this had planned it very well, as the perpetrator left the scene leaving few clues. There didn't appear to be any signs of a break in, which suggests the victim may have known his killer – either that or they possible work at the resort and had access to a key … or, had locksmith skills … like an escape artist –"

"Now *wait* a minute! You're not suggesting that I –"

"No, Mr Fartz, but at this stage, we can't rule anyone out. Especially as you were rivals and had a motive!"

"Yes, but –"

"Where were you between the hours of three and four am this morning, Mr Fartz?" then asked the detective with his pencil poised ready to take down notes.

"I was here in bed asleep," answered Eric, not liking the way the questioning was heading.

"Do you have an alibi – proof of –"

"I know what an alibi is!" quickly said Eric interrupting. He then thought for a moment. "I was alone, b-but there are security camera's *all* around this gated community which will *prove* that I remained here."

"Thank you." There was a pause while the detective wrote something down on his notepad.

"How did you get those scratches on your face, Mr Fartz?" asked the other detective, speaking for the first time.

"Oh, I had an accident while I was rehearsing on stage yesterday!" he quickly answered. The detectives just looked at one another suspiciously.

"And one more question, for now, Mr Fartz." There was a pause. "Would you happen to know the whereabouts of your former assistant, Miss Gloria Henderson? We have not been able to trace her, and it seems that she has left the state?"

"I don't know where she might have gone?" answered Eric. "I remember her telling me that her hometown was Detroit."

"Okay, thank you, Mr Fartz. I understand that she used to have a relationship with the victim. How would you describe her?" Eric hesitated, while he gave it some thought. "I mean, would you describe her as being hot tempered or having violent tendencies? Unfortunately, the best person to have asked that question is now dead, so we are asking people who worked with her and knew her well so as we can form a picture, you understand."

"Yeah," said Eric nodding and shaking slightly. "Well, to begin with, we got on very well, and I liked her. Not in a romantic way – just as friends. I mean, sure, she could be fiery sometimes, but I always thought that she was kind to me – until that is, I found out that she had been sabotaging my magic act and stealing from me …"

"Okay, okay. Well, the main reason we have come here today, Mr Fartz, is to warn you that your life may also be in danger!" said Mark, still with the same grave look as when he first entered the apartment. "One thing we know for sure is that whoever committed this monstrous crime is not a fan of magicians!" There was a pause while Eric stared anxiously at the detective, waiting for the reason. "… His body was set ablaze, and if it hadn't been for the sprinklers putting out the flames, we could have been dealing with a lot more fatalities at the resort. And when forensics removed the charred Duct tape from the victim's mouth, wedged inside was discovered a crumpled-up page torn out from the –" The detective quickly looked down at his notes on the previous page. "… 'King James version of the Bible. More chillingly was a highlighted verse from 'Exodus 22:18', which read: 'Thou shalt not suffer a witch to live'!"

Eric's mouth dropped open with nothing coming out of it.

"It appears that the killer is some religious nut wishing to purge magicians from the face of the earth!"

"*A witch-hunt!*" exclaimed Eric.

"It sure looks that way!" the detective replied soberly, nodding his head. "For anyone to commit this sort of crime – they must have been compelled by madness or hatred! So, be warned Mr Fartz – as you may be next!"

Eric remained silent for a moment while his brain computed what he just said. "… Well, that information should at least help to narrow down your search – shouldn't it?" then innocently asked Eric.

The lead detective broke his plastered serious

look to chuckle cynically. "This is *America* – are you *kiddin'* me!" was the detective's response. Then, in a more serious tone again, said, "But rest assured Mr Fartz that we will do everything in our power to prevent this from happening again. We will be advising the Excalibur resort to step up their security and employ more security guards for your protection, plus ensure that officers are patrolling this area and your place of work twenty-four-seven!"

"Thank you," said Eric, looking slightly less worried, and pleased to hear that.

"Well, we best be getting off," said the lead detective as he started to get up, followed by his partner. "Oh, and if you do hear of the whereabouts of Miss Henderson, then please get in touch immediately!"

"Will do," Eric replied.

Eric thanked the detectives for warning him, and as they were leaving, the lead detective reminded him not to leave the country until they had concluded their investigations. Everyone then said goodbye, and as soon as the detectives were gone, Eric sharply put the bolt across the front door.

As Eric returned to the lounge he started to wonder if the two murders were connected. He just couldn't think who would do such a ghastly thing. He immediately switched on the TV, and sure enough, it was all on the news. He thought, "I must contact Emily right away and tell her not to come out here!"

Then, just as he was about to pick up his phone, it started to ring – it was Emily.

"Hi, sweetheart! It's *me!*" she said excitedly. "I managed to get an earlier flight, and I have just arrived at the airport!"

"What, Heathrow?" said Eric, panicking and forgetting to say hello.

"No. I'm already *here* in Las Vegas!" There was a silence. *"Eric."*

"Yeah, *sorry,* I'm still here – you're at the airport in *Las Vegas?*" repeated Eric, hoping he'd heard it wrong.

"Er, *yeah!*" said Emily. "How many times have I got to say it!"

"Right, I'll come and pick you up – wait there!"

"Well, where else am I gonna go?"

"I should be about half hour, depending on traffic. See ya soon!"

"Okay, *bye! Love* you!" she said excitedly again.

"Love you too!"

Eric quickly ended the call, thinking, "Oh, 'eck! Now what am I gonna do?" rushed out of his apartment, got into his car, then got back out and ran over and grabbed a bunch of pretty flowers from one of the flowerbeds, then got back into the car, and headed straight for the airport.

CHAPTER TWENTY-FOUR

EMILY ARRIVES

Eric arrived at the Mc Carran international airport, Las Vegas, in a fluster. He parked the car, then quickly got out and shut the door and locked it. Then quickly unlocked it again, opened the door and reached inside and grabbed the bunch of flowers he'd forgotten, then once again shut the door, locked it, and dashed off to meet his girlfriend at the arrival's terminal.

There she was standing across the concourse from him, looking beautiful in her pretty yellow summer dress, smiling widely in full makeup. *"Eric!"* she called out joyfully as she whisked back her long, velvety black hair. His eyes met hers, and they immediately ran towards each other and hugged in a warm embrace (just like in the movies). They then started kissing passionately (well, they hadn't seen each other in a long time. But don't worry, I'll save you all the soppy details).

"Mind!" said Eric. "You'll squash the flowers!" which she ignored as they continued to eat each other's faces off (sorry, that might have been soppy).

And after a while of sloppy, soppiness, Eric exchanged the flowers for her two large suitcases and led the way to the car park.

"Oh, the flowers are *beautiful!*" said Emily. "Carnations! My *favourite!* Thank you!"

Eric thought, "That's lucky!" and just smiled.

She then put her nose closer to them to have a stiff. "And they *smell* divine!"

"You look *amazing!*" then said Eric, beaming.

"Thanks!" she replied, delighted. Both were very pleased to see each other – it felt so good to hold one another again. Oh, how he wished he hadn't lost the engagement ring – he would have proposed to her right there and then!

Once, the suitcases were loaded into the boot of his car, Eric and Emily headed back to his apartment, where she planned to stay with him for the next couple of weeks.

On the way there the two of them caught up with one another and didn't stop talking the whole time – there was so much to talk about.

"… Hey, you'll never guess who I met out here?" said Eric, excited.

"Jack, Gary and Bethany and their kids!" answered Emily.

"*Yeah!* How did ya know?"

"Bethany contacted me to see if I wanted to come with them, but I couldn't because of work. She told me to keep it a secret because they wanted to surprise you."

"They certainly did that alright! Mind you, I think they got a bigger surprise," said Eric, suddenly chuckling.

"Oh, *why?*" asked Emily, now curious.

Eric then went on to explain that he had married Gary and Bethany dressed as Elvis Presley, which caused them both to laugh out loud.

"Lucky things getting married!" said Emily, laying a hint. Eric just carried on driving.

He omitted the part after the wedding where he and his friends were chased and shot at by mobsters. And had decided it was probably best, after all, not to mention anything about the serial killer on the loose who may be trying to kill him next – he didn't want to worry her and spoil her holiday (or vacation as they say in the US).

He did tell her that he would be attempting to catch a bullet between his teeth in his new show, though, which immediately worried her, of course. So, it was just as well that he didn't tell her about his accident the day before while rehearsing it. Though, he then had to tell a white lie to explain why he had cuts on his face, which he put down to shaving in a hurry as the cause.

The following week, Eric had arranged with the management to take some time off from his busy schedule – while the theatre was dark/closed to reset the stage for the new show – so that the two of them could do some sightseeing together.

In the meantime, Emily settled into the apartment in Flamingo Heights with Eric, watched his shows, and met most of the cast and crew – except Dirk, Ruben, and a few of his cohort dancers, who remained cold and distant towards them. Eric had already pre-warned Emily about them, so their rudeness wasn't a surprise.

After the late show on Saturday night, Emily appeared at Eric's dressing room doorway, looking a little annoyed and upset.

"What's the matter Em?" asked Eric, seeing that she was not her usual spirited self.

"What's this I hear about you and your previous assistant … *Gloria,* having a fling?" she suddenly asked as she remained at the doorway with her arms folded. She had just been told this by Candy and Rhonda farther along the corridor.

"*What?* That's a *lie!*" protested Eric. "Who told you this?"

"I don't know their names … a couple of the dancers just now in the corridor."

"I bet I know who they are! *Right!* That's it! I'm gonna have a word with them right now!" said Eric furious. He started to head for the door, but Emily moved towards him and stopped him, saying, "I *believe* ya, darling! I *believe* ya! Don't go and have a big row, because that's what they want – they're just trying to cause trouble."

"I know, I know – you're right! It's best to just ignore them," agreed Eric after he calmed down a bit.

And that's just what they did. Both came out

of the dressing room hand in hand, happily chatting to each other, and walked straight passed Candy and Rhonda showing that they weren't bothered in the slightest. Which soon shut the bitter and jealous dancers up! And as Eric and Emily left for a lovely night out, they burst out laughing.

When the pair made their way around to the Strip, Eric noticed that the giant billboard, once advertising the rival magic show, no longer displayed the picture of the magician, Chet Stevenson – but instead a new show featuring a well-known singer. This perturbed Eric and brought the threat of danger crashing back to him. He then noticed the silhouetted shape of a crow appear ominously on top of the billboard. Though it wasn't a crow: it was a parrot. But it was hard to tell from where he was standing.

"Shall we go back to my apartment instead?" asked Eric. "It's very noisy here."

"… Okay, if you want to," said Emily, sounding a little surprised.

On the way back to the car park, she asked him if something was the matter. It seemed strange to her that one moment he was looking forward to going out, and the next he had a complete change of mind. He reassured her that nothing was the matter and told her that he was looking forward to getting away from the area next week and do some sightseeing together.

It was now dark outside and getting late, so he hurried Emily along, keeping a lookout for anyone acting suspiciously. They then got into the car, whereby he immediately locked the doors and drove off back to his apartment.

As the car was approaching the gates to the apartments, Emily noticed a police car parked on the other side of the street with its lights still on.

"I wonder what that police car is doing there?" she said, pointing to it.

Eric shook his head, saying, "I have no idea," knowing full well why it was there.

Eric thought it was good that the detective had been true to his word by having a police presence in the area and felt somewhat reassured by it. What Eric wasn't too sure about, though, was whether the police were there to protect him, or keep an eye on him because they suspected that he was the murderer? Which, when questioning him was something the detective implied. After all, there was a connection some way or another between Eric and the two murder victims.

Back in the relative safety of his apartment, Eric switched on the TV. He'd just remembered that NBC's "The Tonight Show" was on.

"Hey, look, Em!" said Eric, excited. "This is the late-night chat show I was telling you about that I'm a guest on!"

It was about half-way through when they sat down and snuggled-up together on the sofa to watch it. The jovial host was interviewing Eric:

"So, how on earth did ya come up with the unusual name "The Amazing *Fartzini?*" asked the host with a big cheesy grin. "I mean, "Fartzini" is not ya real name, right?" The studio audience laughed.

Eric chuckled. "Well, actually it is my real name," he answered. The audience laughed even more, including the host, who all thought he was joking. When the laughter subsided, Eric then clarified what he meant by saying, "Well, part of it is …"

"Go on!" said the bubbly host, curious.

"Well, I took my mum's European surname, 'Fartz' – spelt with a 'Z' I hasten to add!" Which caused more chuckles, followed by the expression, *'Oh!'* echoing around the studio. "And like my hero, 'Houdini', I added I, N, I to the end of it to make 'Fartzini'."

"Well, I'm glad you cleared that up!" said the host laughing again.

"… So, when did you first become interested in magic?" then asked the host more seriously.

"Well, I was quite a shy kid, and was bullied a lot. Then one day my mum took me to a local Christmas fair where I met a wise old magician demonstrating *amazing* magic tricks *right* before my eyes, and I was hooked!" answered Eric sincerely. The audience fell silent as they listened intently. "And I found that performing magic tricks helped to build my confidence and put a stop to the bullying."

The audience spontaneously applauded Eric's heartfelt and fascinating story, which, no doubt, resonated with many of them.

Then, as Eric and Emily continued to watch the show with their eyes glued to the screen, one of the TV cameras panned around the audience to capture their reaction. And, although it was only very quickly, Eric thought he caught a glimpse of the same man he recognised at the murder scene in downtown Vegas, whose features closely resembled the horrible bully from his childhood days!

"What is it, Eric?" quickly asked Emily, seeing his head suddenly shoot forwards to try and get a closer look. "You're *trembling* Eric – why are you trembling?"

Eric slowly relaxed back into his previous position. "I can't swear it, but I thought I just saw …" Eric paused, struggling to say his name. He'd hoped that he would never have to mention his name ever again. "David Smythe!"

"David Smythe is *dead!*" stated Emily as she stared into her boyfriend's deep blue eyes – the gateway into his troubled mind. "You know that yourself – it was all over the news at the time that there were no survivors of the car crash."

"But this is the *second* time I thought I saw him – what if he survived the crash and somehow managed to escape?" he said with dredged up fear and panic in his voice.

"He's *dead,* darling! He's dead! Now try and put him out of your mind. He can't hurt you anymore!" she told him to try and ease his inner turmoil and pain. But seeing him in this state made her realise that the fear doesn't just go away when the bullying stops but continues in your mind – even after many years. Indeed, sometimes the mental scars can take longer to heal than the physical one's! And it is often something that triggers this emotion as had just happened.

She stroked his long golden main of hair like he was a wounded lion. To her, he was a courageous lion for standing up to the bully and achieving the remarkable things he had done in his life.

They then both began to relax together again and continued watching the interview:

"So, apart from Houdini, who you have already mentioned, who else has been a big influence in your life?" asked the host.

"I have to say my mum, Ingrid, who had to raise me up on her own after she split up from my dad when I was still a child."

"And what was it about your mum that made her so special in your eyes?" continued to ask the host.

"Apart from the love, I suppose it was all the inner strength that she installed in me to believe in myself, to follow my dreams and never give up!" answered Eric to another warm round of applause.

"Sounds like you had a pretty tough time growing up! But that self-belief your mum helped install in you as a kid paid off, because look at you now staring in your *own* magic show at the Excalibur casino resort in *Las Vegas!*" said the host, biggin' him up as they say. This brought the very likeable young magician more applause, and even whoops this time.

Eric just smiled and mouthed 'thank you' as he accepted the warm appreciation from the studio audience.

"This brings me nicely onto my next question: Are you *seriously* going to attempt to catch a *live* bullet between your teeth?" said the host with a look of bewilderment, jokingly adding, "And if so – are you *mad!*"

Eric laughed, as did most of the

audience, though, some of them gasped in shock. "Yes, that's right!" said Eric with enthusiasm and confidence.

"*Yes,* your mad, or *yes,* you are going to attempt the dangerous stunt?" quickly interjected the host, which caused a lot of laughter.

"Yes, to both!" answered Eric with a big smile, which kept the laughter coming.

"… I'm sure that our studio audience and our millions of viewers at home would *love* to see you perform some magic!" said the host enthusiastically. The audience immediately responded by making a lot of noise to show their approval. "Would you care to demonstrate something for us?"

"Yeah, *sure!*" said Eric equally enthusiastic, albeit a little nervous.

The show's producer had already asked Eric to perform a quick spot of magic during his time slot; and like the true showman he is, went along with it, acting as if being asked for the first time.

And, despite feeling the pressure somewhat – after all this was national television and make or break time – he asked the host to lend him a dollar bill.

The host reached into his pocket and plucked out a twenty. "I will get it back, won't I?" asked the host, causing the audience to laugh.

"Yeah, of course!" said Eric chuckling. He took the bill from him and slowly crumpled it into a ball and laid it onto the palm of his outstretched left hand, simply saying, "Watch!" There was a moment when nothing happened. But suddenly the note began to move by itself. Gasps could be heard around the studio. The host's mouth dropped right open. Then slowly the note began to rise, higher and higher in the air, causing more gasps of astonishment. The audience then fell silent as the bill remained hovering in midair, while the master magician encircled his hands around it to prove that there were no means of support. The silence was only broken when the host said, "I'm *this* close folks, and I *still* can't figure out *how* he does it!"

The bill then descended slowly back down into Eric's waiting left hand.

Whereby, he then opened the bill and handed it back to the mesmerized host.

"*Wow!*" said the host excitedly. "Give it up for The Amazing Fartzini!" The audience clapped, cheered, whistled, whooped, and stamped their feet. The then host shook Eric's hand, saying "Well done! That was *incredible!*"

"Thank you very much. That's very kind of you!" said Eric modestly, buzzing from the wonderful reaction he received.

"And, for those of you who would like to see *The Amazing Fartzini* perform *more* amazing magic tricks, he is appearing at the Excalibur hotel and casino resort, *Las Vegas!*" then announced the exuberant host, looking directly into the camera. The audience made a lot of noise again. "*Right now,* folks, we're gonna cut to a commercial break, but we'll be back *real* soon – so stay *right* where you are and *don't* go *anywhere!*"

Eric picked up the remote and switched the TV off, now feeling much more upbeat.

"You came over *really* well, my darling!" said Emily, impressed and kissing him on his cheek.

"Thanks!" Eric replied, delighted with how it all went. So much so that he completely forgot about his childhood bully – at least for the time being.

The next morning, the police car was still there – it may have a been a different police car, but there was one parked in the same position, opposite the gates, as there was last night.

"Oh, look!" said Emily to Eric, spotting it through the gates as both walked towards his car. "The police car is *still* there!"

"Oh, yeah!" said Eric. He then joked, "Maybe we should call the police."

"Ha, ha," said Emily, giving him a friendly shove. "… But don't you think that it's a little strange?"

"Maybe there has been a spate of burglaries in the area?" suggested Eric.

"Yeah, maybe?" said Emily, still looking puzzled.

Both then got into the car and drove off to do a bit of shopping. As Eric drove out of the gates, he recognised the two cops sat inside the patrol car as being Bill and Eddie. "Heaven help us!" he thought.

"Why are those two policemen waving *weirdly* at you like excited little children, Eric?" asked

Emily, noticing the two cops were smiling their heads off and waving frantically through the window towards him.

"I don't know?" answered Eric. "Maybe they have seen my show and are fans?"

"Oh yeah, they probably want your autograph. I keep forgetting what a big star you are now!" said Emily. "To me, you are still the same boy I met all those years ago doing simple card tricks, whom I fell in love with!"

On the way to the shopping mall a little later, Emily suddenly said, "I'm *sure* that's the same police car following us!" after she turned her head around to look once more. "They seem to want your autograph badly!"

Eric smiled and just said, "Nearly there!"

It had been an incredibly stressful time of late, and once the shows were all over that day, Eric and Emily were very much looking forward to being able to spend a lot more quality time together.

CHAPTER TWENTY-FIVE

ERIC AND EMILY GO SIGHTEEING

The weekdays that followed saw the theatre stage at the Excalibur transformed as new scenery replaced the old, and the lighting was reprogrammed in readiness for the opening night on Saturday. And while this was taking place, Eric and Emily made the most of it and went sightseeing.

They visited many tourist spots, including the famous "Welcome to Las Vegas" sign, where they had a lot of fun posing together while taking selfies. They went all the way up to the top of the very tall "Stratosphere"; and once up there, the magnificent views of Las Vegas and the surrounding mountainous areas take your breath away – though Eric didn't want to stay up there too long as he wasn't a fan of great heights. "I can't believe you'll have blades put through your body, have your head twisted around three hundred and sixty degrees, and catch a live bullet between your teeth, but you don't like heights!" said Emily, joking. Eric laughed, but at the back of his mind he was also thinking, that if the killer had followed them, it was a long drop down to the ground, and flying wasn't in his repertoire of magic tricks!

Eric decided to give the "Mobster Museum" in downtown Las Vegas a miss – he'd had his fill of mobsters for the time being and would stick to just watching gangster movies on the telly in the safety of his apartment.

The two of them also went further afield and visited the spectacular Hoover Dam Bypass, which is about half an hour south-east of Las Vegas – amongst other things they discovered that the bright lights of Las Vegas are powered by it.

Another day, they spent the whole day at Red Rock Canyon in the Mohave Desert. What an awe-inspiring place that was! Here Eric felt like he had finally escaped from the stressful hustle and bustle and noise of the Las Vegas Strip: no vehicles honking their horns; no slot machines ringing out; and no hordes of people screaming and shouting. It was just what Eric needed. And what better person to share this wonderful experience with than his one and only true love, Emily, he thought.

"Smell that fresh air!" said Eric after taking a good sniff.

Emily did just that. "I enjoyed the attractions in Las Vegas, but it's so lovely to be outside in the fresh open air amongst nature. And at *least* we don't have anybody following us out here!" said Emily smiling as she turned around full circle to take in the spectacular views of their magnificent surroundings.

Eric agreed and reminded himself that if he'd have had the engagement ring with him, he would've dropped down to his knees right there and then and proposed to her. But alas that was not to be.

"Look up there, Eric! I'm sure that's a Golden Eagle," called out Emily as she pointed to it. It had a huge wingspan and looked so gracious as it glided high above them. Emily was very fond of birds as well as animals.

"Yeah, I think you're right!" Eric replied happily.

They were standing together in the middle of a valley, flanked by tall red stone cliffs and mountains on either side that would even dwarf the Stratosphere they had visited. And in the distance, they could see the Colorado river snake its way through the desert. They had stopped for a break along a tourist trail they were following.

"It's so beautiful!" exclaimed Emily as they stepped over a little stream. "Oh, I'm *so* pleased we came here!"

"Yeah, me too!" replied Eric putting his arms around her.

"What a lovely day we're having!" said Emily, beaming. The two lovebirds then kissed each other tenderly on the lips, feeling full of happiness. But the day would soon turn out to be not so lovely for the happy couple – quite the opposite!

Once they had both taken a large gulp of water from their bottles, they continued along the narrow trail, blissfully unaware that they were now heading in the wrong direction, and dangerously close to an area where loose rocks could fall on top of them at any time.

The trail was supposed to lead them back to where they started, but after a while, Emily noticed that the same mountain range continued to remain to their left-hand side, and the group of tourists who had been behind them were now nowhere in sight.

"… Are you *sure* that we are still following the same trail, Eric?" asked Emily a little concerned.

Eric, who was in front, suddenly stopped in his tracks.

"What's the matter!" asked Emily after she bumped into him from behind.

"Stay still!" calmly, but assertively said Eric, sounding worried.

Peering over Eric's shoulder, she immediately realised why he had suddenly stopped so abruptly. Her worst living nightmare had come true – blocking their path a little way ahead was a huge rattlesnake, raised partially off the ground, staring directly at them with its long-forked tongue weaving in and out of its mouth and the tip of its tail making a loud rattling sound. Emily immediately froze, clinging onto her boyfriend tightly in fear. For although she adored animals and birds: *snakes,* she could live without – especially huge venomous ones.

"What do we do? What do we do?" she asked

rapidly and repeatedly in sheer panic, just about managing to squeeze the air out of her lungs to be heard.

"Keep calm! Keep calm!" said Eric, once again in that calm, self-assured voice – in other words, he hadn't got a clue either!

He then remembered watching a movie once where a snake was about to bite someone. "Move slowly and quietly backwards, Em," he said, consumed with fear himself (well, who wouldn't be). But, with its sensory receptors set on high alert, the agitated snake was still within striking distance. Suddenly its terrifying combat-ready head rose even higher, and it opened its enormous jaws, displaying its sabre-sharp fangs ready to strike! Emily let out a scream.

At that moment, small red-coloured rocks and stones came tumbling down the cliff face to where they were standing, hitting the snake, and sending it scurrying rapidly away to safety. Eric quickly looked up. "QUICK EM! MOVE OUT OF THE WAY!" yelled Eric as he grabbed hold of her arm and assisted her in doing so. A massive boulder was on its way down towards them, gaining speed, and sending other smaller rocks and stones along with it in its wake. The pair of adventures only just moved out of the way in time before the boulder came crashing down to the ground. If it had landed on them, they would have been killed instantly and ended up like squashed tomatoes.

Eric and Emily both looked up, and once the dust had settled a bit, they could see someone standing on top of the high cliff from roughly where the boulder had fallen.

'*Look!* There's someone up there!" said Emily, still in shock from what had just happened. But because the sun's powerful glare shone directly in their faces, they could only see the back-lit person's silhouette – so they couldn't even tell whether the person was male or female, let alone recognise them.

"C'mon, let's go!" exclaimed Eric with urgency in his voice. "It's not safe here!"

The two of them quickly headed back the same way they came. And, before long picked up the original trail again.

"D'ya think that the person we saw on top of the ridge purposely caused that boulder to fall?" asked Emily as they hurried along.

"I doubt it," answered Eric to help calm her down, while at the back of his mind wondering if it *was* the killer – a snake of a different sort, and one even more cunning and deadly. What if the killer had been stalking him? Then climbed up to the top of the cliff and levered the boulder away from the edge? Eric quickly shut the thought out of his mind, and then explained: "Rocks are frequently falling away from the cliffs in this area. If we stick to the trail, we should be alright!"

After hiking for a short while, they soon started to see other hikers up ahead and felt safer. And after a lot more hiking, tired and exhausted, they decided to stop and have a short rest. The sun had finally taken a bow, and as the sky darkened and the shadows grew longer, the intense dry heat of the day was replaced by a cool light breeze, which was a relief after being in the hot sun all day.

"Doesn't the sun look serene!" said Emily as they both watched the dark orange sun disappearing over the horizon.

"Yeah!" answered Eric, equally in awe as he put his arm around her. "Now *that's* what I call a disappearing act!"

In the distance, they could hear coyotes howling and barking.

"C'mon!" said Eric. "We better get going

before it gets too dark."

From there, it didn't take them very long to reach the entrance, and before they knew it, they were soon driving back to Las Vegas. It was on the way back that Eric opened-up about a killer on the loose who may be targeting magicians.

"Oh, my goodness, Eric!" said Emily, as if she hadn't been shocked enough already that day. "Why in *heavens* didn't you tell me this before?"

"Well, I didn't want to worry you – I was gonna advise ya not to travel out here, but you'd already left the UK before I had the chance," he explained.

"Well, I'm glad I did come out here. I've loved the time we've spent together – well, except when we were nearly *bit* by a snake, and when we nearly got *crushed* to death!"

Eric chuckled. "Me too!"

"Though I do wish you'd come back home to Ramsgate so we can be together again, and where you'll be safe!" expressed Emily, feeling more and more worried and concerned.

"I can't love, as I've told ya already, I've committed myself to another six months contract!"

Emily didn't respond, but her face showed disappointment.

"… So *that's* why the police have been following us – for your protection!" then said Emily, putting two and two together.

"Yes!" he replied nodding. "So, don't worry too much – I am sure we'll be safe!"

"I hope so, Eric. I hope so …"

The tired and weary adventurers finally arrived back at the apartment on Wednesday evening at around 9.30 pm, and there as expected were the two policemen sat in their patrol car – much to their relief. The policemen waved at Eric and Emily as they drove through the big iron gates ready for an early night.

CHAPTER TWENTY-SIX

FRIENDS REUNITED

"**I**'ve *got* to go in to rehearse today, Em – they're expecting me. The opening night is only two days away – and besides, they won't let me have any more time off," said Eric the next morning over breakfast.

"… Okay," just replied Emily, slightly upset. "… It's just that we've spent all this time apart, and now that we're together again, at last, I wanted to spend more time with you."

"I understand Em, and I feel the same way. There's nothing more I'd rather do than to spend more time with you, but I'm sorry love, I've gotta go!" Emily didn't respond; just stared at her uneaten plate of food, sulking.

Eric put his mug down, got up from his breakfast table chair, and went and gave Emily a tender kiss on her forehead. "Come with me if ya like," he said to no response. He then headed for the door. "Okay, suit yourself then. I'll see you later!"

She immediately got up, rushed over to him, and gave him a big hug. "I'll stay here, darling – it's alright, you go," she said. "And for *God's* sake, take care of yourself!"

"I will – don't worry!" he replied. Both then kissed each other passionately on the lips as if it were their first kiss – and hoping it wasn't their last. Then as he was going out the door, said, "Anyway, *cheer up* – our friends will be arriving back here tomorrow!"

As Eric drove away, he couldn't help thinking that it was his job that had driven his friends away from him – and hoped that it wouldn't drive Emily away too!

When Eric got to the venue, the first thing he noticed was that the new scenery was now in place. Most of the cast and crew were there already – the dancers were warming-up on stage, the stage crew were in their positions, and the producer, Benjamin, was sat in the auditorium chatting with his choreographer/boyfriend, Ruben, and the marksmen, Rick. Eric figured that the compère, Jim, was probably still in his dressing room having his usual liquid breakfast at this time. Eric was pleased to say that he had quit heavy drinking – and gambling.

"Look! Here comes the star of the show!" said the producer, which Ruben hated.

"Good morning!" Eric called out to the three of them. "Good morning!" they called back – except Ruben, who turned his head the other way.

"Did ya enjoy the sightseeing?" asked Benjamin.

"Yes, thanks," replied Eric. "The scenery looks good!" The scenery represented a shooting range, and Eric was the target!

"D'ya feel nervous about performing the Bullet Catch stunt on Saturday night?" then asked Rick.

"A little bit!" just replied Eric. He had become used to dodging bullets – in more ways than one!"

"Only a *little* bit!" said the producer. "I know if someone pointed a gun at me, I would be as nervous as hell!"

Eric chuckled. "Well, we've rehearsed the

Bullet Catch stunt many times now, and I feel confident that now the glitches have been dealt with I'm in safe hands!" expressed the new daredevil magician in town, hiding any doubts he had very well. Then with a serious look on his face, quietly addressed the marksman. "We should run through it several times today!"

The following day, Gary, Bethany, Jack, and the children arrived back in the magic kingdom for big kids, Las Vegas, after spending a fabulous time in the magic kingdom for little kids, Disneyland.

Upon their arrival back at the Treasure Island resort hotel that afternoon, Eric and Emily greeted them in the lobby.

"Uncle Eric!" screamed the excited children as they rushed over and hugged him tightly.

Eric laughed. *"Hiya!* Well, it looks like you've all had a good time!" he said to them.

"Yeah! It was *awesome!"* they all screamed out together. Immediately followed by: 'Show us a trick! Show us a trick!'

"Leave him be, you little rascals!" said their mum. "I'm sure Uncle Eric will show you some tricks later … *if* ya behave yourselves!"

Lots of warm greetings and even hotter hugs later.

"… We met Mickey Mouse!" said one of the little children to Eric and Emily, all excited.

"*Did Ya!*" said Emily smiling widely and acting all surprised.

"*Cool!*" said Eric.

"And Minnie Mouse, and Donald Duck, and Goofy, and –" said another excited child, interrupted before she could complete the entire list of Walt Disney characters.

"They had to close one of the rides because daddy got stuck in his seat on the 'Thunder Mountain' ride and couldn't get back out for ages!" said Tracey, one of the older children. All the children then started giggling and laughing.

"Oh dear, oh dear!" expressed Eric and Emily, who couldn't help but laugh along with them.

"Children, why don't you all play something nice and quietly together!" said their mum with a smile.

"Congratulations on getting married! I'm so sorry I couldn't make your wedding!" expressed Emily.

"Oh, don't worry about it, we understand – don't we Gary … *Gary! I said* we understand *don't* we!" said Bethany, having to give him a nudge.

Gary was too busy listening to Eric and Jack's conversation about guns. "Understand what?" he said to her, looking puzzled.

"Oh, nevermind!" Bethany responded, shaking her head.

"… I heard it went with a bang!" said Emily.

"You can say that again!" answered Bethany raising her eyebrows (Eric hadn't told Emily about being shot at by mobsters on the day of the wedding, so perhaps "bang" wasn't the best choice of words). Bethany didn't explain about what happened either – she preferred to leave that to Eric to do.

"Eric told me that he married you both dressed up as *Elvis!*" then said Emily with a big grin.

Bethany laughed. "Yeah! He did a good job to be fair, though his singing leaves a lot to be desired!" Both the ladies laughed out loud.

"What ya laughing at?" suddenly said Eric, whose ears must have pricked.

"Never you mind!" said Bethany jokingly. "We're are talking about ya, not to ya. You just carry on with your conversation, and we'll carry on with ours."

"… I quite envy you getting married," then

said Emily, not worried if Eric did hear this time. "I wish my man would propose to me!"

"Oh, don't worry – I'm sure that will happen one day!" said Bethany, trying to reassure her friend. "And I'd like to be one of your bridesmaids when it does!"

Emily scoffed. "Chance would be a fine thing!"

Soon afterwards, while Bethany went over to the reception to check-in, Eric, Emily, Jack, and Gary, plonked themselves on a couple of plump cushioned sofas nearby and continued chatting. They all thought it was so lovely to be reunited again – it felt just like old times.

And, once Gary and Jack had finished telling Eric and Emily about their adventures in Disney Land, Eric and Emily told them all about their adventures – and misadventures at Red Rock Canyon.

"*A snake!*" said Gary wide-eyed, making him suddenly shudder.

"*Yeah!* A great big *Rattle Snake!*" said Eric.

"What a *real* one?" asked Gary, still wide-eyed.

"Well, of course, it was! It wasn't Disney Land, *Dopey!*" said Jack jokingly, laughing.

"Well, *you're* the one who thought the Statue

of Liberty in Las Vegas was the *real* one!" Gary then said to Jack, laughing back at him. "… Everyone knows it's in Florida!"

Everyone, except Jack, gave Gary a blank look.

"Now, now, you two!" said Emily, putting a stop to their childish bickering (it certainly did feel like old times again).

Just then Bethany returned. "What's that about a snake?" she asked as she sat down to join them.

"When we went to Red Rock Canyon, we came across a snake. It was as long as my arms width!" said Emily stretching out her arms. "I was terrified!"

"I bet you were!" said Bethany grimacing. "I would be terrified too!"

"I wouldn't have been!" boasted Gary, puffing out his chest.

"*Sure,* Gary!" everybody said in unison, chuckling.

"… So, what happened next then?" inquired Jack. "Did it slither away?"

"*No,* it didn't!" said Emily. She then started to tell them about the huge boulder that came hurtling down the cliff face towards them.

"Wait! *Sorry* Emily!" said Bethany, suddenly

interrupting her. "Gary, where are the children?" Everybody quickly looked around, but they were no longer in sight. Bethany looked annoyed at her husband and tutted. "Gary, you were supposed to be looking after them!"

"Look, there they are – over there in the corner!" said Eric spotting them all gathered around together looking as if they were talking with someone.

"KIDS!" Bethany shouted at the top of her voice.

Suddenly lots of kids turned their heads around in the lobby. Bethany then caught her kid's attention and indicated for them to come back.

Gary and Bethany and their friends couldn't see who the children were talking to because their bodies were shielding the person sat down from view. Then even as the children turned and started making their way joyfully back to their parents, the person had raised a newspaper in front of their face, so they still weren't able to discover their identity – especially in the crowded room.

"*Kids,* what have we told you about running off like that without telling us where you're going!" said their mum crossly, reminding them.

"*And* never to talk to strangers!" added Gary, also displeased.

"Sorry, Mummy and Daddy!" sheepishly said all the children with their heads lowered.

"– Well, we'll leave you to it, and catch up with you later!" said Eric, seeing that their friends Gary and Bethany had their hands full with the children. So, Eric and Emily said goodbye and left through the main entrance.

"What's that in your hands?" Bethany suddenly asked the children, noticing for the first time that they were each clutching hold of something.

"The kind person gave them to us, Mummy!" said Tracy smiling.

"Let us see," said their mum as Gary and Jack watched on. They then each opened their hands displaying cheap Rosary bead necklaces with a crucifix attached.

When Bethany looked over to where the person was sitting again – they were gone. She thought it was a little odd but just saw it as a sweet gesture.

"C'mon, let's go to our room!" said Bethany.

CHAPTER TWENTY-SEVEN

SHOWTIME!

The large double doors to the Excalibur theatre venue opened, welcoming in hordes of eager and excited people, keen to witness the new magic show in town on opening night – and to see whether the magician would get his brains blown out or not.

The show was a complete sell-out. And as well as members of the public, there were also VIP's – including celebrity guests, and the press. All the planning, promotion, and rehearsals had led up to this very moment.

The star of the show, The Amazing Fartzini, was sat at his dressing table all alone, staring at himself in the mirror. Outside in the corridor, he could hear the usual din of excited showgirls moving about to and fro – only this time, they were more joyous and excited than ever.

But, as they say: 'The mirror never lies', and the image it reflected of Eric was *not* of joy and excitement: it was of someone in turmoil. Not because he was about to perform the most dangerous and infamous magic trick stunt ever created for the first time in front of a live audience – bizarrely, he remained calm about that. It was because once the show was over, he would have to say goodbye to his sweetheart, Emily, and his close friends; and didn't know when he would get the chance to see them again – if ever!

And, as the mirror reflected his sad image, he reflected upon his life and the big dilemma he now faced as to whether he should stay in Las Vegas or leave and travel back to the UK with his friends. He certainly wasn't happy with the life he led in Vegas!

Eric's girlfriend and his friends were due to fly back to the UK in the early hours of Sunday morning. Why not just get on the plane and fly back home with them? What was to stop him just leaving? Well, there was the small matter of the new contract he had agreed to, which, of course, meant that if he broke the terms and conditions thereof, would face a civil court battle and be ordered to pay compensation – money he didn't have.

Before Eric came out to Las Vegas, he had promised Emily that he would only stay for the duration of his six-month contract. He had broken that promise – which he felt bad about – and he certainly didn't want to lose her over it. But was he now prepared to give up his childhood dream of staring in Las Vegas? He felt trapped in a world that he had created – compelled to – but maybe it was now time to make his most challenging escape yet? Perhaps it was time for him to grow up? *Naah!* That would be *boring!*

Well, dear reader, sometimes fate lends a helping hand when it comes to making decisions – as you will soon find out when you read on.

Earlier during the afternoon, Eric and Emily met up with their friends and had a lovely time together. Everyone said how quick the time seemed to have gone, and that they couldn't believe that it would be their last day together in Las Vegas. They all felt quite sad about having to say goodbye to their good friend, Eric, especially Emily.

Meanwhile, as they were making the most of their limited time together, unbeknownst to Eric, things were beginning to hot up in the murder case enquiry into the death of magician Chet Stevenson.

Much earlier in the day, the Las Vegas Metropolitan Police Headquarters received a report of a murder victim found slain in his RV on a trailer park over on the Indian reservation. As it turned out, the victim was Rob Maloney, the old, retired magician whom Eric had met a few weeks back – and judging by the state of the corpse found, could have been lying there for just as long. The police report described a horrendous smell, which was what prompted other RV owners living on the site to eventually call 911. The report also described the victim as suffering the same fate and method of execution like that of the other murdered magician. There was also evidence at the scene to suggest that the killer had intended to set fire to the RV but was probably disturbed and had to abandon his attempt. And according to eyewitness accounts, the last person to visit the old magician was Eric Fartz!

The forensics team had also discovered a long strand of blonde wavy hair attached to Chet Stevenson's blood-stained silk bed sheet by his congealed blood – on one of the few areas of fabric not destroyed by the fire. Which along with the other circumstantial evidence, immediately now pointed the finger directly at Eric Fartz as being the prime murder suspect.

"He's our man. I'm *sure* of it!" said detective Mark Hitchcock to his superior. "It's usually the *quiet* one's!"

"Okay, *quickly* collect all the evidence together you can, and I will arrange a warrant for his arrest!" said the authoritative voice of the Chief of Police. "We need to get him into custody for a DNA test ASAP before he brutally murders any more rival magicians in this city!"

There was a loud banging on the stars dressing room door, which immediately startled Eric.

"OPEN UP! IT'S THE POLICE!" yelled Gary jokingly on the other side of the door to subdued laughter from Jack and Emily, who thought it was funny. Bethany had remained with the children at the hotel as the evening show wasn't suitable for young children.

Eric recognized Gary's Welsh accent immediately and went and unlocked the door.

"Ha, ha, very funny!" said Eric upon opening the door to greet them.

"Hi!" they all said at once.

"Come in!" said Eric, pleased to see them and feeling a lot more cheered up because of it.

"We all just wanted to wish you good lu—" said Jack before being cut off by Eric.

"Thanks!" he quickly said to Jack, who was unaware of the age-old superstition that it was unlucky to say "good luck" to performers in a theatre. "It's *great* to see you all!"

Eric got a bit emotional – though, he tried not to show it – and started giving them all a big hug. Emily felt emotional too, but she thought she'd save her tears for when she says goodbye to him at the airport.

Gary laughed. "But we've only just seen you a short while ago!"

After giving each of his friends a warm and friendly hug, Eric continued chatting while he finished buttoning-up his red stage shirt. He then went and sat back down at his dressing table and started combing his long blonde wavy hair; now and again casually plucking out the odd strand of hair from his comb and disposing of it on the carpet.

After a little while, Jack went off to the toilet, leaving the others to continue chatting.

"Jack's been gone a long while," said Emily, wondering where he'd got to.

"If he ate as much free buffet as I did, he's probably still doing a *massive* dump!"

"*Oh, please!*" immediately said Emily, disgusted. "Too much information!"

But it didn't take long to find out why Jack had been gone for so long: as soon as Gary and Emily poked there head out into the corridor; there he was outside the dancers dressing room, busy chatting up the pretty dancer from the UK, Sasha.

The noise outside increased as did the cast and crews nerves as the auditorium started to fill up. Then, "Ten minutes till showtime!" was repeatedly heard as the deputy stage manager moved briskly along the corridor, rapping his knuckles loudly on each of the artiste's doors.

Eric's friends said goodbye for now and left him to finish getting ready. "Take great care, darling!" said Emily, kissing him on the lips before she followed the others out.

Eric's friends then hurriedly made their way out into the noisy auditorium and went and sat down in their seats. There was a real buzz of excitement in the air, and as the last people took their seats, the lights went down, and the dramatic overture started to signal the start of the new show.

One of the last people to take their seat when the lights went down, was a young woman of striking appearance. She was in full make-up and wore a stylish figure-hugging leopard skin style all in one outfit, and matching Jimmy Choo heels. You will remember her as Gloria – though I doubt that was her real name. Not that anyone could see who she was in the dark – which was preciously what she wanted, as she had been barred from the premises, and was wanted by the police. But Gloria being Gloria – looking her best was far more important than being arrested. Mind you, her hairstyle was completely different.

"Hi! Have you seen The Amazing Fartzini perform before?" asked a friendly lady sat next to Gloria.

Gloria didn't want to get into a conversation, but answered, "Just once or twice."

"Oh, he's *amazing* – isn't he?" then expressed the lady enthusiastically.

"Yeah!" just said Gloria.

"My husband and I watched him on the television, and we both said, we *must* come and watch him … I'm Debbie Jackson by the way!"

There was an awkward moment of silence while the lady waited for the leopard-woman to say her name.

"Rebecca!" answered Gloria with a strained attempt at a smile before turning her head back towards the stage.

By now all the dancers were ready in their positions on stage waiting for curtain-up. Ruben was in the wings flapping about as usual. Eric was still in his dressing room. And the compère, Jim, was chatting to the marksman, Rick, in the corridor.

Rick was dressed in a long black hooded gown to represent the Grim Reaper – which the producer thought would add to the drama of the finale – holding his skull mask in his hand.

Pacing up and down in the corridor was an armed security guard, who's name badge said, Daniel. He was there as an extra security measure to protect Eric from the magician-slayer lest he strikes again. He also had the responsibility of escorting the marksman while he carries the musket and the live ammunition back and forth from the storeroom and the stage.

Meanwhile, stepping into a taxi was a very tall, well-built, bearded man, dressed in the uniform of a security guard and wearing black leather gloves and a cap, strapped with a .44 Magnum revolver around his waist, whilst also armed incongruously with a copy of the Holy Bible, clenched firmly in his hand. "The Excalibur! And hurry!" called out the passenger in a sharp and unfriendly tone, which immediately informed the driver that he didn't want to engage in small talk – so he kept quiet. His passenger had a transatlantic accent, which suggested that he wasn't from the US.

The rear-view mirror revealed the man's face more closely, which caused the driver to grimace at first. He looked like somebody out of a horror movie. His ugly and scary face looked leatherier than the gloves he was wearing and was a mishmash of old scars and burn marks that would frighten anyone. It was no wonder the poor soul had grown a beard to help mask himself – though, the beard and the hair on his head were very patchy where, due to the many scars, facial hair could no longer grow. And due to his disfigurement, he looked a lot older than he was. The unnerved driver was glad that he had a screen between him and his passenger.

As the taxi driver quickly tore in and out of traffic along the busy Vegas Strip, his passenger quickly tore a page out from his Bible.

Back at the Excalibur, the stage tabs began to open, revealing a scintillating star curtain as a backdrop. Then a moment or two later, on came the gorgeous Excalibur showgirls dancing to a high-octane number to thumping music and colourful flashing lights. The audience immediately started to whistle and applaud. The routine certainly got the dancer's hearts racing – and most of the guys in the audience!

"Gary! Cover your eyes!" whispered his newlywed wife half-jokingly, after seeing him ogling at the dancers with a huge grin on his face and eyes that looked like they were about to pop out of their sockets! Which he pretended not to hear. Jack had his eyes on only one dancer – Sasha.

Backstage, Mr Goldberg, Eric's manager, popped by to see him. Before he arrived, Eric knew it was him by all the gold he wore jangling about as he walked along the corridor.

The door was already half-open (which Eric didn't bother to lock after his friends left. But with the extra security guard outside, he felt it would be safe). Mr Goldberg, being his usual pushy self, pushed the door wide open. "Is the star of the show in?" he called out as he entered uninvited. He was sweating profusely again even though the air conditioning was working fine.

"Hi, Mr Goldberg," said Eric from his armchair in the corner of the room. He'd been running over his new magic show to himself before being disturbed.

"How are ya doin'?" asked Mr Goldberg. "Are you all set?"

Eric just nodded.

"I can't stay long because I've gotta get back to my VIP guests!"

"Good!" thought Eric.

"I just thought I'd let ya know that the press is in – so give it your best!"

"Yes, *of course!*" Eric replied. "Well, I really must now focus on my –"

Mr Goldberg cut him off. "We don't want cha to die a death tonight like the *last* time the press was here!" he said with a chuckle – though Eric could see he meant it.

Eric just smiled, feeling now even more pressurised.

Eric then remembered something he wanted to ask his manager. "By the way, my last month's wages are now overdue – when will I get them?"

As if suddenly developing a hearing problem, Mr Goldberg quickly said, "Well, I *must* go – see you after the show!" and before Eric could repeat his words, turned on his heels and was out the door.

Eric just shook his head, annoyed. He didn't have time to chase after him. He had to concentrate on putting on the best show of his life.

The showgirls came off stage to a rousing response from the audience; and as they made their exit, Jim quickly went out on stage to greet the smiling crowd and bask in all that warmth before the enthusiastic applause fizzled out. And as the last dancer came bounding into the wings, the tabs closed for the stagehands to re-set the stage with The Amazing Fartzini's magic props and scenery, while Jim entertained out front.

Shortly after Jim went on stage, Eric waited for the dancers to pass by his dressing room, and then made his way into the wings where his assistant was waiting for him.

Just then, a security guard entered the building via the rear stage door. Unsmiling, he flashed his security badge towards Tom at the security desk, who was more interested in watching the baseball game on his portable TV and quickly waved him through.

"*Brrr!*" murmured Tom, feeling a sudden chill as the giant of a man passed by him.

"Who the *devil* is that?" asked Tom's colleague, Mary, catching sight of his horrifically scarred and twisted face. "I've never seen him before."

If Tom had cared to look, his badge read: "James".

"He must be one of the recruits hired to protect Eric!" answered Tom, momentarily looking up from the TV screen and then quickly back again so as not to miss the action.

Or was this security guard the Devil incarnate?

"Did ya see his face?" asked Mary to no answer. "He must have been in a horrific fire!"

"HOME RUN!" Tom suddenly hollered enthusiastically.

"No one's gonna mess with him!" continued

Mary, talking to herself. "Eric will be *safe* with him!"

The compère immediately got the crowd laughing.

"Jim's going down well!" commented Eric to his assistant, Laura.

Jane looked a bit nervous.

"You'll be alright, Jane!" said Eric reassuringly to her. "We've rehearsed many times – just be sure to check that the live bullet is extracted from the musket after you remove the ramrod!"

"Yes, I will!" she reassured him.

The scary-looking security guard approached the other security guard, Daniel, towards the end of the corridor.

"Watcha!" said James. "The Chief has ordered me to relieve you of your post and wants you to guard the entrance to the auditorium instead!"

"Oh, *really?*" replied Daniel, a bit surprised and hesitant. "… Okay then, buddy."

"Quick! Hurry!" growled James.

Now in this crazy world, there are scary-guys, and there are scary-guys; but *this* scary-guy, would even scare the *scariest* of scary-guys if you know what I mean! And Daniel *certainly* didn't want to get into an argument with *him*. So, after handing James the keys to the where the musket and ammunition were locked away, he made haste for the door leading into the auditorium. At least he would now be able to watch the show, he thought, pleased.

Behind the tabs, Eric quickly checked that all his magic props were in position correctly. Then made himself disappear into his appearance box illusion ready for the start of his show, relieved not to have to wear that ridiculous Merlin costume.

In the corridor, the new security guard, James, was acquainting himself with the backstage layout.

"Excuse me, where's the other guy?" asked the marksman as he approached James from behind; getting a sudden shock as he turned around showing his face.

"Oh, he had to leave because he felt unwell. And I've replaced him," answered James, very matter of fact.

A dancer started to come out of her dressing room, screamed, and then quickly went back inside upon seeing James for the first time. Shortly afterwards, while the two men were talking, curious dancers' heads started to appear out of the doorway.

"Oh, dear!" said Rick. "I hope he'll be okay!"

"Probably just something he ate," quickly said James.

"I'm Rick, the marksman. I guess then you'll be the one escorting me to the stage with the musket and ammunition."

James just nodded and walked off; leaving Rick, thinking, he's not very friendly, I much prefer the other guy.

Jim finished his short spot and began introducing the star of the show.

"That's good! He's not waffling on as much as usual," thought Eric from the confines of his secret compartment. "Benjamin must have had a word with him."

"… Ladies and Gentlemen prepare to be amazed!" dramatically announced the compère as the tabs opened; smoke, filled the dimly lit stage, and mysterious music started playing.

And after a few dizzying spins inside the previously shown empty box, The Amazing Fartzini made his magical appearance, conjuring up a spontaneous mix of ooh's and aah's, applause, whistles, stamping of feet, and a good measure of whoops from the mesmerized audience. Then to the delight of the audience, he continued to amaze them throughout the first part of his show.

As Eric performed, he tried to spot his friends among the packed auditorium, but the follow spot was too bright and prevented him from doing so. One person that he did think he recognized on the front row was Gloria. "Surely, that *can't* be, *her?*" he said to himself. And, while he was thrusting a gruesome-looking blade through the lower torso area of his assistant, whose head was poking out through a hole in the top section of the cabinet, he asked her. "Hey, is that *Gloria* on the front row over to the right?"

While still smiling widely, she turned her head slightly to look. "Yes, it looks like her!" she voiced, delivering a good impression of a not so good ventriloquist.

Then as Eric turned round to face the audience again; he noticed, marching down the aisles on each side of the auditorium, were cops in uniform, with presumably plain-clothed detectives leading them. There were also many police officers positioned outside on the street by the rear stage door.

Eric's first thoughts were: 'I know that I asked for police protection, but this is taking it a bit *too* far!' Then, as the police officers stopped and lined themselves up along each side of the auditorium, he suddenly thought: "Ah, they've *probably* come to arrest Gloria!" Not knowing that they had come to arrest him as soon as the show was over. The audience just assumed it was all part of the show.

Peering through the stage left wings watching Eric perform was the new security guard. He must have been the only person watching the show that wasn't smiling – just a cold unemotional stare.

"Oh, *there* you are!" said Rick, the marksman, who'd been looking for the security guard. "It won't be long now before The Amazing Fartzini performs the Bullet Catch, so we'd better go now and fetch the musket and ammunition!"

"Okay," just answered the security guard with a nod.

Rick led the way; he'd made this trip many times during the rehearsals. When they reached the stage manager's office, the security guard removed the keys from his pocket, found the right key, and unlocked the door. He then pushed it wide open.

"After you!" said the security guard, James,

whose cold expression hadn't changed.

Rick stepped inside the office when suddenly, "CRACK!" made the bone-crunching sound as the butt of the security guards .44 Magnum landed on the top of Rick's head. Rick immediately collapsed to the floor, knocked out cold!

The resort security had been so concerned about protecting the star of the show that nobody thought about the marksman's protection!

Mercilessly, without even checking to see if the elderly man was still alive, the security guard immediately disrobed him and put on his Grim Reaper costume. They were both about the same height, so it fitted him okay – albeit a little tight.

The security guard then quickly located where the musket, gunpowder, and ammunition were stored, and immediately unlocked the cabinet and removed it. He could hear the audience applauding, and then the compère's voice beginning to announce The Amazing Fartzini's finale. So, as quickly as he could, he reached down and grabbed the skull mask, which was still in the marksman's hand, put it on and made for the door armed to the teeth with weaponry, including a loaded .44 Magnum hidden down the rear of his trousers, a hunting knife strapped to his calf, and a can of lighter fluid for *his* finale. He closed the door behind him, locked it, and then made haste for the stage left wings.

Eric had just a moment ago come off stage after taking a well-deserved bow and was stood anxiously by the stage right wings preparing himself to go back on again very soon to perform his finale – the Bullet Catch.

CHAPTER TWENTY-EIGHT

FINALE

The massive theatre stage was now in complete darkness (the perfect setting for a killer to strike!), and the compère was making his introductory speech to the Bullet Catch from the stage left wings.

"… What you are about to witness, Ladies and Gentlemen, has already claimed the lives of *many* magicians!" dramatically announced Jim. He had a superb theatrical-type voice and had the audience gripped and hanging on to every word he uttered. "The Amazing Fartzini will now put his life in *danger* and attempt to catch a *live* bullet shot from an old-fashioned musket between his *teeth!*" Upon saying this, the spellbound audience gasped. "Ladies and Gentlemen, would you please welcome back onto the stage, *The Amazing Fartzini!*"

Dramatic music then began to play, and splashes of deep-red stage lighting gradually spilled out upon the stage until it looked soaked in blood to reveal a shooting range. Then amidst a multitude of stars twinkling in the background, the star of the show walked confidently back out on stage to loud applause. As Eric stood in position, a God light's powerful white beam shone down on him from directly above, lighting him up.

The compère then introduced the masked marksman and invited him onto the stage. "Ladies and Gentlemen, given the unenviable task of firing the musket is retired police officer and marksman, Rick Poplowski. So, will you now please give him a big round of applause as he joins The Amazing Fartzini on stage!" announced Jim.

To the sound of applause, the masked marksman slowing walked out on stage carrying the musket, gunpowder, and ammunition and stood in the correct position, easily identified by a large "X", facing The Amazing Fartzini opposite.

The sight of this huge man dressed as the Grim Reaper sent shivers down the backs of people's spines.

"Oh my God, how scary!" commented Emily sat in the audience watching the show with her friends.

"It doesn't scare me!" Gary replied, whose face didn't agree.

"Yeah, *right!*" said Jack chuckling.

When the marksman was stood in his position, also under a brightly lit beam of light from the God's, Eric's sleuth-like mind noticed that his shoes were different. And he now seemed much stockier – like he'd just had a workout at the gym and was pumped-up. "Maybe he had changed his shoes from earlier? And possibly he had been doing some exercises before he came out on stage?" thought Eric. But there was something strange about him that did not quite sit right with Eric.

The compère then announced that the magician's assistant will now come down into the audience in search of a volunteer to choose a musket ball and put their name or some identifying mark on it using an indelible marker pen.

The atmosphere in the theatre felt extremely

tense. And there was an eerie silence as the assistant stepped down the centre steps, carrying a small box of musket balls in one hand and a marker pen in the other, while the follow spot stalked her as she went into the auditorium. Somebody on the front row soon raised their hand and volunteered; and after choosing a musket ball, promptly wrote their name across it (luckily it wasn't a long name!). And then, while still in the gaze of the follow spot, the assistant held the signed bullet aloft in one hand as she made her way back upon the stage along with the volunteer to where the marksman was standing.

"Oh, I don't feel good about this!" said Emily, starting to feel very uneasy.

"He'll be fine!" said Jack trying to reassure her. "Don't worry!"

Next, the compère commanded the marksman to prime the musket with gunpowder in the traditional way. The audience then watched with bated breath as he removed a horn of gunpowder and loaded a small amount into the pan and the barrel.

"The assistant will now load the signed musket ball into the muzzle, while the volunteer checks that everything is above board, then ram it home ready for firing!" continued to announce Jim. Even he now had a slight nervousness to his voice!

Now with the musket ball loaded, the compère generated applause for the volunteer as he made his way back to his seat. All the while, Eric remained still, with his legs apart and his arms down by his sides, playing the part, looking solemn, and bracing himself in anticipation – and hoping that it all goes to plan.

Having stolen the signed live bullet surreptitiously from out of the musket, his trained assistant then handed The Amazing Fartzini the gimmicked dinner plate, whilst at the same time secretly slipping him the bullet. The assistant then exited, leaving only The amazing Fartzini and the marksman on stage.

"Prepare to fire!" then commanded the compère.

Upon hearing this, the audience let out another gasp – louder this time than before. The marksman immediately followed the order and raised the musket into the firing position, cocked the hammer, and pointed it directly at The Amazing Fartzini ready for the final command to fire. It was all beginning to feel very real for the audience – a few people got up and left, and one lady even fainted.

Now, even though Eric had rehearsed this routine many times now and knew that the gun would only fire a blank: there is always something very unsettling about having someone pointing a gun at you. And as Eric stared down the barrel of the gun, he couldn't help but feel nervous.

But his nerves, along with the members of the audience, were about to get a whole lot worse!

Eric slowly and dramatically raised the dinner plate momentarily in front of his handsome face, secretly loading the signed bullet into his mouth before extending his arms out in front of him in readiness to perform the dangerous stunt. And, with his heart racing and sweat pouring down his face, he peered over the top of the dinner plate at the scary figure stood before him, while some members of the audience peeped over the tops of their shaking hands (including Gary), braced himself, and took a deep breath.

Then just as Eric was about to shout, "Fire!" suddenly the pseudo marksman raised the musket high into the air and fired, causing a loud noise, and making everyone jump. He then whipped off his skull mask and yelled to Eric, "SURPRISE! SURPRISE!"

Eric stumbled backwards in shock (he was certainly surprised all right – he nearly swallowed the bullet!). The audience immediately gave out a loud scream in horror – the marksman's face was even scarier than his disguise!

Eric couldn't believe his eyes. "David!" he mouthed. Eric knew who it was instantly, despite his arch-enemy wearing a beard and his face being severely burnt and scared. He would recognise that haunting voice anywhere!

David Smythe Jr then tossed the musket on the stage and swiftly reached inside his cloak and pulled out his massive .44 Magnum revolver. He immediately pointed it at Eric. "Let's see ya try and catch one of *these* bullets then, Fartz!" he snarled.

It felt to Eric like David was speaking to him again in the school playground! But strangely, apart from the initial surprise, Eric remained calm and unnerved.

"Who's that? Where's Mr Poplowski?" said the stage manager to Jim, who was standing in the wings next to him.

"Don't ask me – I've never seen him before in my life!" answered Jim.

While in the audience, the producer was shaking his head, saying to himself, "I wish they'd stick to the script!"

"Is that David … Smythe Jr?" asked Emily once the ringing in her ears had gone away.

"My *God,* I think it might be!" said Jack leaning forwards.

"Nah, it *can't* be!" said Gary as shocked as they were. For he too recognized that terrifying resurrected voice.

"Why is Eric just *standing* there?" then said Emily, deeply concerned.

Apart from Emily, Jack, and Gary, the rest of the audience thought it was all part of the act. Even the police weren't sure what was happening and remained where they were awaiting instructions to arrest Eric.

Meanwhile on stage, Eric and David were deep in conversation.

"… You thought I was dead, didn't ya!" said David with a sickly grin, seemingly pleased that this time he had fooled the magician. Eric didn't respond. "I know it was your *evil* witchcraft that caused the car I was travelling in to crash, *killing* my dear mother and father

… Well, by the grace of the God I survived that horrific car crash, and destiny has brought me here to *rid* the world of *heretics* like *you!* So, *prepare* to *die!*" David cocked the hammer.

Eric quickly disposed of the bullet by coughing into his hand in case he choked on it like he nearly did before. "The same way you also killed the other innocent magician, Chet Stevenson, and your girlfriend?" asked Eric, unafraid as he stared into the killer's stone-cold eyes.

"You missed out that old magician living on the trailer park," then said David grinning. "His magical powers were no match for the Almighty's! I can hear his *pitiful* voice now, pleading with me to spare his life."

"*What?*" said Eric surprised.

"Oh, didn't cha know? Yes, I killed him, too!" exclaimed David, as if proudly.

"You're *sick* – you need help!" responded Eric, also questioning his own sanity as to whether this was all real.

"Oh, but I *enjoyed* it!" said David with an even bigger grin.

"WHY YOU –!" screamed Eric full of rage as he spun the plate towards David like a Frisbee to try and distract him and charged courageously towards him. Or it could have been that he threw the musket ball at him instead? Or maybe both?

Anyway, by this time Eric's friends were already up out of their seats, frantically trying to draw attention to the danger he was in, while at the same time trying to squeeze their way passed peoples legs to reach the centre aisle so they could run to his aid. But they found themselves trapped in the middle of their row!

However, at the same time Eric made his move towards David, realising that Eric was in grave danger, Gloria kicked off her Jimmy Choo's, and like a powerful wildcat, she sprang up onto the stage and leaped towards Eric. And just as David fired at Eric, she pushed him out of harm's way. Gloria screamed at the top of her voice and fell to the stage as the bullet caught her instead. It ripped right through the soft flesh of her upper right arm! Lots more terrified screams immediately followed from among the audience – some remained frozen to their seats in shock, while other panicked audience members scrambled for the exit. Acting quickly, the stage manager, Dirk, and the compère, Jim, ran out from the wings and grabbed the imposter from behind, wrapping their arms around his to prevent him from firing at anyone again. The Frankenstein-like monster spun them both dizzily around like they were on a merry-go-round – only this was no amusement ride!

By this time, the police had seen and heard everything they needed to know and quickly came running onto the stage to arrest the killer. It took several police officers to grapple the crazed gunman facedown onto the stage floor and disarm him before locking him in handcuffs.

At the same time the lead detective, Mark Hitchcock, was giving the confessed killer his rights, Eric was kneeling in a pool of blood beside Gloria, trying to prevent her from losing more blood. "MEDIC! MEDIC!" he kept calling out.

An announcement finally came at last for everyone to evacuate the auditorium in an orderly manner (half the audience had already gone by then!). Eric's worried and concerned friends ignored it and continued to try and reach him, but the police prevented them from doing so. It was sheer pandemonium!

Hearing the continual terrified screams, followed by the announcement, the dancers locked themselves in their dressing room, frightened and wondering what on earth was happening. Ruben was nowhere to be seen (And it wasn't until much later after this story ends that someone would find him cowering inside one of The Amazing Fartzini's illusion boxes too frightened to come out!).

As Eric knelt beside Gloria waiting for the ambulance to arrive, he tried his best to comfort her. "You saved my *life*, Gloria! You are my guardian angel!" he said to her amid all the noise and confusion.

She smiled weakly. "No, you are *mine!*" she replied as she lay centre stage in pain, passing in and out of consciousness. "… I'm sorry I treated you wrongly."

"Don't worry! I forgive you! You just relax – the ambulance will be here shortly!" said Eric to comfort her as he held her hand. How could he not forgive her: she had bravely risked her life to save his.

The stage manager, Dirk, came over with his first aid kit to assist Gloria as soon as he had untangled himself from the bogus marksman.

Soon afterwards, staggering onto the stage came the real marksman, Mr Poplowski, holding his sore head – the bangs from the gunfire probably woken him up, and after banging on the door someone must have heard him and unlocked it. Eric and Jim quickly rushed over to the dazed and disorientated man and helped him sit down and arranged for one of the waitresses to fetch some ice.

Once Mr Poplowski had been taken care of, feeling exhausted, Eric went and sat down on the edge of the stage.

"It's okay, Officer – they're with me!" Eric called out to the police officer who was preventing his friends from getting any closer.

The officer let them through, and Emily immediately rushed over to her boyfriend and gave him a loving hug. His other friends followed close behind her and did the same.

"I can't *believe* what just happened!" said Emily, relieved as the rest of them were that Eric was okay.

"Me neither!" replied Eric, like them still in shock.

"After everything that's happened, you should come *home* with us!" expressed Emily, hoping he would say, yes. The others agreed.

"Aye, I will! I had already made up my mind to do that even before this happened. But first, I will need to check that it's okay with the police," answered Eric to their great delight.

Meanwhile, David Smythe Jr was being escorted to the rear exit of the building by several police officers. All with firearms pointing directly at him in case he tried to escape.

The ambulance teams then arrived in the auditorium to take care of Gloria and Mr Poplowski.

"Is she gonna be alright?" Emily asked Eric, referring to Gloria.

"I'm sure she will!" answered Eric with a reassuring smile. "I'm lucky to be alive, thanks to her!" Eric and his friends all then had another group hug.

A little while later, the lead detective on the case, Mark Hitchcock, came over and spoke to Eric. He briefly asked Eric a few questions relating to David Smythe Jr, which Eric answered as best he could. Then reassured Eric it will be a cold day in hell before the deranged killer is released on bail, and the likelihood is he would spend the rest of his days behind bars – probably in a secure psychiatric hospital. The detective also told Eric that now they have the self-confessed killer in custody, he would be at liberty to leave Las Vegas and travel wherever he wanted.

Oh, and in case you were wondering about the long strand of wavy blonde hair? It turned out that it didn't belong to Eric as the police first thought: the strand of hair was from the blonde wig recovered at the murder scene of David Smythe Jr's ex-girlfriend, which most likely transferred from his clothing onto Chet Stevenson's bedsheet, linking the killer to her murder as well!

After speaking to the detective, Eric and his friends all went backstage to his dressing room. There, he booked Emily, Sasha, and himself on the same flight back to the UK as the others – it wasn't a busy flight, and he even managed to arrange for them all to sit together. Then as quickly as he could, he packed his personal belongings into his sports bag.

"What about all your magic equipment?" asked Emily.

"Oh, I'm not too worried about that – I can always replace it in the UK," Eric replied. "C'mon! Let's get out of 'ere!"

"Hey, where's Jack?" then asked Emily.

"I bet I can guess!" said Gary, grinning widely.

Sure enough, when they all came out of his

dressing room, there Jack was, talking to Sasha further along the corridor.

"Sasha's coming home with us too!" said Jack, beaming and smiling from ear to ear as the others approached them.

"Great!" they all said.

Then just as they all started to head happily for the backstage exit, Eric heard his manager's irritating voice calling him from farther back along the corridor.

"Eric! Oh, *Eric!"* beckoned Mr Goldberg.

Eric turned around and walked assuredly towards him.

"Despite the unfortunate event that happened this evening, the show must go on as they say, and we expect you still to perform tomorrow evening!" said Mr Goldberg unsympathetically as Eric approached him. There was no "How are you?" or "How are you feeling after that terrible ordeal?" Nothing like that – it was straight down to business as usual.

"I quit!!" responded Eric assertively.

"Quit?!" Mr Goldberg let out a cynical laugh, causing his gold jewellery to jangle. "Don't be ridiculous! You can't *quit* – you've *signed* a contract!"

"Yes, I can – if you check the contracts, you'll find my signatures are no longer there!"

"But I saw you sign them!"

Eric laughed. "I used 'Vanishing Ink' to sign my name!"

"But – think of all the money you will lose if you leave now!" desperately said his manager.

It's true, Eric could've done with the money, as he only had just enough money left to pay for the return flights home, but he didn't care.

"If there's one thing that becoming a star in this furnace of a place has taught me, Mr Goldberg," passionately expressed Eric, "it's that money and fame aren't everything – and that there are far more important things in life! So, you can stick your contract where the sun doesn't shine!"

Then, to the sound of his friends cheering, Eric started walking away from his shocked manager.

"Mr Constantino won't be very happy about this!"

Eric ignored his last comment, stopped, turned his head around and said, "Oh, yeah! And you're *fired!*" Then carried on walking back to his friends.

"*Fired!*" repeated his ex-manager,

flabbergasted.

"*Yeah,* you *heard* him!" called out Gary. *"I'm* his manager now!

"You are?" said Eric to Gary chuckling. "C'mon, gang! Let's go!"

And so, Eric, Emily, Gary, Jack, and Sasha headed for the exit.

As Eric began signing out of the Excalibur resort for the final time, the security guard, Tom, suddenly remembered something. "Oh, I've just remembered. Earlier today somebody left a small package for you!"

Tom reached below the counter and handed it over to Eric.

"Oh, thanks, Tom!" said Eric, wondering what it could be. Eric quickly shoved it in his new sports bag and hurriedly caught up with his friends who were now outside trying to hail a cab.

They all then went back to their hotel rooms and apartments to pack their suitcases and collect their passports – and in Gary's case to also collect his wife and kids – and then headed straight for the airport where they had arranged to meet up.

It was now 12.55 am USA time according to Jack's watch, and their British Airways flight to

London Heathrow was due to leave in less than an hour. Everybody had checked in, except Eric and Emily, who still hadn't shown up.

"Try ringing them again, Gary," said Bethany panicking. Gary tried again, as did Jack; but there was no answer, and they were all beginning to worry that something was up, and they weren't going to make it in time. The children were all fast asleep on sofas none the wiser.

Fifteen minutes later, Eric and Emily still hadn't arrived.

"They are calling our gate number!" said Bethany, sounding even more in a panic. "We need to go through passport control now, or we'll miss our flight!"

The others agreed, and with a heavy heart, Jack, Sasha, Gary, Bethany, and the children went through passport control to the departures lounge. There was no time to look at the duty-free shops; they headed straight for their departure gate, where passengers were already starting to board.

As they showed their boarding passes at the gate, Eric and Emily's friends could hear over the public address system: 'This is the last call for passengers on the British Airways flight to

London Heathrow departing from gate thirteen. Please would you now make your way there!'

On the plane, they quickly located where they were sitting in economy class. *"Bagsy,* I sit next to the window!" said Gary like the big kid he was. And after stowing away their hand luggage in the compartments above, they all sat down in their allocated seats. Gary and Bethany and their children took up two whole rows, and Jack and Sasha sat next to each other in the row in front nearest the window. Next to them were two empty seats where Eric and Emily should have sat.

They all felt a mixture of excitement and disappointment.

"I don't think they are gonna make it in time!" said Jack glumly to the others.

"No, me neither," said Gary, sounding the same way. Then suddenly sparking up and saying randomly, "I *wonder* what's on the menu!"

"Oh, *Gary,* stop thinking of your stomach for once!" bemoaned Bethany, followed by her tutting.

"What?" Gary just replied as he picked up the menu from the seat pocket in front.

But just when the large door on the Boeing 747 was about to be closed, and Eric and Emily's friends had given up hope of the pair of them boarding on time, two people came bounding onto the plane waving their boarding passes – it was Eric and Emily.

"There they are!" said Jack, spotting them as they walked briskly down the aisle towards their friends. All their friends cheered and applauded them as they approached.

"Hiya!" said Eric and Emily, much relieved to have made it on board in time as were their friends.

"We thought you weren't gonna make it!" said Jack, smiling.

"Us neither!" replied Eric chuckling.

"Talk about cutting it fine!" commented Bethany while at the same time feeding the youngest child with a bottle of milk.

"What took ya so long?" asked Gary, curious as ever.

"We got abducted by *aliens!"* answered Eric keeping a straight face and trying not to laugh.

"Really?" replied Gary.

The others all burst out laughing.

"Well, they could have *been!* I've seen a UFO before!" stated Gary, all serious-like, causing more laughter.

"We just got waylaid," said Emily once she could stop laughing.

"Yeah, I had to tie up a few loose ends. I had to return the rent-a-car and so on," briefly explained Eric.

"We did try to call ya," said Jack. "How come ya didn't answer?"

"Well, Eric's battery had died, and silly me left my mobile in my hand luggage which was in the boot of the car," answered Emily. Eric and Emily then both apologised.

"Well, the main thing is ya made it!" said Bethany.

"Yeah, I *can't* believe we are all going home together! It's wonderful!" expressed Emily delighted as everyone else was.

Well, it wasn't long before the gigantic metal bird took to the skies, and everyone settled down for the long flight home.

Eric felt such a relief to be leaving Las Vegas after everything that happened and settled down into his seat feeling well and truly worn out.

Gary slipped off his size twelve trainers and slid them under the seat in front of him.

"Hold ya noses kids!" called out Bethany.

"Daddy's taken his shoes off!"

"Pooh!" screamed the kids, who had come to life again with all the anticipation and excitement of the plane taking off.

"Can ya pass me my slippers, please, my love?" asked Gary with a smile.

Bethany reached into her large handbag and pulled out his pink furry slippers, which he then slipped on, feeling at once much more comfortable and relaxed.

Once the plane had reached an altitude of 35,000 ft, Eric suddenly felt a cold chill. He glanced out of the frosted window and could see snow and ice forming on the plane's lit-up wing. Soon Eric began to shiver, and his breath became more and more visible as the temperature plummeted and freezing-cold air now enveloped the cabin turning it into a giant popsicle with wings. "The heating must have packed up!" he thought to himself. There was then an announcement from the cockpit: "Ladies and Gentlemen, this is your captain David Smythe Jr welcoming you onboard flight BA666 and wishing you all a bumpy and terrifying ride to hell!" followed by insane laugher. The plane then started to nose-dive at great velocity back towards Earth!

Eric suddenly let out a loud, terrified, scream!

"Eric, wake up, *wake up!*" said Emily, shaking him gently. He opened his eyes, still half asleep, dripping with sweat. "You must have been having a nightmare!"

"Oh, *thank* God!" he murmured, immensely relieved – and feeling nice and warm.

"What was it about?" she asked, curious.

"Oh, nothing – goodnight," he managed to say before drifting off to sleep again.

Jack and his new girlfriend Sasha were still wide awake and busy getting more acquainted with one another – letting their lips do all the talking.

Several hours of broken sleep later, and somewhere over Europe, the group of friends were gradually awakened by the sound of clatter here and there, and daylight bursting through the sides of the cabin window blinds.

And soon, most cabin window blinds were raised to let the early morning sunshine in and fill the cabin with light.

"It won't be long now!" said Emily peering out of the window at the mass of land below. "I think we must be somewhere over Europe!"

Eric and Emily gave each other a morning kiss. "Your mum will be pleased to see you,

Eric!" said Emily cheerfully.

"Yeah, I can't wait to see her!" Eric replied, smiling at the thought.

Gary's tummy started rumbling. "I hope it won't be long before they serve breakfast!" he said. "I'm *starving!* I could *murder* a Full English!"

"The stewardess is starting to work her way down the aisle now, Gary," Bethany informed him. He immediately lowered his tray in anticipation.

"Oh, it's gonna take *ages* for her to reach us!" then moaned Gary a bit frustrated.

"Well, you'll just have to be patient and wait your turn like the rest of us!" she then told him forthrightly – feeling a bit ratty after a restless night. "Honestly, it's like having another child with me!"

The other's chuckled.

"Look out the window Gary!" suddenly said, Jack. *"There's a flying saucer!"*

"Where!" said Gary, excited.

The chuckles then turned into laughter as Gary peered out of the window, believing him.

"Oh, *very* funny!" then said Gary, realising he had been had and joining in with the laughter.

Soon after, Emily excused herself and went

off to the toilet at the back of the plane to freshen up. Eric then removed his sports bag from the overhead compartment, and once he'd sat down again, unzipped it in search of his book. And there, resting on top of everything, was the small package handed to him at the Excalibur resort security desk. He had completely forgotten all about it.

Gary and Bethany were busy chatting with the kids, while Jack and Sasha were busy getting more acquainted again.

Eric started to open the package, then paused suddenly, thinking, "Wait! What if David Smythe Jr planted a bomb inside? And this was his ultimate revenge!" He wouldn't put anything past his sick and evil nemesis.

Feeling slightly nervous, he carefully brought the parcel up to his ear and listened for a ticking noise. But he couldn't hear anything. He then cautiously continued to open it. And when he had, a big smile suddenly appeared on his face, and he let out a shriek of joy. Wrapped inside the parcel was the sparkling diamond engagement ring, still inside its original box that he thought he had lost forever. He recognised it immediately! There is faith in humanity, after all, thought Eric! There was no message, but he guessed that the Elvis impersonator who he switched clothes with must have recognised him and did the decent and honest thing and returned it.

"Oh, *look*, Gary!" said Bethany excitedly, giving him a nudge upon catching a glimpse of a sparkling diamond ring shining brightly in the light through the gap between the headrests. "I reckon it's the engagement ring Eric lost!"

"Oh yeah," responded Gary with much less enthusiasm. He was too preoccupied watching the trolley of hot food getting closer and closer; picturing, plump juicy sausages, crispy bacon, scrambled eggs, baked beans, tinned tomatoes, hash browns, mushrooms, and toast smothered in creamy butter – drooling at the thought.

Bethany got up from her seat and leaned over the headrest in front of her. "It's *beautiful!*" she called out to Eric. Then asked, "Is that the engagement ring you lost?"

"Yeah!" replied Eric, still smiling.

"I was *right!* It is the engagement ring he lost!" she told Gary. Then exclaiming, "Now *that's* magic!"

Jack and Sasha heard the excitement and prised their lips apart; then seeing Eric had got the ring back, said how pleased they were for him. "Are ya gonna propose?" asked Jack. Eric nodded enthusiastically.

"Quick! Emily's coming back!" then quickly said, Bethany.

Eric quickly shoved the ring box in his front trouser pocket and put his bag under his seat. Then pretended everything was the same as usual. Though, he found it extremely hard to contain his excitement.

As Emily approached, Eric got out of his seat and let her sit back down. "You seem unusually happy for this time of the morning. How come?" she asked inquisitively.

"Oh, no reason," he answered coolly. "Just pleased we are travelling back home together, that's all."

"Yeah, me too!" she said, smiling and giving him a peck on the cheek.

Just then the friendly stewardess stopped by with the food trolley and started serving Eric's row with their trays of hot food.

"Oh, I haven't had a full English breakfast in ages!" commented Eric, looking forward to tucking in.

Gary peered through the gap between the headrests and started licking his lips at the sight and smell of the scrumptious-looking cooked breakfasts.

The stewardess then moved the trolley down to the next row which Gary's family occupied. Gary's face was beaming with joy. The children were all served first and started tucking into their cooked breakfast's straight away. The stewardess then served Bethany next. Then just as she was about to hand Gary his long-awaited full English breakfast, Bethany immediately held her palm up towards her and said, "He can't eat that – he's a vegetarian!"

"Oh, sorry!" said the stewardess; and much to Gary's dismay promptly put it away and brought out the cold vegetarian meal choice for Gary instead.

Eric and Jack heard what was said and burst out laughing. For once, Gary was speechless and just stared at the strange and alien food in front of him.

"Well, you agreed if ever Eric got the ring back, you'd become a vegetarian!" said his wife, quietly reminding him so Emily couldn't hear.

"Yeah, but –" just mumbled Gary in a state of shock.

"Yeah, but nothing!" said his wife grinning. "It's what you agreed!"

"I know, but … can I have one of your sausages?" pleaded Gary. She shook her head – she was enjoying this.

"Well, can I have a *bite* at least!"

Then after an agonising pause, she laughed and said, "I was only kiddin'! Go on then, have mine, and I'll have yours – which I prefer anyway." She knew if she didn't swap the meals over, he'd only be grumpy and sulk all day.

Eric gulped down his breakfast as fast as he could. He was so excited and couldn't wait to propose to his longtime girlfriend at last. And as soon as everyone had finished their breakfasts and everything was all cleared away, he could wait no longer; feeling slightly nervous, he got up from his seat and standing in the aisle, said to his friends, "Can I have your attention please!" All his friends, except Emily, watched on excitedly, knowing what he was about to do. Eric then reached into his pocket, pulled out the ring box and got down on one knee beside Emily. He opened the ring box revealing the beautiful engagement ring inside. He looked lovingly into her eyes, which sparkled as brightly as the diamonds before her, and said, "Emily Ryan – will you marry me?"

And happier than she's ever felt, she replied, "*Yes!*"

THE END.

Acknowledgements

I thank the artist Shelley Ashkowski for bringing my vision of the book cover, beautifully to life!

And, as always, thank my wonderful wife, Angela, and our son Jake for their much-appreciated love and support!

ABOUT THE AUTHOR

Shane Robinson was born in Ramsgate, Kent, in 1963. Before he became a children's author, he was a professional magician. His interest in magic started at the young age of ten. He went on to become a successful magician under the stage name of "Zane", performing at top venues around the world, including cruise liners such as the world-famous QE2.

And, as well as still performing magic, he is also the owner of an internet magic shop called www.zanesmagicshop.com and is the creator of several marketed magic trick products sold around the world.

He has also appeared in two critically acclaimed movies performing magic: *Funny Bones* and *Magicians*.

He regularly trades at various public events in the UK, demonstrating and selling beginners magic tricks and books to delighted children, and inspiring the next generation of magicians.

He is very happily married to Angela, and they have a son named Jake and a granddaughter named Holly.

www.ingramcontent.com/pod-product-compliance
Lightning Source LLC
Chambersburg PA
CBHW030951190726
48285CB00004BB/1304